Praise for

Anne Perry's Christmas Mysteries

A Christmas Journey

"One of the best books to brighten up the joyous
season."
—*USA Today*

A Christmas Visitor

"[Perry] has a flair for humor, and the names she
chooses for her characters are so wondrous it's a
pity to kill any of them off."
—*Richmond Times-Dispatch*

A Christmas Guest

"[A] satisfying tale."
--*The Wall Street Journal*

A Christmas Secret

"Anne Perry has crafted a finely written Christmas
puzzle that has a redemptive seasonal message
woven within its solution."
—*The Wall Street Journal*

Anne Perry's Christmas Mysteries

Anne Perry's Christmas Mysteries

Two Holiday Novels

A CHRISTMAS GUEST

A CHRISTMAS SECRET

Anne Perry

BALLANTINE BOOKS · NEW YORK

2008 Ballantine Books Trade Paperback

A Christmas Guest copyright © 2005 by Anne Perry
A Christmas Secret copyright © 2006 by Anne Perry
Excerpt from *A Christmas Grace* copyright © 2008 by Anne Perry

Published in the United States by Ballantine Books, an imprint of The Random House Publishing Group, a division of Random House, Inc., New York.

BALLANTINE and colophon are registered trademarks of Random House, Inc.

Originally published as two separate works as *A Christmas Guest* and *A Christmas Secret* by Ballantine Books in 2005 and 2006 in hardcover.

This book contains an excerpt from the forthcoming edition of *A Christmas Grace*. This excerpt has been set for this edition only and may not reflect the final content of the forthcoming edition.

ISBN 978-0-345-49642-3

Printed in the United States of America

www.ballantinebooks.com

2   4   6   8   9   7   5   3   1

A Christmas Guest

To all those who are still
hoping and still learning

PART ONE

. . . .

"*I* DO NOT ACCEPT IT!" MARIAH ELLISON SAID indignantly. It was intolerable.

"I am afraid there is no alternative," Emily replied. She was wearing a beautiful morning dress of pale water green with fashionably large sleeves and a sweeping skirt. With her fair coloring, it made her look prettier than she was, and having married money she had airs above her station.

"Of course there is an alternative!" Grandmama snapped, staring up at her from her chair in the withdrawing room. "There is always an alternative. Why in heaven's name should you wish to go to France? It is only a week and a half until Christmas!"

3

Emily sighed deeply. "We have been invited to spend Christmas in the Loire valley."

"*Where* in France is immaterial. It is still not England. We shall have to cross the Channel. It will be rough and we shall all be ill."

"I know it would be unpleasant for you," Emily conceded. "And the train journey from Paris might be tedious, and perhaps cold at this time of year . . ."

"What do you mean *perhaps*?" Grandmama snapped. "There is no possible doubt."

"So perhaps it is as well that you were not invited." Emily gave a very slight smile. "Now you will not have to worry how to decline with grace."

Grandmama had a sharp suspicion that Emily was being sarcastic. She also had an unpleasant and surprisingly painful realization. "Do I take it that you are going to leave me alone in this house for Christmas while you go visiting wherever you said it was, in France?" She tried to keep her voice angry rather than betraying her sudden sense of being abandoned.

"Of course not, Grandmama," Emily said cheerfully. "It would be quite miserable for you. But apart from that, you can't stay here because there will be nobody to care for you."

"Don't be absurd!" Grandmama regained her temper with asperity. "There is a houseful of servants." Emily's Christmas parties were among the few things Grandmama had been looking forward to, although she would have choked rather than admit it. She would have attended as though it were a duty required of her, and then loved every moment. "You have sufficient housemaids for a duchess! I have never seen so many girls with mops and dusters in my life!"

"The servants are coming with us and you cannot stay here alone at Christmas. It would be wretched. I have made arrangements for you to go and stay with Mama and Joshua."

"I have no desire to stay with your mother and Joshua," Grandmama said instantly.

Caroline had been her daughter-in-law, until Edward's death a few years ago had left her a widow of what Grandmama referred to as "an unfortunate age." Instead of settling into a decent retirement from society, as the dear Queen had done, and as everyone had expected of her, Caroline had married again. That in itself was indiscreet enough, but instead of a widower with means and position, which might have had considerable advantages and been looked upon with approval, she had married a man nearly two decades younger than herself. But worse than that, if anything could be, he was on the boards—an actor! A grown man who dressed up and strutted around on the stage, pretending to be someone else. And he was Jewish, for heaven's sake!

Caroline had lost what wits she had ever had, and poor Edward would be turning in his grave, if he knew. It was one of the many burdens of Grandmama's life that she had lived long enough to see it. "No desire at all," she repeated.

Emily stood quite still in the middle of the withdrawing room, the firelight casting a warm glow on her skin and the extravagant coils of her hair. "I'm sorry, Grandmama, but as I said, there really is no choice," she repeated. "Jack and I are leaving tomor-

6

row, and there is a great deal of packing to do, as we shall be gone for at least three weeks. You had best take a good supply of warmer gowns, and boots, and you may borrow my black shawl if you would care to?"

"Good gracious! Can they not afford a fire?" Grandmama said furiously. "Perhaps Joshua should consider a more respectable form of employment? If there is anything else on earth he is fitted for?"

"It has nothing to do with money," Emily retorted. "They are spending Christmas in a house on the south coast of Kent. The Romney Marshes, to be exact. I daresay the wind will be chill, and one often feels the cold more when away from home."

Grandmama was appalled! In fact she was so appalled it was several seconds before she could find any words at all to express her horror. "I think I misheard you," she said icily at last. "You mumble these days. Your diction used to be excellent, but since your marriage to Jack Radley you have allowed your standards to slip . . . in several areas. I thought you said that your mother is going to spend

7

Christmas in some bog by the sea. As that is obviously complete nonsense, you had better repeat yourself, and speak properly."

"They have taken a house in Romney Marsh," Emily said with deliberate clarity. "It is near the sea, and I believe the views will be very fine, if there is no fog, of course."

Grandmama looked for impertinence in Emily's face, and saw an innocence so wide-eyed as to be highly suspicious.

"It is unacceptable," she said in a tone that would have frozen water in a glass.

Emily stared at her for a moment, regathering her thoughts. "There is too much wind at this time of the year for there to be much fog," she said at last. "Perhaps you can watch the waves?"

"In a marsh?" Grandmama asked sarcastically.

"The house is actually in St. Mary in the Marsh," Emily replied. "It is very close to the sea. It will be pleasant. You don't have to go outside if it is cold and you don't wish to."

"Of course it will be cold! It is on the English

Channel, in the middle of winter. I shall probably catch my death."

To give her credit, Emily did look a little uncomfortable. "No you won't," she said with forced cheer. "Mama and Joshua will look after you very well. You might even meet some interesting people."

"Stuff and nonsense!" Grandmama said furiously.

*N*evertheless the old lady had no choice, and the next day she found herself sitting with her maid, Tilly, in Emily's carriage. It made slow progress out of the city traffic, then sped up as it reached the open road south of the river and proceeded toward Dover, roughly a hundred and forty-five miles southeast of London.

Of course she had known the journey would be dreadful. To make it in one day she had set out before dawn, and it would be late before they reached whatever godforsaken spot in which Caroline had chosen to spend Christmas. Heaven alone knew what it would be like! If they were in trying circumstances it might be no more than a cottage without civilized facilities, and so cramped she would spend the entire time forced into their company. It was going to be the worst Christmas of her life!

Emily's thoughtlessness in gallivanting off to France, of all places, at this time of year, was beyond belief! It was an outrage against all family loyalty and duty.

The day was gray and still, and mercifully the rain was no more than a spattering now and then. They stopped for luncheon, and to change the horses, and again a little after four o'clock for afternoon tea. By that time, naturally, it was dark and she had not the faintest idea where she was. She was tired, her legs were cramped from the long sitting, and un- avoidably she was rattled and jolted around with the constant movement. And of course it was cold— perishingly so.

They stopped again to inquire the way as lanes grew narrower and even more rutted and overhung.

When at last they arrived at their destination she was in a temper fit to have lit a fire with the sheer heat of her words. She climbed out with the coachman's assistance, and stood on the gravel drive of what was obviously a fairly large house. All the lights seemed to be blazing and the front door was decorated with a magnificent wreath of holly.

Immediately she was aware of the smells of smoke and salt, and a sharp wind with an edge to it like a slap in the face. It was damp, so no doubt it was straight off the sea. Caroline had obviously lost not only her money but the last vestige of her senses as well.

The door opened and Caroline came down the steps now, smiling. She was still a remarkably handsome woman in her fifties, her dark mahogany hair only lightly sprinkled with the odd silver at the temples, which had a softening effect. She was dressed in deep, warm red and it gave a glow to her skin.

"Welcome to St. Mary, Mama-in-law," she said a trifle guardedly.

The old lady could think of nothing whatever

11

that met the situation, or her feelings. She was tired, confused, and utterly miserable in a strange place where she knew perfectly well she was unwanted.

It was several months since she had seen her erstwhile daughter-in-law. They had never been genuinely friends, although they had lived in the same house for over twenty years. During her son Edward's lifetime there had been a truce. Afterward Caroline had behaved disgracefully and would listen to no advice at all. It became necessary for Grandmama to find other accommodations because Caroline and Joshua moved around so much, as his ridiculous profession dictated. There was never a question of Grandmama living with Charlotte, the elder granddaughter. She had scandalized everyone by marrying a policeman, a man of no breeding, no money, and an occupation that defied polite description. Heaven only knew how they survived!

So she had had no choice but to live with Emily, who at least had inherited very considerable means from her first husband.

"Come in and warm yourself." Caroline offered her arm. Grandmama briskly declined it, leaning heavily on her stick instead. "Would you like a cup of tea, or hot cocoa?" Caroline continued.

Grandmama would, and said so, stepping inside to a spacious and well-lit hall. It was a trifle low-ceilinged perhaps, but floored with excellent parquet. The stairs swept up to a landing above and presumably several bedrooms. If the fires were kept stoked and the cook were any good, it might be endurable after all.

The footman carried her cases in and Tilly followed behind him. Joshua came forward and welcomed her, taking her cape himself. She was escorted into the withdrawing room where there was a blazing fire in a hearth large enough to have accommodated half a tree.

"Perhaps you would enjoy a glass of sherry after such a long journey?" Joshua offered. He was a slender man of little above average height, but possessed of extraordinary grace, and the suppleness and beauty of an actor's voice. He was not hand-

13

some in a traditional sense—his nose was rather too prominent, his features too·mobile—but he had a presence one could not ignore. Every prejudice in her dictated that she dislike him, yet he had sensed her feelings far more accurately than Caroline had.

"Thank you," she accepted. "I would."

He poured a full glass from the crystal decanter and brought it to her. They sat and made conversation about the area, its features, and a little of its history. After half an hour she retired to bed, surprised to find it was still only quarter past ten, a perfectly reasonable hour. She had imagined it to be the middle of the night. It felt like it, and it was irritating to be wrong.

*S*he awoke in the morning after having slept all night almost without moving. From the amount of light coming through the curtains it appeared to be quite late, possibly even after breakfast. She had barely bothered to look at her surroundings when she arrived. Now she saw that it was an agreeable room if a trifle old-fashioned, which normally she approved of. The modern style of having less furniture, making far too much open space—no tassels, frills, carvings, embroidered samplers, and photographs on the walls and on every available surface—she found too sparse. It made a place look as if no one lived there, or if they did, then they had no family or background they dared to display.

But here she was determined not to like anything. She had been put upon, dismissed from such home as she had, and packed off to the seaside like a maid who had got herself with child, and needed to be removed until it all could be dealt with. It was a cruel and irresponsible way to treat one's grandmother. But then all respect had disappeared in modern times. The young had no manners left at all.

She rose and dressed, with Tilly's assistance, then went downstairs, more than ready for something to eat.

Then she found to her fury that Caroline and

Joshua had risen early and gone for a walk toward the beach. She was obliged to have toast and marmalade and a lightly boiled egg, sitting by herself in the dining room at one end of a finely polished mahogany table surrounded by fourteen chairs. It was agreeably warm in the house, and yet she felt cold, not of the body so much as of the mind. She did not belong here. She was acquainted with no one. Even the servants were strangers about whom she knew nothing at all, nor they of her. There was nothing to do and no one to talk to.

When she had finished she stood up and went to the long windows. It looked bitterly cold outside: a wind-ragged sky, clouds torn apart and streaming across a bleached blue as if the color had died in it. The trees were leafless; black branches wet and shivering, bending at the tops. There was nothing in the garden that looked even remotely like a flower. An old man walked along the lane beyond the gate, his hat jammed on his head, scarf ends whipped around his shoulders and flapping behind him. He did not even glance in her direction.

She went into the withdrawing room where the fire was roaring comfortably, and sat down to wait for Caroline and Joshua to return. She was going to be bored to weeping, and there was no help for it. It was a bitter thing to be so abandoned in her old age.

Might there be any sort of social life at all in this godforsaken spot? She rang the bell and in a few moments the maid appeared, a country girl by the look of her.

"Yes, Mrs. Ellison?" she said expectantly.

"What is your name?" Grandmama demanded.

"Abigail, ma'am."

"Perhaps you can tell me, Abigail, what people do here, other than attend church? I presume there is a church?"

"Yes, ma'am. St. Mary the Virgin."

"What else? Are there societies, parties? Do people hold musical evenings, or lectures? Or anything at all?"

The girl looked dumbfounded. "I don't know, ma'am. I'll ask Cook." And before Grandmama could excuse her, she turned and fled.

17

"Fool!" Grandmama said under her breath. Where on earth was Caroline? How long would she walk in a howling gale? She was besotted with Joshua and behaving like a girl. It was ridiculous.

It turned out to be another hour and a half before they came in cheerful, windblown, and full of news about all kinds of local events that sounded provincial and desperately boring. Some old gentleman was going to speak about butterflies at the local church hall. A maiden lady intended to discuss her travels in an unknown area of Scotland, or worse than that, one that had been known and forgotten— doubtless for very good reasons.

"Does anyone play cards?" Grandmama inquired. "Other than Snap, or Old Maid?"

"I have no idea," Caroline replied, moving closer to the fire. "I don't play, so I have never asked."

"It requires intelligence and concentration," Grandmama told her waspishly.

"And a great deal of time on your hands," Caroline added. "And nothing better to fill it with."

"It is better than gossiping about your neighbors," Grandmama rejoined. "Or licking your lips over other people's misfortunes!"

Caroline gave her a chilly look, and controlled her temper with an effort the old lady could easily read in her face. "We shall be having luncheon at one," she observed. "If you care to take a walk, it's wintry, but quite pleasant. And it might rain tomorrow."

"Of course it might rain tomorrow," Grandmama said tartly. "In a climate like ours that is hardly a perspicacious remark. It might rain tomorrow, any day of the year!"

Caroline did not try to mask the irritation she felt, or the effort it cost her not to retaliate. The fact that she had to try so hard gave the old lady a small, perverse satisfaction. Good! At least she still had some semblance of moral duty left! After all, she had been Edward Ellison's wife most of her adult life! She owed Mariah Ellison something!

"Maybe I shall go for a walk this afternoon," she

19

said. "That maid mentioned something about a church, I believe."

"St. Mary the Virgin," Caroline told her. "Yes, it's attractive. Norman to begin with. The soil is very soft here so the tower has huge buttresses supporting it."

"We are on a marsh," Grandmama sniffed. "Probably everything is sinking. It is a miracle we are not up to our knees in mud, or worse!"

*A*nd so it passed for most of the next two long-drawn-out days. Walking in the garden was miserable; almost everything had died back into the earth, the trees were leafless and black and seemed to drip incessantly. It was too late even for the last roses, and too early for the first snowdrops.

There was nothing worth doing, no one to speak to or visit. Those who did call were excruciatingly boring. They had nothing to talk about except people Grandmama did not know, or wish to. They had never been to London and knew nothing of fashion, society, or even current events of any importance in the world.

Then in the middle of the second afternoon a letter arrived for Joshua. He tore it open as they were having tea in the withdrawing room, the fire roaring halfway up the chimney, rain beating on the window in the dark as heavy clouds obscured even the shreds of winter light. There was hot tea on a silver tray and toasted crumpets with butter melted into them and golden syrup on top. Cook had made a particularly good Madeira cake and drop scones accompanied by butter, raspberry jam, and cream so thick one could have eaten it with a fork.

"It's a letter from Aunt Bedelia," Joshua said, looking at Caroline, a frown on his face. "She says Aunt Maude has returned without any warning, from the Middle East, and expects them to put her up for Christmas. But it's quite impossible. They have another guest of great importance whom they cannot turn out to make room for her."

"But it's Christmas!" Caroline said with dismay.

"Surely they can make room somehow? They can't turn her away. She's family. Have they a very small house? Perhaps a neighbor would accommodate her, at least overnight?"

Joshua's face tightened. He looked troubled and a little embarrassed. "No, their house is large, at least five or six bedrooms."

"If they have plenty of room, then what is this about?" Caroline asked, an edge to her voice, as if she feared the answer.

Joshua lowered his eyes. "I don't know. I called her Aunt Bedelia, but actually she is my mother's cousin and I never knew her very well, or her sister Agnes. And Maude left England about the time I was born."

"Left England?" Caroline was astounded. "You mean permanently?"

"Yes, I believe so."

"Why?"

Joshua colored unhappily. "I don't know. No one will say."

"It sounds as if they simply don't want her there,"

22

Grandmama said candidly. "As an excuse it is tissue-thin. What on earth do they expect you to do?"

Joshua looked straight at her and his eyes made her feel uncomfortable, although she had no idea why. He had fine eyes, a dark hazel-brown and very direct.

"Mama-in-law," he replied, using a title for her to which he had no right at all. "They are sending her here."

"That's preposterous!" Grandmama said more loudly than she had intended. "What can you do about it?"

"Make her welcome," he replied. "It will not be difficult. We have two other bedrooms."

Caroline hesitated only a moment. "Of course," she agreed, smiling. "There is plenty of everything. It will be no trouble at all."

Grandmama could hardly believe it! They were going to have this wretched woman here! As if being banished herself, like secondhand furniture, were not bad enough, now she would have to divide what little attention or courtesy she received with some miserable woman, whose own family could not endure her. They would have to cater to her needs and no doubt listen to endless, pointless stories of whatever benighted spot she had been in. It was all really far too much.

"I have a headache," she announced, and rose to her feet. "I shall go and lie down in my room." She stumped over to the door, deliberately leaning heavily on her stick, which actually she did not require.

"Good idea," Caroline agreed tartly. "Dinner will be at eight."

Grandmama could not immediately make up her mind whether to be an hour early, or fifteen minutes late. Perhaps early would be better. If she were late they were just rude enough to start without her, and she would miss the soup.

*M*aude Barrington arrived the following morning, alighting without assistance from the carriage that had brought her and walking with an easy step up to the front door where Joshua and Caroline were waiting for her. Grandmama had chosen to watch from the withdrawing room window, where she had an excellent view without either seeming inquisitive, which was so vulgar, or having to pretend to be pleased and welcoming, which would be farcical. She was furious.

Maude was quite tall and unbecomingly square-shouldered. A gentle curve would have been better, more feminine. Her hair appeared to be of no particular color but at least there was plenty of it. At the moment far too much poked out from underneath a hat that might have been fashionable once, but was now a disaster. She wore a traveling costume that looked as if it had been traipsed around most of the world, especially the hot and dusty parts, and now had no distinguishable shape or color left.

Maude herself could never have been pretty—her features were too strong. Her mouth in particular was anything but dainty. It was impossible to judge accurately how old she was, other than between fifty and sixty. Her stride was that of a young woman—or

25

perhaps a young man would have been more accurate. Her skin was appalling! Either no one had ever told her not to sit in the sun, or she had totally ignored them. It was positively weather-beaten, burned, and a most unfortunate shade of ruddy brown. Heaven only knew where she had been! She looked like a native! No wonder her family did not want her there at Christmas. They might wish to entertain guests, and they could hardly lock her away.

But it was monstrous that they should wish her on Joshua and Caroline, not to mention their guests!

She heard voices in the hallway, and then footsteps up the stairs. No doubt at luncheon she would meet this miserable woman and have to be civil to her.

And so it turned out. One would have expected in the circumstances that the wretched creature would have remained silent, and spoken only when invited to do so. On the contrary, she engaged in conversation in answer to the merest question, and where a word or two would have been quite sufficient.

"I understand you have just returned from

abroad," Caroline said courteously. "I hope it was pleasant?" She left it open for an easy dismissal if it were not a subject Maude wished to discuss.

But apparently it was. A broad smile lit Maude's face, bringing life to her eyes, even passion. "It was marvelous!" she said, her voice vibrant. "The world is more terrible and beautiful than we can possibly imagine, or believe, even after one has seen great stretches of it. There are always new shocks and new miracles around each corner."

"Were you away long?" Caroline asked, apparently forgetting what Joshua had told her. Perhaps she did not wish to appear to Maude as if they had been discussing her.

Maude smiled, showing excellent teeth, even though her mouth was much too big. "Forty years," she replied. "I fell in love."

*C*aroline clearly did not know what to make of that. Maude's hands were innocent of rings and she had introduced herself by her maiden name. The only decent thing to do would have been to avoid the subject, but she had made that impossible. No wonder they had found it intolerable to have her at home. Really, this imposition was too.much!

Maude glanced at Grandmama, and cannot have failed to see the disapproval in her face. "In love with the desert," she explained lightly. "And cities like Marrakech. Have you ever been to a Muslim city in Africa, Mrs. Ellison?"

Grandmama was outraged.

"Certainly not!" she snapped. The question was ridiculous. What decent Englishwoman would do such a thing?

Maude was not to be stopped. She leaned forward over the table, soup forgotten. "It is flat, an oasis facing the Atlas Mountains, and stretches out from the great red tower of the Koutoubya to the blue-palmed fringes and the sands beyond. The Almoravid princes who founded it came with their hordes from the black desert of Senegal,

28

and built palaces of beauty to rival anything on earth."

Caroline and Joshua forgot their soup also, though Grandmama did not.

"They imported masters of chiseled plaster, gilded cedar, and ceramic mosaics," Maude continued. "They created garden beyond garden, courts that led to the other courts and apartments, some high in the sunlight, others deep within walls and shadows and running water." She smiled at some inner delight. "One can walk in the green gloom of a cypress garden. Or breathe in the cool sweetness of a tunnel of jasmine where the light is soft and ever whispering with the sound of water and the murmur of pigeons as they preen themselves. There are alabaster urns, light through jeweled glass, and vermilion doors painted with arabesques in gold." She stopped for a moment to draw breath.

Grandmama felt excluded from this magic that Maude had seen, and from the table where Joshua and Caroline hung on every word. She was totally unnecessary here. She wanted to dismiss it all as foreign, and completely vulgar, but deeply against her will she was fascinated. Naturally she would not dream of saying so.

"And you were allowed to see all these things?" Caroline said in amazement.

"I lived there, for a while," Maude answered, her eyes bright with memory. "It was a superb time, something marvelous or terrible every week. I have never been more intensely alive! The world is so beautiful sometimes I felt as if I could hardly bear it. One gazes at things that hurt with the passion of their loveliness." She smiled but her eyes were misted with tears. "Dusk in a Persian garden, the sun's fire dying on the mountains in purple and umber and rose; the call of the little owls in the coolness of the night; dimpled water over old stones; the perfume of jasmine in the moonlight, rich as sweet oil and clear as the stars; firelight reflected on a copper drum."

She pushed her soup away, too filled with emotion to eat. "I could go on forever. I cannot imagine boredom. Surely it is worse than dying, like some terrible, corroding illness that leaves you neither the joy and the hunger of life nor the release of death. Even that exquisite squeezing of the heart because you cannot hold the light forever is better than not to have seen it or loved it at all."

Grandmama had no idea what on earth she was babbling about! Of course she hadn't. At least not more than a needle-sharp suspicion, like a wound too deep to feel at first, narrow as a blade of envy, cutting almost without awareness.

What would anyone reply to such a thing? There ought to be something, but what was there that met such a . . . a baring of emotion? It was unseemly, like taking off one's clothes in public. No taste at all. That was what came of traveling to foreign parts, and not only foreign but heathen as well. It would be best to ignore the whole episode.

But of course that was quite impossible. The afternoon was cold but quite clear and sunny, although the wind was sharp. Escape was the only solution.

"I shall go for a walk," she announced after luncheon was over. "Perhaps a breath of sea air would be pleasant."

"What an excellent idea," Maude said with enthusiasm. "It is a perfect day. Do you mind if I come with you?"

What could she say? She could hardly refuse. "I'm afraid there will be no jasmine flowers or owls, or sunset over the desert," she replied coolly. "And I daresay you will find it very chilly . . . and . . . ordinary."

A shadow crossed Maude's face, but whether it was the thought of the lonely marsh and sea wind, or the rejection implicit in Grandmama's reply, it was impossible to say.

Grandmama felt a jab of guilt. The woman had been refused the comfort or sanctuary of her own home. She deserved at least civility. "But of course you are welcome to come," she added grudgingly. Blast the woman for putting her in a position where she had to say that.

Maude smiled. "Thank you."

They set out together, well wrapped up with capes and shawls, and of course strong winter boots. Grandmama closed the gate and immediately turned to the lane toward the sea. In the summer it would be overhung with may blossom and the hedgerows deep with flowers. Now it was merely sparse and wet. If the wind were cold enough, after all her living in the desert and such places, the very damp of it alone should be sufficient to make Maude tire of the idea within half an hour at the most.

But Maude was indecently healthy and used to walking. It took Grandmama all her breath and strength to keep up with her. It was roughly a mile to the seashore itself and Maude did not hesitate in her stride even once. She seemed to take it for granted that the old lady would have no difficulty in keeping up, which was extremely irritating and quite thoughtless of her. Grandmama was at least fifteen years older, if not more, and of course she was a lady, not some creature who gallivanted all over the world and went around on her feet as if she had no carriage to her name.

The sky above them was wide and wild, an aching void of blue with just a few clouds like mares' tails shredded across the east on the horizon above the sea. Gulls, dazzling white in the winter sun, wheeled and soared in the air, letting out their shrill cries like noisy children. The wind rippled the grass, flowerless, and everything smelled of salt.

"This is wonderful!" Maude said happily. "I have never smelled anything so clean and so madly alive. It is as if the whole world were full of laughter. It is so good to be back in England. I forgot how the spirit of the land is still so untamed, in spite of all we've done. I was in Snave so short a time I had no chance to get out of the house!"

She is not sane, Grandmama thought to herself grimly. No wonder her family wants to get rid of her!

They breasted the rise and the whole panorama of the English Channel opened up before them, the long stretch of sand, wind, and water bleached till it gleamed bone pale in the light. The surf broke in ranks of white waves, hissing up the shore, foaming like lace, consuming themselves, and rushing back again. Then a moment later they roared in inches higher, never tired of the game. The surface was cold, unshadowed blue, and it stretched out end-lessly till it met the sky. They both knew that France was not much more than twenty miles away, but today the horizon was smudged and softened with mist that blurred the line.

Maude stood with her head high, wind unravel-ing the last of her hair from its pins and all but tak-ing her shawl as well.

"Isn't it glorious?" she asked. "Until this moment I had forgotten just how much I love the sea, its width, its shining, endless possibilities. It's never the same two moments together."

"It always looks the same to me," Grandmama said ungraciously. How could anyone be so point-lessly joyous? It was half-witted! "Cold, wet, and only too happy to drown you if you are foolish enough to give it the chance," she finished.

Maude burst into laughter. She stood on the

shore with her eyes closed, her face lifted upward, smiling, and the wind billowing her shawl and her skirts.

Grandmama swiveled around and stamped back onto the tussock grass, or whatever it was that tangled her feet, and started back along the lane. The woman was as mad as a hatter. It was unendurable that anyone should be expected to put up with her.

$\mathcal{T}$he following day was no better. Maude usurped every moment by regaling them with tales of boating on the Nile, buffalo standing in the water, unnameable insects, and tombs of kings who worshipped animals! All very fashionable, perhaps, but disgusting. Both Caroline and Joshua took hospitality too far, and pretended to be absorbed in it, even encouraging her by asking questions.

Of course the wretched woman obliged, particularly at the dinner table. And all through the roast beef, the Yorkshire pudding and the vegetables, followed by apple charlotte and cream, her captive audience was made to listen to descriptions of ruined gardens in Persia.

"I stood there in the sand of the stream splashing its way over the blue tiles, most of them broken," Maude said, smiling as her eyes misted with memory. "We were quite high up and I looked through the old trees toward the flat, brown plain, and saw those roads: to the east toward Samarkand, to the west to Baghdad, and to the south to Isfahan, and my imagination soared into flight. The very names are like an incantation. As dusk drew around me and the pale colors deepened to gold and fire and that strange richness of porphyry, in my mind I could hear the camel bells and see that odd, lurching gait of theirs as they moved silently like dreams through the coming night, bound on adventures of the soul."

"Isn't it hard sometimes?" Caroline asked, not in criticism but perhaps even sympathy.

"Oh yes! Often," Maude agreed. "You are thirsty, your body aches, and of course you can become so tired you would sell everything you possess for a good night's sleep. But you know it will be worth it. And it always is. The pain is only for a moment, the joy is forever."

And so it went on. Now and then she picked at the macadamia nuts she had brought to the table to share, saying that her family had given them to her, knowing her weakness for them.

Only Joshua accepted.

"Indigestible," Grandmama said, growing more and more irritated by it all.

"I know," Maude agreed. "I daresay I shall be sorry tonight. But a little peppermint water will help."

"I prefer not to be so foolish in the first place," Grandmama said icily.

"Do you have peppermint water?" Caroline asked. "I can give you some, if you wish?"

"I prefer to exercise a little self-control in the first place," Grandmama answered, as if the offer had been addressed to her.

Maude smiled. "Thank you, but I have one dose,

and I'm sure that will be sufficient. There are not so many nuts, and I can't resist them."

She offered the dish to Joshua again and he took two more, and asked her to continue with her tales of Persia.

Grandmama tried to ignore it.

It seemed as if morning, noon, and night they were obliged to talk about or listen to accounts of some alien place, and pretend to be interested. She had been right in the very beginning: This was going to be the worst Christmas of her life. She would never forgive Emily for banishing her here. It was a monstrous thing to have done.

*S*he awoke in the morning to hear one of the maids screeching and banging on the door. Was there no end to the lack of consideration in this house? She sat upright in bed just as the stupid girl burst through into the room, face ashen white, mouth wide open, and eyes like holes in her head.

39

"Pull yourself together, girl!" Grandmama snapped at her. "What on earth is the matter with you? Stand up straight and stop sniveling. Explain yourself!"

The girl made a masterful attempt, took a gulping breath, and spoke in between gasps. "Please ma'am, somethin' terrible 'as 'appened. Miss Barrington's stone cold dead in 'er bed, she is."

"Nonsense!" Grandmama replied. "She was perfectly all right at dinner yesterday evening. She's probably just very deeply asleep."

"No, ma'am, she in't. I knows dead when I sees it, an' when I touches it. Dead as a skinned sheep, she is."

"Don't be impertinent! And disrespectful." Grandmama climbed out of bed and the cold air assailed her flesh through her nightgown. She grasped a robe and glared at the girl. "Don't speak of your betters like farmyard animals," she added for good measure. "I shall go and waken Miss Barrington myself. Where is Tilly?"

"Please, ma'am, she's got a terrible chill."

"Then leave her alone. You may fetch Miss Barrington's tea. And mine also. Fresh, mind. No leftovers."

"Yes, ma'am." The girl was happy to be relieved of responsibility, and of having to tell the master and mistress herself. She did not like the old lady, nor did any of the other servants, miserable old body. Let her do the finding and the telling.

Grandmama marched along the corridor and banged with her closed hand on Maude's door. There was no answer, as she had expected. She would rather enjoy waking her up from a sound, warm sleep, for no good reason but a maid's hysterics.

She pushed the door open, went in, and closed it behind her. If there were going to be a bad tempered scene over the disturbance, better to have it privately.

The room was light, the curtains open.

"Miss Barrington!" she said very clearly.

There was no sound and no movement from the figure in the bed.

"Miss Barrington!" she repeated, considerably more loudly, and more peremptorily.

Still nothing. She walked over to the bed.

Maude lay on her back. Her eyes were closed, but her face was extremely pale, even a little blue, and she did not seem to be moving at all.

Grandmama felt a tinge of alarm. Drat the woman! She went a little closer and reached out to touch her, ready to leap back and apologize if her eyes flew open and she demanded to know what on earth Grandmama thought she was doing. It was really inexcusable to place anyone in this embarrassing position. Gadding about in heathen places had addled her wits, and all sense of being an Englishwoman of any breeding at all.

The flesh that met her fingers was cold and quite stiff. There could be no doubt whatsoever that the stupid maid was correct. Maude was quite dead, and had been so probably most of the night.

Grandmama staggered backward and sat down very hard on the bedroom chair, suddenly finding it difficult to breathe. This was terrible. Quite unfair.

42

First of all Maude had arrived, uninvited, and disrupted everything. Now she had died and made it even worse. They would have to spend Christmas in mourning! Instead of reds and golds, and carol singing, feasting, making merry, they would all be in black, mirrors covered, whispering in corners and being miserable and afraid. Servants were always afraid when there was a death in the house. Most likely Cook would give notice, and then where would they be? Eating cold meats!

She stood up. She had no reason to feel sad. It would be absurd. She had barely met Maude Barrington, certainly she had not known her. And there was nobody to feel sorry for. Her own family had not wanted her, even at Christmas, for heaven's sake! Perhaps they were tired of the endless stories about the bazaar at Marrakech and the Persian gardens or the boats on the Nile and the tombs of kings who had lived and died a thousand years or more before the first Christmas on earth, and worshipped gods of their own making, who had the heads of beasts.

But then her family could not have been nice

43

people or they would not have turned Maude away at Christmas. They would have listened with affectation of interest, as Caroline and Joshua had done. Indeed, as she had done herself. She could imagine the water running over blue tiles in the sun. She did not know what jasmine smelled like, but no doubt it was beautiful. And to give her credit, Maude had loved the English countryside just as much, even in December. It was wretched that she should have died among people who were veritable strangers, taking her in out of charity because it was Christmas. Her own had not loved or wanted her.

Grandmama stood still in the middle of the bedroom with its flowered chintzes, heavy furniture, and dead ashes in the grate, and a hideous reality took her breath away. She herself was here out of charity as well, unloved and unwanted by anyone else. Caroline and Joshua were good people; that was why they had taken her in, not because they cared for her. They did not love her, they did not even like her. No one did. She knew that as well as she knew the feel of ice on her skin and the cold wind that cut to the bone.

She opened the door, her fingers fumbling on the handle, breath tight in her chest. Outside in the passage, she walked unsteadily to the other wing of the house, and Joshua and Caroline's room. She knocked more loudly than she had intended, and when Caroline opened the door to her she found her voice caught in her throat.

"The maid came and told me Maude died in the night." She gulped. Really this much emotion was ridiculous! She had barely known the woman. "I am afraid it is true. I saw her myself."

Caroline looked stricken, but she could see from the old lady's face that there was no doubt. At her age she had seen enough death not to mistake it.

"You had better come into the dressing room and sit down," Caroline said gently. "I'll have Abby fetch you a cup of tea. I'm so sorry you had to see her." She held out her arm to support Grandmama as she stumbled across the room and into the wide, warm dressing room with its seats and wardrobes and one of Caroline's gowns already laid out for the day. Grandmama was angry with herself for being so close to weeping. It must be the shock. It was most unpleasant to grow old. "Thank you," she said grudgingly.

Caroline helped her into one of the chairs and looked at her for a moment as if to make sure she were not going to faint. Then, as Grandmama glared back at her, she turned and went out to set in motion all the endless arrangements that would have to be made.

The old lady sat still. The maid brought her tea and poured it for her, encouraging her to drink it. It was refreshing, spreading warmth from the inside. But it changed nothing. Why was Maude dead? She had been in almost offensively good health the short time she had been here. What had she died of? Certainly not old age. Not any kind of wasting away or weakening. She could march like a soldier, and eat like one, too.

She closed her eyes and in her mind she saw

46

Maude again, lying motionless in the bed. She did not look terrified or disturbed, or even in any pain. But there had been an empty bottle on the table beside her. Probably the peppermint water. The stupid woman had given herself indigestion guzzling all the nuts, just as Grandmama had told her she would. Why were some people so stupid? No self-control.

She drank the last of her tea and stood up. The room swayed around her for a moment. She took several deep breaths, then went out of the dressing room and back along the corridor to Maude's bedroom. There was no one else in sight. They must all be busy, and Caroline would be doing what she could to settle the staff. Staff always behaved erratically when someone died. At least one maid would have fainted, and someone would be having hysterics. As if there were not enough to do!

She opened the door and slipped inside quickly, closing it after her, then turned to look. Yes, she had been quite right, there was an empty bottle on the bedside table. She walked over and picked it up. It

47

said "peppermint water" on the label, but just to be certain she took out the cork and sniffed it experimentally. It was quite definitely peppermint, clean and sharp, filling her nose.

Maude had brought it with her, with only one dose left. She must use it regularly. Stupid woman! If she ate with any sense it would not be necessary. Curious that they should have it even in Arabia, or Persia, or wherever it was she had come from most recently. And the label was in English, too.

She looked at it again. It was printed with the name and address of a local apothecary in Rye, just a few miles away around the Dungeness headland.

But Maude had said she had not left Snave, in fact not had the chance to go out at all. So someone had given it to her, with one dose in it. Presumably that was to treat the result of eating the macadamia nuts! But one dose? How very odd. Especially when they could have been all but certain that she would require it. Surely no household would be short of so ordinary a commodity, especially over Christmas, when it could be guaranteed that people would overindulge? There was something about it that was peculiar.

She picked up the bottle again and, keeping it concealed in the folds of her skirt, returned to her room, where she hid it in the drawer with her underclothes.

Then, with Tilly's assistance, she dressed in the darkest clothes she had with her—not quite black, but a gray that in the winter light would pass for it. She went downstairs to face the day.

Caroline was in the withdrawing room before the fire. Joshua had gone to fetch the local doctor so that the necessary authorities could be satisfied.

"Are you all right, Mama-in-law?" she asked anxiously. "It is a terrible experience for you."

"It was a much worse experience for Maude!" Grandmama replied with tart candor. There were troubling thoughts in her mind, but she was not quite certain exactly what they were. She could not share them, especially with Caroline, who had never detected anything, as far as she knew. She might even wish to avoid scandal, and refuse even to consider it, and Maude deserved better than that! Perhaps it rested with Mariah Ellison, and no one else, to face the truth.

A few minutes later the doctor arrived and was taken upstairs.

"Heart failure," he informed them when he came down again. "Very sad. She seemed in excellent health otherwise."

"She was!" Grandmama said quickly, before anyone else could reply. "She was a world traveler, walked miles, rode horses, and even camels. She never spoke of any ailment at all."

"It can come without warning," the doctor said gently.

"An attack that kills?" Grandmama demanded. "She did not look as if she were in that kind of agony!"

"No," he agreed with a slight frown. "I think it more likely that her heart simply slowed and then stopped."

"Slowed and then stopped?" Grandmama said incredulously.

50

"Mama-in-law!" Caroline remonstrated.

"I think it may well have been peaceful," the doctor said to Grandmama. "If that is of comfort to you? Were you very fond of her?"

"She barely knew her!" Caroline said tartly.

"Yes, I was fond of her." Grandmama contradicted her, equally tartly.

"I'm very sorry." The doctor was still gentle. He turned to Joshua. "If I can assist with arrangements, of course I shall be happy to."

"Thank you," Joshua accepted.

"We shall have to inform the rest of her family," Grandmama said loudly. "Bedelia whatever-her-name-is."

"I have been thinking how on earth I can write such a letter," Caroline acknowledged. "What to say that will make it . . . *better* sounds absurd. If I simply say that we are terribly sad to inform them, will that be best?" She looked worried, and "sad" would be no exaggeration. There was a grief in her face that was quite genuine.

Grandmama's mind was racing. What was she

51

allowing herself to think? Heart slowing down? Nuts that everyone knew were indigestible? One dose of peppermint water? Had Maude been murdered? Preposterous! That's what came of allowing one's daughter to marry a policeman. This was Caroline's fault. If she had been a mother of the slightest responsibility at all she would never have permitted Charlotte to do such a thing! Thomas Pitt, as a law enforcement official, was not a suitable husband. He had absolutely nothing to commend him, except possibly height?

But if someone like Pitt could solve a crime, then most certainly Grandmama could. She would not be outwitted by a gamekeeper's son, half her age!

And if Maude Barrington had been murdered, then Mariah Ellison would see that whoever had done so was brought to justice and answered to the last penny for such an act. Maude might have been an absurd woman, and a complete nuisance, but there was such a thing as justice.

Grandmama felt as if a light and a warmth had

gone out of the air and a heaviness settled in its place, which she did not understand at all.

"You should not write," she said firmly to Caroline. "It is far too dreadful and sudden a thing to put in a letter, when apparently they live so near. Snake, isn't it? Or something like that."

"Snave," Caroline corrected. "Yes. It's about four or five miles away. Still well within the Marsh. Do you think I should go over and tell them myself?" Her face tightened. "Yes, of course you're right."

"No!" Grandmama said quickly. "I agree it should be done personally. After all, she was their sister, however they treated her. Perhaps they will even feel an overwhelming guilt now." She thought that extremely unlikely. They were obviously quite shameless. "But I will go. You have arrangements to make for Christmas, and Joshua would miss you. And I imagine I actually spent more time with Maude than you did anyway. I may be able to be of some comfort, inform them a little of her last days." She sounded sententious and she knew it. She watched

53

Caroline's expression acutely. It would be a disaster if she were to come, too; in fact it would make the entire journey a waste of time. In order to have a hope of accomplishing anything she would be obliged to tell Caroline what she suspected with increasing certainty the more she considered it.

A spark of hope lit in Caroline's eyes. "But that is a great deal to ask of you, Mama-in-law."

Of course she was dubious. Mariah Ellison had never in her life been known to discomfort herself on someone else's behalf. It was totally out of character. But then Caroline did not know her very well. For nearly twenty years they had lived under the same roof, and for all of it Grandmama had lived a lie. She had hidden her misery and self-loathing under the mantle of widowhood. But how could she have done anything else? The shame of her past continually burned inside her as if the physical pain were still raw and bleeding and she could barely walk. She had had to lie, for her son's sake. And the lie had grown bigger and bigger inside her, estranging her from everyone.

54

"You did not ask it of me," she said more sharply than she meant to. "I have offered. It is the answer that makes the greatest sense." Should she add that Caroline and Joshua had made her welcome here and it was a small repayment? No. Caroline would never believe that. They had allowed her in, she was not welcome, nor was she stupid enough to imagine that she could be. Caroline would be suspicious.

"I have nothing else to do," she added more realistically. "I am bored." That was believable. She was certainly not about to admit to Caroline, of all people, that she actually had admired Maude Barrington and felt a terrible anger that she should have been abandoned by her family, and very possibly murdered by one of them. She waited for Caroline's reaction. She must not push too hard.

"Are you certain you would not mind?" Caroline was still unconvinced.

"Quite certain," she replied. "It is still a pleasant morning. I shall compose myself, have a little luncheon, and then go. That is, if you can spare the carriage to take me there? I doubt there is any other way of travel in this benighted spot!" A sudden idea occurred to her. "Perhaps you fear that . . ."

"No," Caroline said quickly. "It is most generous of you, and I think entirely appropriate. It shows far more care than any letter could do, no matter how sincere, or well written. Of course the coachman will take you. As you say, the weather is still quite clement. This afternoon would be perfect. I do appreciate it."

Grandmama smiled, trying to show less triumph than she felt. "Then I shall prepare myself," she replied, finishing her tea and rising to her feet. She intended to remain at Snave for as long as it required to discover the truth of Maude's death, and to prove it. Knowing alone was hardly adequate. Her visit might well stretch into several days. She must succeed. It was not a matter of sentimentality, it was a matter of principle, and she was a woman to whom such things mattered.

PART TWO

. . . .

$\mathcal{T}$HE JOURNEY WAS BUMPY AND COLD, EVEN
with a traveling rug wrapped around from the waist
downward. There was a bitter, whining wind coming in off the sea, though now and again it cleared
the sky of clouds. The light was chill and hard over
the low-lying heath. This was the invasion coast
where Julius Caesar had landed fifty-five years before the birth of Christ. No such thing as Christmas
then! He had gone home and been murdered the following year. That had been by his own people too,
those he had known and trusted for years.

Eleven centuries after that, William, Duke of
Normandy, had landed with his knights and bow-
men and killed King Harold at Hastings, just around
the coast from here. Somehow she was faintly satis-

fied with Caesar coming. Rome had been the center of the world then. England had been proud to be part of that Empire. But William's invasion still rankled, which was silly, since it was the best part of a thousand years ago! But it was the last time England had been conquered, and it annoyed her.

King Philip of Spain's armada would probably have landed here too, if the wind had not destroyed it. And Napoleon Bonaparte. Only he went to Russia instead, which had proved to be a bad idea.

Was this a bad idea, too? Arrogant, stupid, the result of a fevered imagination? But how could she possibly turn back? She would look like a complete fool! To be disliked was bad enough. To be despised as well—or worse, pitied—would be unendurable.

Looking out of the carriage window as the sky darkened and the already lowering sun was smeared with gray, she could not imagine why anyone would choose to be here if they did not have to. Except Maude, of course! She thought these flat, wide spaces and wind-raging skies were beautiful with their banners of cloud, marsh grasses, and air that always smelled of salt.

Perhaps she did not remember it frozen solid, or so shrouded in fog that you could not make out·your hand in front of your face! That was exactly what would be useful now, some dreadful weather, so she could not return to St. Mary in the Marsh for several days. She had undertaken a very big task, and the more she thought of it the bigger it seemed, and the more hopeless. It was in a way a comfort that she could not turn back, or she might have. She had no idea what these people were like, and not a shred of authority to back up what she was intending to do. Or to try. It might have been better after all if Charlotte were here. She had meddled so often surely she had acquired a knack for it by now?

But she wasn't here. Grandmama would have to make the best of it by herself. Forward regardless. She had intelligence and determination, which might be enough. Oh—and right on her side as well, of course. It was monstrous that Maude Barrington should have been murdered, if she had been. But whatever the truth of that, they had still turned her away, and at Christmas. That in itself was an unforgivable offense, and on Maude's behalf, she felt it to the core.

The distance was covered far too quickly. It was only a handful of miles, forty minutes' journey at a brisk trot, far less as the crow flew. Every lane seemed to double back on itself as if to circumnavigate each field and cross every ditch twice. The sky had cleared again and the light was long and low, making the shivering grass bright and casting networks of shadow through the bare trees when the carriage drove into the tiny village of Snave. There was really only one big house. The rest seemed to be cottages and farm buildings. Why in heaven's name would anyone choose to live here? It was no more than a widening in the road.

She took a deep breath to steady her nerves and waited with pounding heart for the coachman to open the door for her. A dozen times she had rehearsed what she was going to say, and now when

62

she needed it, it had gone completely out of her mind.

Outside in the driveway the wind was like a knife-edge and she found herself rocking on her feet in the strength of it. She grasped onto her cloak to keep it from flying away, and stamped up to the front door, leaning heavily on her stick. The coachman pulled on the doorbell for her, and stood back to wait.

It was answered almost immediately. Someone must have seen the carriage arrive. An extremely ordinary-looking butler spoke to her civilly enough.

"Good afternoon," she replied. "I am Mrs. Mariah Ellison. Mr. Joshua Fielding, with whom Miss Barrington was staying, is my son-in-law." The exact nature of their relationship could be explained later, if necessary. "I am afraid I have extremely distressing news to bring to the family, the sort of thing that can really only be told in person."

He looked alarmed. "Oh, dear. Please do come in, Mrs. Ellison." He opened the door wider for her and backed away a little.

"Thank you," she accepted. "May I ask you the favor of a little warmth and refreshment for my coachman also, and perhaps water for the horses, and at least in the meantime, shelter from this rather cutting wind?"

"Of course! Of course! Do you . . ." He swallowed. "Do you have Miss Barrington with you?"

"No, indeed not," she replied, following him inside after a brief glance behind her to make certain that the coachman had heard, and would drive around to the stables and make himself known.

Inside the hall she could not help but glance around. It was not a house of London fashion; nevertheless it was well furnished and extremely comfortable. The floor was very old oak, stained dark with possibly centuries of use. The walls were paneled, but lighter, and hung with many paintings, mercifully not the usual portraits of generations of forebears with expressions sour enough to turn the milk. Instead they were glowing still lifes of fruit and flowers, and one or two pastoral scenes with enormous skies and restful cows. At least some-

64

one had had very good taste. It was also blessedly warm.

"The family is all together, ma'am," the butler continued gravely. "Would you perhaps prefer to tell Mrs. Harcourt this news in private? She is Miss Barrington's elder sister."

"Thank you. She will know best how to inform the rest of the family."

The butler thereupon led her to a doorway off to the side. He opened it to show her into a very agreeable room, lighting the lamps for her and poking up a fire, which had almost gone out. He placed a couple of pieces of coal on it judiciously, then excused himself and left. He did not offer her tea. Perhaps he was too alarmed at the news, even though he did not yet know what it was. Judging by his manner, he expected a disgrace rather than a tragedy—which in itself was interesting.

She stood by the fire, trying to warm herself. Her heart was still thumping and she had difficulty keeping her breath steady.

The door opened and a woman of great beauty

came in, closing it behind her. She was perhaps sixty, with auburn hair softening to rather more gold than copper, and the clear, fair skin that so often goes with such coloring. Her features were refined, her eyes large and blue. Her mouth was perfectly shaped. She bore little resemblance to Maude. It was not easy to think of them as sisters. No one would have called Maude beautiful. What had made her face so attractive was intelligence, and a capacity for feeling and imagination, a soul of inner joy. There was no echo of such things in this woman's face. In fact she looked afraid, and angry. Her clothes were up to the moment in fashion, and perfectly cut with the obligatory shoulders and high crowned sleeves.

"Good afternoon, Mrs. Ellison," she said with cool politeness. "I am Bedelia Harcourt. My butler tells me that you have driven all the way from St. Mary in the Marsh with unfortunate news about my sister. I hope she has not"—she hesitated delicately—"embarrassed you?"

Grandmama felt a fury of emotion rise up inside

her so violently she was overwhelmed by it, almost giddy. She wanted to rage at the woman, even slap her perfect face. However, that would be absurd and the last way to detect anything. She was quite sure Pitt would not have been so . . . so amateur!

"I'm so sorry, Mrs. Harcourt." She controlled herself with a greater effort than she had ever exercised over her temper before. "But the news I have is very bad indeed. That is why I came personally rather than have anyone write a letter to you." She watched intently to see if there were the slightest betraying foreknowledge in Bedelia's face, and saw nothing. "I am afraid Miss Barrington passed away in her sleep last night. I am so very sorry." That at least was sincere. She was amazed how sorry she was.

Bedelia stared at her as if the words had no meaning that she could grasp. "Passed away?" she repeated. She put her hand up to her mouth. "Maude? But she never even said she was ill! I should have known! Oh, how terrible. How very terrible."

"I am sorry," Grandmama said yet again. "The maid knocked on my door. I was in the same part of the house. I went to her immediately, but Miss Barrington must have died early in the night. She was . . . quite cold. We called a doctor, naturally."

"Oh, dear." Bedelia stepped backward and almost folded up into the chair behind her. It was a collapse, and yet it was oddly graceful. "Poor Maude. How I wish she had said something. She was too . . . too reticent . . . too brave."

Grandmama remembered Bedelia's letter to Joshua saying that she would not have Maude in the house because they had other important guests, and she found it extremely difficult not to remind her of that. But to do so would make an enemy of her, and then gaining any knowledge would be impossible. Really, this detecting required greater sacrifices than she had foreseen.

"I am deeply sorry for coming bearing such painful news," she said instead. "I cannot imagine what a shock it must be for you. I spent a little time with Miss Barrington and she was a delightful person. And I admit that to me she appeared to be in the most excellent health. I can understand your shock."

Bedelia raised her eyes and looked up at her. "She . . . she had lived abroad for some time, in very harsh climates. It must have affected her more than we appreciated. Possibly more than she appreciated herself."

Grandmama sat down in the other chair opposite Bedelia. "She spoke somewhat of Marrakech, and I believe Persia. And Egypt also. Was she there for some time?"

"Years," Bedelia replied, straightening up. "Since she left, shortly before I was married, and that is all but forty years ago. She must have lived in a style far more . . . injurious to her health than we had realized. Perhaps she did not fully know it herself."

"Perhaps not," Grandmama agreed. Then a thought occurred to her. Sitting here being pleasant and questioning nothing was unlikely to gain her any knowledge. Pitt would have done better. "Or maybe she was only too well aware that she was not in good health, and that is why she returned to England, and her family, the people to whom she was closest in the world?"

Bedelia's magnificent eyes opened wider and were momentarily as hard and cold as the midwinter sea.

Grandmama looked back at her without so much as blinking.

Bedelia let out her breath slowly. "I suppose you could be right. No such thought had crossed my mind. Like you, I imagined her to be in the most excellent health. It seems we were both tragically mistaken."

"She said nothing that could lead you to expect this?" Grandmama felt most discourteous to press the matter, but justice came before good manners.

Bedelia hesitated, as if she could not make up her mind how to answer. "I can think of nothing," she said after a moment. "I confess I am utterly devastated. My mind does not seem to function at all. I have never lost anyone so . . . so very close to me before."

"Your parents are still alive?" Grandmama said in amazement.

"Oh, no," Bedelia corrected herself quickly. "I meant of my own generation. My parents were excellent people, of course! But distant. A sister is . . . is very dear. Perhaps one only realizes it when they are gone. The void left behind is greater than one can conceive beforehand."

You are overplaying it, Grandmama thought to herself. You wouldn't even have her in the house! Outwardly she smiled. It was a totally artificial expression.

"You are very naturally suffering from shock," she commiserated. "When one's own generation passes away it is a reminder of mortality, the shadow of death across one's own path. I remember how I felt when my husband died." So she did—the most marvelous liberation of her life. Even if she could tell no one, and had to pretend to be devastated, and wear mourning for the rest of her days, like the Queen.

"Oh, I am sorry!" Bedelia said quickly. "You poor

71

soul! And now you have come all the way in this weather to bring this news to me personally. And I am sitting here without even offering you tea. My wits are completely scattered. I still have my beloved Arthur, how can I complain of anything? Perhaps poor Maude has gone to a better place. She was never a happy creature. I shall allow that to be my comfort." She rose to her feet a trifle unsteadily.

"Thank you, that is most kind of you," Grandmama accepted. "I must admit it has been a dreadful day, and I am quite exhausted. I am so glad you have your husband. He will no doubt be a great strength to you. One can be very . . . alone."

Bedelia's face softened in concern. "I can scarcely imagine it. I have always been so fortunate. This room is a little chill. Would you care to come through to the withdrawing room where it is far warmer? We shall all take tea and consider what must be done. Of course if you prefer to return to St. Mary in the Marsh as soon as possible, we shall understand."

"Thank you," Grandmama said weakly. "I should

be most grateful for as long a rest as I may take, without imposing upon you. And certainly tea would be very welcome." She also rose to her feet, as unsteadily. as she could without risking actually falling over, which would be ridiculous, and only to be resorted to if all else failed.

Bedelia led the way back across the hall to the withdrawing room, and Grandmama followed, refusing to offer her arm to the younger woman. She must be consistent about her own exhaustion or she might be disbelieved.

The withdrawing room was spacious also and the warmth from the enormous fire engulfed them both as soon as they entered. There was too much furniture for more modern tastes; carved sideboards, heavily stuffed sofas and chairs with antimacassars on all of them. There were also hard-backed chairs by the walls with fat leather-upholstered seats and slightly bowed legs, and several footstools with tassels around the edges. A brightly colored Turkish rug was worn duller where possibly generations of feet had passed. On the walls were embroidered samplers, paintings of every variety large and small, and several stuffed animals in glass cases, even a case full of butterflies as dry as silk. The colors were mostly hot: golds, browns, and ocher reds. Caroline would have thought it oppressive. Grandmama was annoyed to find it very agreeable, indeed almost familiar.

The people in it were entirely another matter. She was introduced to them, and Bedelia was obliged to explain her presence to them.

"My dears." Everyone turned to her. "This is Mrs. Ellison, who has most graciously come in person rather than send a message to tell us some terrible news." She turned to Grandmama. "I am certain you would prefer to sit down, perhaps by the fire? May I introduce you to my sister, Mrs. Agnes Sullivan." She indicated a woman whose superficial resemblance to her was explained by the relationship. They appeared of a similar height, although Mrs. Sullivan did not rise as the three men had done. Her coloring had probably been similar to Bedelia's in youth, but now it was scattered with more gray and the dark areas were duller. Her features were less finely chiseled, and her expression, apart from a certain sadness, was much gentler. Her clothes, although well cut, managed to look commonplace.

"How do you do, Mrs. Sullivan," Grandmama said formally.

"And her husband, Mr. Zachary Sullivan," Bedelia continued.

Zachary bowed very slightly. He was a slender man with brown hair, now graying at the temples. His face also was pleasant, but marked by a certain sense of loss, as if he had failed to achieve something that mattered to him too much to forget.

"My daughter-in-law, Clara, and my son, Randolph," Bedelia continued, indicating in one sweep a young man whose coloring resembled hers, although his features did not, being considerably stronger and blunter. The woman beside him was handsome enough in a powerful way, dark-haired, dark-eyed, and with brows rather too heavy.

Bedelia smiled, in spite of the occasion. "And my husband Arthur," she finished, turning to a remark-

75

ably handsome man whose dark hair was now iron gray. His eyes held a wit and life that captured attention instantly, and his smile at Grandmama showed perfect teeth.

"Welcome to Snave, Mrs. Ellison," he said warmly. "I am sorry it is distressing news that brings you. May I offer you tea, or would you prefer something more robust, such as a glass of sherry? I know it is early, but the wind is miserable and you have to be chilled, and perhaps tired also."

"That is most generous of you, and understanding." Grandmama made her way over to the fire, and the seat Zachary had left vacant for her. Whoever was guilty of having killed Maude, if indeed someone had, she hoped it was not Arthur Harcourt.

"What is it you have to tell us, Mrs. Ellison?" Agnes Sullivan asked with a tremor in her voice.

"I am afraid Miss Barrington passed away in her sleep last night," Grandmama replied solemnly. "I believe it must have been peaceful, and she seemed to be in excellent health and spirits right until the last moment. She made no remark as to feeling unwell. I am so sorry." She glanced rapidly from one to the other of them, trying to judge their reactions. Not that she was sure she could tell guilt from shock anyway, or from grief for that matter.

Zachary looked least surprised, rather more puzzled, as if he had not fully understood the meaning of her words.

Agnes gave a gasp and her hand flew to her mouth in a gesture of stopping herself from crying out, oddly like Bedelia's five minutes before. She was very pale.

"Poor Aunt Maude," Randolph murmured. "I'm so sorry, Mama." He looked at Bedelia with concern.

Clara Harcourt said nothing. Perhaps as one who had barely known Maude she felt it more appropriate not to speak.

Arthur Harcourt's olive complexion was a muddy color, neither white nor gray, and his eyes seemed to have lost focus. What was he feeling? Was that the horror of guilt now that the act was real and not merely dreamed?

"I am sorry to bring you such news." Grandmama

77

felt compelled to fill in the silence that seemed to choke the room. The mere flickering of the fire sounded like a sheet torn in the wind.

"It . . . it was good of you," Agnes stammered. "Such a terrible thing for you . . . a guest in your house . . . a virtual stranger."

Suddenly a quite brilliant idea lit in Grandmama's mind. It went up like a flare of light. She could almost feel the heat of it in her face. "Oh, not at all!" she said with feeling. "We talked for hours, Maude and I." She was stunned at her own audacity. "She told me so much about . . . oh, of any number of things. Her feelings, her experiences, where she had been and the people she had met." She waved her hands for emphasis. "Believe me, there are those I have been acquainted with for years about whom I know far less. I have never made such excellent friends with anyone so rapidly, or with such a natural affection." That was a monstrous lie—wasn't it? "I must admit her trust in me was most heartwarming, and that was a great deal the reason why I could not possibly allow anyone else to come to you now," she hurried on. "I shall never forget Maude, or the confidence she placed in me regarding her life and its meaning." It was an extraordinary feeling to have made such statements as if they were true, as if she and Maude had become instant and total friends.

She realized with a flutter of absurdity, even of sweetness, that it was not completely a lie. Maude had told her more of meaning in a couple of days than most of her acquaintances had in years, although not the personal details she implied to her wretched family!

And grudgingly, like the lancing of a boil, she admitted that she had actually liked Maude, at least more than she had expected to, considering the gross imposition of having her in Caroline's home for Christmas—uninvited!

Bedelia stared at her incredulously. "Really? But you knew her for barely a day . . . or two!"

"But we had little to do but talk to each other. She was fascinating at the luncheon and dinner table, but even more so when we were out walking,

79

just the two of us. I was very flattered that she should tell me so much. I found myself speaking equally frankly to her, and finding her most gentle and free from critical judgment. It was a quite . . . quite wonderful experience," she added too quickly. She said it purely to frighten them into believing she knew something of whoever it was who had murdered Maude, if indeed they had. This was a deviousness added to her new grief. She intended them to think her too desolate to consider the long carriage ride in the dark to go home again!

She also found, to her dismay, that she wished quite painfully that it were all true. She had not been anything like such friends with Maude. Nor had she confided in her the agonies of her own life, the shame she had carried for years that she had not had the courage to leave her abusive husband and flee abroad as his first wife had done!

But it was startlingly sweet to think that Maude might have sympathized rather than despising her for a coward, as she despised herself. There would have been nothing in the world more precious than a friend who understood. But that was idiotic! Maude would never have submitted herself to such treatment.

"Then you grieve with us," Arthur said gently, intruding across her thoughts. "Please feel welcome here, and do not consider the journey back to St. Mary tonight. It will be dark quite soon, and you must be both tired and distressed. I am certain we can supply anything you might need, such as a nightgown and toiletries. And of course we have plenty of room."

"Since Lord Woollard has left, the guest room is perfectly available," Clara put in quickly.

"Oh yes, the guest who was staying with you before, when poor Maude arrived," Grandmama noted. "How very kind of you. I really should be most grateful. May I inform my coachman of your generosity, so he can return to St. Mary? It is possible Mr. and Mrs. Fielding may require the coach tomorrow. And of course if they do not hear, they may worry that something has happened to me."

"Naturally," Arthur agreed. "Would you care to

tell him yourself, or shall I have the butler inform him?"

"That would be very kind of you," she accepted. "And ask him to tell Mrs. Fielding of your graciousness, and that I am perfectly well . . . just . . . just so grieved."

"Of course." Now the die was cast. What on earth was she thinking of? Her stomach lurched and her mouth was dry.

She sipped the excellent sherry she had been given and allowed herself to bask for a moment in its delicious warmth. She had embarked upon an adventure. That is the way she must look at it. She was still angry that Maude had been treated so appallingly, whether it included murder or not, although she really thought it might! And she was tired and grieved, quite truly grieved. Maude had been too full of life to die, too joyous in tasting every good experience to give it up so soon. And no one should be unwanted by their own, whatever the reason.

What was the reason? Who in this comfortable

82

room with its roaring fire, its silver tea tray and overstuffed sofas, had wanted Maude out of the house? And why had the rest of them allowed it? Were they all guilty of something? Secrets so terrible they would kill to hide them? They looked so perfectly innocuous, even ordinary. Good heavens, what wickedness can lie beneath a smiling exterior as commonplace as a slice of bread!

Later a maid showed her to the spare bedroom. It was warm and agreeably furnished with a four-poster bed, heavy curtains of wine brocade, another red Turkish carpet, and plenty of carved oak furniture. A very fine ewer with painted flowers on it held fresh water. There was a matching bowl for washing in and on the stand beside them plenty of thick towels with which to dry oneself. There was no way of telling whether Lord Woollard, or anyone else, had occupied it recently. But she would take the opportunity to see how many guest rooms there were so she would know whether Maude could have been accommodated had they wished to. She tiptoed along the corridor, feeling like a sneak thief, and cautiously tried the handles and opened the doors of the two other rooms. They were both bedrooms, and both presently unoccupied. So much for that lie.

She returned to her own room, her hands trembling a little and her knees weak. She sat down. Then another idea struck her. She opened the small cupboard beside the bed, and found lavender water, a vial with a couple of doses of laudanum, and a full bottle of peppermint water! The cork was jammed in tightly, but more telling than that, there was a film of dust over it. It had not been purchased in the last couple of days since Maude had left! So much for being out of it! That put a new complexion on Maude's single dose! Had there been something else in it, disguised by the pungent taste? And the macadamia nuts to make her require it? She closed the cupboard door and sat down heavily on the bed. So far everything had gone quite marvelously. But there was a great deal to do. She must ascertain if Maude had indeed been murdered, if so by whom, precisely how—and it would hardly be complete if she did not also know why! How could she possibly do all that before they politely sent her home? Pitt had no challenge of mere hours in which to solve his cases! He went on for days! Sometimes even weeks! And he had the authority to ask questions and demand answers—not necessarily true ones, of course. She was going to have to be much cleverer than he was! It might not be quite so easy as she had assumed.

Still, so far, so good. And she was much too angry to give up.

$\mathcal{H}$owever, later on, when in ordinary circumstances she would have been changing for dinner, she was overwhelmed by the strangeness of her surroundings and all the events that had occurred in the last few days. This time last week she had been in London with Emily and Jack, as usual. Then she had been upheaved and sent to St. Mary in the Marsh. She had barely settled to accepting that when Maude Barrington had arrived. That was almost accommodated, and Maude died, without the slightest warning of any sort!

Grandmama had been the only one to perceive that it might well not be natural, but a crime, the most appalling of all crimes, and there was no one else but herself to find justice for it. And here she was sitting quite alone in a house full of strangers, at least one of whom she was now convinced was, a murderer. Added to that she had not even fresh underclothes or a nightgown to sleep in. They had offered to lend her something, but all the women in the family were at least three or four inches taller than she was, and thinner as well, by more inches than that! She must have taken leave of her wits. Certainly she could never admit any of this to Caroline! Or anybody else. They'd have her locked up.

There was a knock on the door and she started so violently she gulped and gave herself hiccups.

"Come in!" she said, hiccuping again.

It was the housekeeper, to judge from her black dress, lace cap, and the cluster of keys hanging from her waist. She was short and rather stout, exactly Grandmama's own build.

"Good evening, ma'am," she said very agreeably. "I'm Mrs. Ward, the housekeeper. It was very good of you to come personally with the sad news. It must have inconvenienced you very much."

"Her death grieved me," Grandmama answered frankly, relieved that it was a servant, not one of the family. "To come and tell you personally seemed no more than the obvious thing to do. She died among strangers, even if they were people who liked her immediately, and very much."

Mrs. Ward's face colored as if with considerable emotion she felt obliged to hide. "I'm very glad you did," she said with a tremble in her voice. She blinked rapidly.

"You knew her," Grandmama deduced. She made herself smile. "You must be grieving as well."

"Yes, ma'am. I was a maid here when I was a girl. Miss Maude would have been sixteen then."

"And Mrs. Harcourt?" Grandmama asked shamelessly. She must detect! Time would not wait upon niceties.

"Oh, eighteen she was. And such a beauty as you've never seen.".

Grandmama looked at the housekeeper's face. There was no light in it. She might respect Bedelia Harcourt, even be loyal to her, but she did not like her as she had Maude. That was something to remember. Servants said little, good ones seldom said anything at all, but they saw just about everything.

"And Mrs. Sullivan?"

"Oh, she was only thirteen, just a schoolgirl, all ink and books and clumsiness, but full of enthusiasm, poor girl. The governess was always trying to get her to walk with the dictionary on her head, but she kept losing it."

"Dictionary?"

"Only for the weight of it! Miss Agnes was perfectly accurate with her spelling. But that's all in the past. Long ago." She blinked rapidly again. "I just came to say that if there is anything I can get for you, I should be happy to." She had an air of sincerity as if her words were far more than mere politeness, or even obedience to Bedelia's request.

"Thank you," Grandmama replied. "I . . . I'm afraid I have none of the usual necessities with me." Dare she ask for a clean petticoat or chemise?

Mrs. Ward looked embarrassed. "There is no difficulty in the least finding you toiletries, Mrs. Ellison. I was thinking of . . . of more personal things. If you'll forgive my saying so, it seems to me that you and I are much the same height. If you would not be offended, ma'am, you might borrow one or two of my . . . my clothes. It would give us the chance to . . . care for yours and return them to you?" She was very pink; as if afraid already that she had presumed.

Grandmama was suddenly touched by the woman's kindness. It seemed perfectly genuine, and perhaps added to because she had cared for Maude. "That is extremely generous of you to offer," she said warmly. "I would be most grateful. I have nothing but what I stand up in. It was the last thing on my mind as I left this morning."

Mrs. Ward colored even more, but most obviously with relief. "Then I shall see that they are brought. Thank you, ma'am."

"It is I who thank you," Grandmama said, startled by her own courtesy, and rather liking it. It flashed into her mind that in a way Maude's death had given her the opportunity to begin a new life herself, even if only for a day or two. No one here in Snave knew her. She could be anything she wanted to be. It was a dizzying sort of freedom, as if the past did not exist. She suddenly smiled at the housekeeper again. "You have extraordinary courtesy," she added.

Mrs. Ward blushed again, then she retreated. Fifteen minutes later she returned carrying two black dresses, an assortment of undergarments, and a nightgown.

With the assistance of one of the maids assigned to help her, a most agreeable girl, Grandmama was able to dress for dinner in very respectable black bombazine, well cut and modest in fashion, as suited an elderly lady or a housekeeper. She put on her own jet and pearl jewelry, serving the double purpose of lifting the otherwise somberness of the attire, and also being classic mourning jewelry. She had a lot of such things; from the period when she had made a great show of being a widow.

Added to which they were really very pretty. The seed pearls made them dainty.

She went down the stairs and across the hall to the withdrawing room. She could hear lively conversation from inside, amazingly so, but she did not know the voices well enough to tell who they belonged to.

She opened the door, and they all ceased instantly, faces turned toward her. The gentlemen rose to their feet and welcomed her. The ladies looked at her, made polite noises, observed the change of gown but did not remark on it.

Conversation resumed, but stiffly, with a solemnity completely different from that before she had come in.

"I hope you are comfortable, Mrs. Ellison?" Bedelia inquired.

"Very, thank you," Grandmama replied, sitting in one of the overstuffed chairs. "You are most generous." Again she smiled.

"It is fortunate Lord Woollard left when he did," Clara observed.

Grandmama wondered whether that remark was made to convince her that they had not had sufficient accommodation for more than one further guest at a time, hence the need to turn Maude away. If so, it was ridiculous. She knew there were at least two more rooms unoccupied. And family should be first, most particularly when they were returning from a long time away.

"Indeed," she said, as if she were agreeing. "Is he a close friend? He will be very sad to hear of Maude's demise."

"He never met her," Bedelia said hastily. "I do not think we need to cloud his Christmas by telling him bad news that can scarcely be of concern to him."

So they had entertained a mere acquaintance in Maude's place!

"I thought perhaps he was a relative," Grandmama murmured.

Arthur smiled at her. "Not at all. A business acquaintance." He sounded tired, a strain in his voice, a kind of bitter humor. "Sent actually to assess whether I should be offered a peerage or not. See if I am suitable."

"Of course you are suitable!" Bedelia said sharply. "It is a formality. And I daresay he was pleased to get out of the city and visit us for a day or two. Cities are so . . . grubby when it snows."

"It isn't snowing," he pointed out.

She ignored him. "At least his visit was not marred by tragedy."

"Or anything else," Clara added quietly.

"I think it will snow," Agnes offered, glancing toward the curtained windows. "The wind has changed and the clouds were very heavy before sunset."

Grandmama was delighted. Snow might mean she could not leave tomorrow, if it were sufficiently deep. "Oh dear," she said with pretended anxiety. "I did not notice. I do hope I am not imposing on you?"

"Not in the slightest," Bedelia assured her. "You say you were a friend of Maude's, even on so short an acquaintance. How could you not be welcome?"

"Of course," Agnes agreed again, echoing Bedelia. "You said Maude spoke to you a great deal? We saw her so little, perhaps it would not be too distressing if we were to ask you what she told you of her . . . travels?" She looked hastily at Bedelia. "That is . . . if it is seemly to discuss! I do not wish to embarrass you in any way at all."

What on earth was Agnes imagining? Orgies around the campfire?

"Perhaps . . . another time," Arthur said shakily, his voice hoarse. "If indeed it does snow, you may be here with us long enough to . . ." He trailed off.

"Quite," Bedelia agreed, without looking at him.

Zachary apologized. "We are all overwrought," he explained. "This is so unexpected. We hardly know how to . . . believe it."

"We had no idea at all that she was ill." Randolph

spoke for the first time since Grandmama had come into the room. "She seemed so . . . so very alive . . . indestructible."

"You no more than met her, my dear," Bedelia said coolly.

Grandmama turned to her in surprise.

"Maude left before my son was born," Bedelia explained, as if an intrusive question had been asked. "I think you do not really understand what an . . . an extraordinary woman she was." Her use of the word *extraordinary* covered a multitude of possibilities, most of them unpleasant.

Grandmama did not reply. She must detect! The room was stiff with emotion. Grief, envy, anger, above all fear. Did she detect the odor of scandal? For heaven's sake, she was not achieving much! She had no proof that it had been murder, only a certainty in her own suspicious mind.

"No," she said softly. "Of course I didn't know how extraordinary she was. I spoke with her and listened to her memories and feelings, so very intense, a woman of remarkable observation and understanding. But as you say, it was only a short time. I have no right to speak as if I knew her as you must have, who grew up with her." She let the irony of the forty-year gap hang in the air. "I imagine when she was abroad she wrote wonderful letters?"

There was an uncomfortable silence, eloquent in itself. So Maude had not written to them in the passionate and lyrical way she had spoken at St. Mary. Or she had, and for some reason they chose to ignore it.

She plowed on, determined to stir up something that might be of meaning. "She had traveled as very few people, men or women, can have done. A collection of her letters would be of interest to many who do not have such opportunities. Or such remarkable courage. It would be a fitting monument to her, do you not think?"

Agnes drew in her breath with a gasp, and looked at Bedelia. She seemed helpless to answer without her approval. A lifetime habit forged in childhood? Perhaps forged was the right word, it seemed to fetter her like iron. It made Grandmama furious, with Agnes and with herself. It was a coward's way, and she knew cowardice intimately, as one knows one's own face in the glass.

Clara turned to her husband, then her mother-in-law, expecting some response.

But it was Arthur who answered.

"Yes, it would," he agreed.

"Arthur!" Bedelia said crisply. "I am sure Mrs. Ellison means well, but she really has no idea of the extent or the nature of Maude's . . . travels, or the unsuitability of making them public."

"Have you?" Arthur asked, his dark brows raised.

"I beg your pardon?" Bedelia said coolly.

"Have you any idea of Maude's travels?" he repeated. "I asked you if she wrote, and you said that she didn't." He did not accuse her of lying, but the inevitability of the conclusion was heavy in the air. She sat pale-faced, tight-lipped.

It was Clara who broke the silence. "Do you think it will still be acceptable for us to have the Matlocks and the Willowbrooks to dine with us on Christmas Eve, Mama-in-law? Or to go to the Watch

Night services at Snargate? Or would people think us callous?"

"I don't suppose we can," Agnes said sadly. "I was looking forward to it too, my dear." She looked at Clara, not at Zachary who had drawn in his breath to say something.

"Death does not alter Christmas," Bedelia responded after a moment's thought. "In fact Christmas is the very time when it means least. It is the season in which we celebrate the knowledge of eternity, and the mercy of God. Of course we shall go to the Watch Night services in Snargate, and show a bond of courage and faith, and solidarity as a family. Don't you think so, my dear?" She looked at Arthur again, as if the previous conversation had never taken place.

"It would seem very appropriate," he answered to the room in general, no discernible emotion in his voice.

"Oh I'm so glad," Agnes responded, smiling. "And we have so much to be grateful for, it seems only right."

Grandmama thought it an odd remark. For what were they so grateful, just now? The fact that Lord Woollard had considered Arthur suitable for a peerage? Could that matter in the slightest, compared with the death of a sister? Of course it could! Maude had not been home for forty years, and they had considered her absent permanently. She had chosen to return at a highly inconvenient time, otherwise they would not have dispatched her to stay with Joshua and Caroline. Was there really some family scandal she might speak of, and ruin such a high ambition?

Any further speculation on that subject was interrupted by the announcement of dinner. The meal was excellent, and richer than anything Caroline had offered.

Conversation at the table centered on other arrangements for Christmas, and how they might be affected either by Maude's death, or the weather. They skirted around the issue of a funeral, and when or where it should be conducted, but it hung in the air unsaid, like a coldness, as if someone had left a door open.

Grandmama stopped listening to the words and concentrated instead upon the intonation of voices, the ease or tension in hands, and above all the expression in a face when the person imagined they were unnoticed.

Clara appeared relieved, as if an anxiety had passed. Perhaps the visit of Lord Woollard had made her nervous. She might be less confident than she appeared. Had she been socially clumsy or otherwise unacceptable? Since her husband was the only heir, that would have been a serious problem. Perhaps she came from a more ordinary background than the rest of the family and had previously made errors, or her mother was one of those women ruthlessly ambitious for their daughters, and no achievement was great enough?

Zachary did not say a great deal, and she saw him look at Bedelia more often than she would have expected. There was an admiration in him, a sense of awe. For her beauty? She was certainly far better looking than poor Agnes. She had a glamour, an air of femininity, mystery, almost power, that confidence gave her. Grandmama watched her as well, and in spite of herself.

What was it like to be beautiful? There were not many women so blessed, certainly she had never been so herself, and neither were Agnes nor Maude. Clara was no more than handsome. Luminous, heart-stopping beauty was very rare. Even Bedelia did not have that.

Grandmama had seen it once or twice, and one did not forget it. Emily's great-aunt by her first marriage, Lady Vespasia Cumming-Gould, had possessed it. Even in advanced years it was still there, unmistakable as a familiar song—one note, and the heart brings it all back.

Why did Zachary still watch Bedelia? Ordinary masculine fascination with beauty? Or good manners, because this was her house?

Arthur did not watch her the same way.

Agnes looked at both of them, and seemed to see it also. There was a sadness in her eyes. Was it an awareness that she could never compete? Perhaps that was the sense of failure Grandmama detected, and understood. She knew it well: a plain face, no magic in the eyes or the voice, above all the knowledge of not being loved.

Envy? Even hate, over the years? Why? Simply beauty? Could it matter so much? Very few women were more than pleasing in their youth, and perhaps gaining a little sense of style, or even better, wit, in their maturity. And she had not been left on the shelf. But sisters did compete. It was inevitable. Was money also involved, and now a peerage, too?

The conversation continued around her, concern for those who would be alone over the Christmas period and possibly in need, those whose health was poor, anyone to whom they could or should give a small gift. Would the weather deteriorate?

"Do you often get shut in by the snow?" Grandmama inquired with interest. "It must be a rather frightening experience."

"Not at all," Zachary assured her. "We will be quite safe. We have food and fuel, and it will not be for more than a day or two. But please don't concern yourself. If it happens at all, it will be in January and February. You know the old saying 'As the days get longer, the weather gets stronger.'" He smiled, transforming his face from its earlier gravity to a surprising warmth.

She smiled back, enjoying the sudden and inexplicable sense of freedom it gave her. "I have found it very often true," she agreed. "And I am sure you are quite wise enough to guard against any possible need. It was rather more such things as someone falling ill that I was thinking of. But I daresay that is a difficulty for all people who live in the wilder and more beautiful country areas."

She continued being charming. It was like having a new toy. She turned to Bedelia. "You know, Mrs. Harcourt, I would never have seen Romney Marsh as anything more than a very flat coast, rather vulnerable, with a permanent smell of the sea, until I met Miss Barrington. But on our walks I saw how she was aware of so much more! She spoke of the wildflowers in the spring, and the birds. She knew the names of a great many of them, you know, and their habits. The water birds especially." She

103

was inventing at least part of this as she was going along. It was exhilarating. The surprised and anxious faces around her increased her sense of adventure.

She drew in her breath and went on. "I had never realized before how perfectly everything fits into its own place in the scheme of things."

"Really?" Bedelia said, her voice almost expressionless. "It is an interest she had developed recently. In fact, since she left England altogether. She must have gained it from reading. Except perhaps in her early childhood, she never saw them in life."

"She did not go walking a great deal?" Grandmama asked innocently.

"She was only here for a matter of hours," Bedelia informed her. "She did not have time to go out at all. Surely she told you that she arrived without giving us any prior warning, and we were thus unable to accommodate her. Do you imagine we would have asked Joshua Fielding to offer his hospitality were it possible for us to do so ourselves?"

So she was correct! Maude had been given the single dose of peppermint water by someone in the house. She must think very rapidly. Better to retreat than to cause an argument, much as the words stuck in her mouth. Was it better to be considered a fool and of no danger at all, or as a highly knowledgeable woman who needed to be watched? She must decide immediately. She could not be both, and time was short.

Bedelia was waiting. They were all looking at her. A brilliant idea flashed into her mind. She could be both apparently stupid, and extremely clever—if she affected to be a little deaf!

She drew in a breath to say so, and apologize for it. Then just before she did, she had another thought of infinitely greater clarity. If she were to claim to be deaf then any evidence she gained could later be denied!

She smothered her pride, a thing she had never done before, except on that unmentionable occasion when her own past had loomed up like a corpse out

105

of the river. But if she had survived that, then nothing this family could do to her would ever make a dent in her inner steel.

"You are quite right," she said meekly. "I had forgotten she had been away so very long. If she had no interest before, then it must have been acquired entirely by reading. Perhaps she was homesick for the wide skies, the salt wind, and the sound of the sea?"

There was a flash of victory in Bedelia's eyes, a knowledge of her own power. Grandmama felt it as keenly as if it had been a charge of electricity between them such as one is pricked by at times if one touches certain metals when the air is very dry. She had read that predatory animals scented blood in the same way, and it gave her a shiver of fear and intense knowledge of vulnerability, which made life suddenly both sweet and fragile.

Was that what Agnes had known all her life? Or was she being fanciful? What about Maude? Was she crushed, too? Was that really why she had left England, and everything familiar that she unquestionably loved, and gone to all kinds of ancient, bar-

baric, and splendid other lands, where she neither knew anyone nor was known? A desperate escape?

Perhaps there was very much more here, beneath the surface, than she had dreamed, even when she had stood in the bedroom beside Maude's dead body this morning?

Bedelia was smiling. "Perhaps she was," she agreed aloud. "But she could have chosen to live by the sea if she had wished to. Poor Maude had very little sense of how to make decisions, even the right ones. It is most unfortunate."

"We were hoping to go out far more, later, when she returned . . ." Agnes glanced at Bedelia. "In the New Year . . . or . . . or whenever we were certain . . . ," she trailed off, knowing that somehow she had put her foot in it.

Grandmama stared at her, willing her to explain.

Bedelia sighed impatiently. "Agnes, dear, you really do let your tongue run away with you!" She turned to Grandmama in exasperation. "You had better know the truth, Mrs. Ellison, or you will feel that we are a cruel family. And it is not so at all.

107

Maude is our middle sister, and she was always unruly, the one who had to draw attention to herself by being different. It happens in families at times. The eldest have attention because they are first, the youngest because they are the babies, the middle ones feel left out, and they show off, to use a common term."

"Maude was not a show-off," Arthur corrected her. "She was an enthusiast. Whatever she did, it was with a whole heart. There was nothing affected or contrived in her."

Bedelia did not look away from Grandmama. "My husband is a man of extraordinarily generous spirit. It is his work for the less fortunate for which Her Majesty is offering him a peerage. I am immensely proud of him, because it is for the noblest of reasons, nothing tawdry like finance, or political support." She smiled patiently. "But occasionally his judgment is rather more kind than accurate. It was apparent as soon as she arrived that Maude had traveled in places where manners and customs are quite different from ours. I'm afraid that even her language was not such that we could subject our other guests to her . . . her more colorful behavior. We knew that Joshua, being on the stage, might be more tolerant of eccentricity. Of course we could not know that you also would be staying with him, and if Maude has shocked you or made you uncomfortable, then we are guilty of having caused that, and on behalf of all of us, I apologize. Our inconsidera-. tion in that regard is what has been disturbing Agnes."

Agnes smiled, but there were tears in her eyes.

"I see." Grandmama tried to imagine Maude as an embarrassment so severe as to be intolerable. She did not know Lord Woollard. Perhaps he was insufferably pompous. There certainly were people so consumed by their own emotional inadequacy and imagined virtue as to take offense at the slightest thing. And the Maude she had met would find a certain delight in puncturing the absurd, the self-important, and above all the false. It would be a scene to be avoided. If Arthur Harcourt had done as much for others as Bedelia said, then he was deserving of recognition, and more importantly the added power to do more good that such an accolade would offer him.

"I'm sure you do," Bedelia said gently.

"All families seem to have their difficult members," Zachary added ruefully.

Grandmama had an unpleasant feeling that in her family it was she herself. Although Caroline was now giving her some competition, marrying an actor so much younger than herself! And there was Charlotte, of course, and her policeman!

A short while later the ladies retired to the withdrawing room and she learned little more of interest. She considered inquiring after people's health, but could think of no way of approaching the subject without being catastrophically obvious. She was extremely tired. It had been one of the longest days of her life, beginning with tragedy and horror, and ending with mystery, and the growing certainty in her mind that someone in this house had altered Maude's medicine. Exactly how it had been achieved, and with what, she had yet to ascertain.

Even more important to her was why. Maude had been successfully sent to stay with Joshua. Lord Woollard had been and gone. What was the element so precious, or so terrible, that it was worth murder?

She excused herself, thanked them again for their hospitality, and went up to her room. Please heaven it would snow tonight, or in some other way make it impossible for her to leave. There was so much she had to learn. This detection matter was more difficult than she had supposed, and against her will she was being drawn into other people's lives. She cared about Maude, there was no use denying that anymore. She disliked Bedelia and had felt the strength of her power. She was sorry for Agnes without knowing why. Arthur intrigued her. In spite of all that was said about him, his success and his goodness to others, she felt an unnamed emotion that disturbed her. It did not fit in.

Randolph and Clara were still too undefined, except that Clara had great social ambitions! Could that possibly be enough to inspire murder?

It was all swirling around in her head as she put

on the housekeeper's nightgown and climbed into the bed, intending to weigh it all more carefully, and instead fell asleep almost immediately.

$\mathcal{T}$ he following morning she slept in, and was embarrassed to waken with the chambermaid standing at the foot of the bed with tea on a tray, and an inquiry as to what she would care for, for breakfast.

Would two lightly boiled eggs and some toast be possible?

Indeed it would, with the greatest pleasure.

After enjoying it, in spite of the circumstances and the thoughts that occupied her mind, she rose and washed. She dressed in the housekeeper's other black gown, again with the chambermaid's assistance, and found she rather enjoyed talking to her. Then she made her way downstairs.

She met Agnes in the hall. She was wearing outdoor clothes and apparently about to leave.

"Good morning, Mrs. Ellison," she said hastily. "I

do hope you slept well? Such a distressing time for you. I hope you were comfortable? And warm enough?"

"I have never been more comfortable," Grandmama replied with honesty. "You are most generous. I do not believe I stirred all night. Are you about to go out?"

"Yes. I have a few jars of jams and chutneys to take to various friends. Nearby villages, you know? I am afraid the weather does not look promising."

Grandmama had another burst of illumination, of double worth. She could catch Agnes alone, unguarded by Bedelia, and if the weather did not oblige by snowing them in, she could affect to have caught a slight chill to prevent her returning to St. Mary in the Marsh tomorrow, or worse, this afternoon.

"May I come with you?" she asked eagerly. "I am not here beyond this brief Christmas period, and I would so love to see a little of the outside. It is quite unlike London. So much wider . . . and cleaner. The city always seems grubby when the snow has been trodden, and everything is stained with smoke from so many chimney fires."

"But of course!" Agnes said with pleasure. "It would be most agreeable to have your company. But it will be cold. You must wear your cape, and I will have another traveling rug brought for you."

Grandmama thanked her sincerely, and ten minutes later they were sitting side·by side in the pony trap, with Agnes holding the reins. It was, as Agnes had warned, extremely cold. The wind had the kiss of ice on it. Clouds streamed in from the seaward side and the marsh grasses bent and rippled as if passed over by an unseen hand.

The trap was well sprung and the pony inexplicably enthusiastic, but it was still not the most comfortable ride. They left the village of Snave and moved quite quickly in what Grandmama presumed to be a westerly direction, and slightly south. It was all a matter of judging the wind and the smell of the sea. Agnes began by companionably telling her something about the village of Snargate and its inhabitants, and then explaining that from Snargate they would continue to Appledore. Then if there were time, to the Isle of Oxney as well, which of course was not an island at all, simply a rise from the flat land of the coast. However, if there were floods, then it would live up to its name.

Grandmama thought that possibly the history of these ancient villages might be quite interesting, but at present it was the history of the Barrington sisters that demanded her entire attention. She must direct Agnes to it, and not waste precious time, of which there was far too little as it was.

"You speak of the land so knowledgeably," she began with flattery. It always worked. "Your family has its roots here? You belong here?" People always wanted to belong. No one wished to be a stranger, as Maude must have been all her adult life.

"Oh, yes," Agnes said warmly. "My great-great-grandfather inherited the house and added to it a hundred and fifty years ago. It is Bedelia's of course. We had no brothers, unfortunately. And then it will be Randolph's. But then it would have been his any-way, because I have no sons either." She turned her face forward so Grandmama could see no more than a fleeting moment of her expression, and the moisture in her eyes could have been from the east wind. It was certainly cold enough.

"You are fortunate to have sisters," Grandmama told her. "I grew up with only brothers, and they were a great deal older than I. Too much so to be my friends."

"I'm sorry." There was no expression in Agnes's face, no lift of memory that made her smile.

Grandmama lied again. "You must have Christmas memories, and traditions in the family?" She looked at the baskets of jars covered with dainty cloth and tied with ribbons. "You do those so very well." More flattery, even if true.

"We always have," Agnes answered, still no lift in her voice.

Grandmama continued to probe, and finally drew a few more specific answers. In heaven's name, it was hard work! Did Pitt always have such a struggle? It was worse than pulling out teeth. But she was determined. Justice might depend upon this.

"I imagine you all did this together, when you were girls," she said with what she knew was tact-lessness. "Or perhaps you were courting? I can think of nothing more romantic." Had she gone too far?

"Zachary did, with Bedelia," Agnes replied. "It was this season, and terribly cold. Several of the streams froze that year. I remember it." She remained looking forward, her expression bleak as the wind pulled strands of her hair loose and whipped them across her face.

Grandmama was momentarily lost. Zachary was Agnes's husband. She would dearly like to let this go. She heard pain in Agnes's voice, and old griefs were none of her affair. But Maude was dead. She could not feel the sting of salt in the air or see the wild flight of seabirds skittering down the wind and whirling back up again, high and wide, wheeling far out over the land.

"Mrs. Harcourt is very beautiful, even now," she tested the verbal knife. "She must have been quite breathtaking then. I have a distant relative who was like that."

117

"Yes." Agnes's hands were tight on the reins, the leather of her gloves strained. "Half the young men in the county were in love with her."

"And she chose Mr. Harcourt?" It was a stupid question, and probably entirely irrelevant to Maude's death, but she had nothing better to pursue.

"Yes." For a moment it seemed as if Agnes was going to say no more. Then she drew in her breath, wanting to speak after all. "Although it was not so simple as that."

"Really? I suppose things seldom are," Grandmama said sympathetically. "And even less often are they what they seem to be on the surface. People make very hasty judgments, sometimes."

"They are the easiest," Agnes agreed. She negotiated a sharp turn in the lane and Grandmama saw the village of Snargate ahead. This was proving very difficult indeed. They were almost at the village green. The inn, the church with ancient yew trees and graveyard, and the lych-gate covered with the bare vines of honeysuckle lay beyond.

118

They made their first delivery of Christmas fare, and the second, and then left Snargate and continued the short distance to Appledore.

"I suppose there is always speculation where there are sisters, and one is as beautiful as Bedelia," Grandmama said as soon as they were on their way again, blankets carefully tucked around shivering knees. The sky cleared a little and banners of blue appeared bright between the clouds.

As if deliberately hurting herself, Agnes told the story. "Maude didn't know about it, not really. She was away that Christmas. Aunt Josephine was ill and alone, and Maude went to look after her. Zachary was courting Bedelia. He was so in love with her. They went everywhere together, to the balls and the dinners and the theater in Dover, even through the snow. That was when the Queen was young and happy, and Prince Albert was so dashing. We saw drawings of them in the newspapers. It was before the Crimean War. I expect you remember?"

"I do." It had been a nightmare time. Her own husband had been alive, charming, persuasive, privately brutal, demanding things no decent woman ever imagined. She could still taste the wool of the carpet in her mouth and remember his weight on top of her, forcing her down. In public it had been all contentment, the glamour of endless crinoline skirts on a figure unrecognizable now in her too ample waist and hips. And at home a hell she could not think of without a hot shame making her feel sick. How could she, of all people, criticize anyone's cowardice? It stirred in her rage and pity, and a hunger to avenge it so sharp she could feel it. The bitter wind was almost a comfort.

But Agnes was lost in her own passions and did not even glance to see if her companion was with her mentally. "Then Arthur Harcourt arrived," she went on. "I think it was early March. The beginning of spring. The days were getting longer and everything was coming into bud. Arthur was not only handsome but charming and funny and kind. He could make us all laugh so hard we were embarrassed to be caught at it. One did not enjoy things so openly then. It was thought to be unladylike.

He didn't care. And he could dance like an angel. Everything seemed worth doing when he was with us."

Grandmama thought she could guess the rest. Bedelia fell out of love with Zachary and in love with Arthur, who was a much better catch. A far better catch. Poor Zachary was cast aside, and in time took second best, the duller, plainer Agnes. And Agnes accepted.

Without thinking, Grandmama reached across and put her hand on Agnes's where it rested above the edge of the rug, holding the reins tightly. She did not say anything. It was a silent understanding, a pity without words.

For a few moments they rode through the lanes toward Appledore in silence.

Then suddenly Agnes spoke again. "Of course we thought then that Bedelia and Arthur would marry. It seemed inevitable."

"Yes, it would," Grandmama agreed.

"But Aunt Josephine died, and Maude came back home. Everything changed," Agnes said.

121

"Indeed?" Grandmama had almost forgotten about Maude. "How?"

"Arthur and Maude just . . ." Agnes gave a tiny shrug. "Just seemed to . . . to fall so in love it was as if Bedelia ceased to exist. It didn't seem like a flirtation. Bedelia was . . . unable to believe it at first. I mean Maude, of all people? Goodness knows what she told him!"

"Told him?" Grandmama said before she could stop herself.

"Well, she must have told him something terrible about Bedelia to have caused him to abandon her like that! And of course untrue. Jealousy is . . . a very unkind thing. It eats the heart out of you, if you allow it to."

"Oh, that is true," Grandmama agreed sincerely. "It can be an instant passion, or a slow-growing one, but it is certainly deadly. But it seems as if Arthur saw through it, whatever it was." She hated saying that because it blamed Maude, and she was far from prepared to do that, but she must keep Agnes telling the story.

122

"Oh, yes," Agnes agreed. "It lasted perhaps a month, then Arthur came to his senses. He realized that he truly loved Bedelia. He broke off the silly business with Maude, and asked Bedelia to marry him. Of course she forgave him, and accepted."

"I see." She did not see at all.

Three sisters, two men. Someone had to have lost. Grandmama resented that it should have been Maude. Or had it really been all of them, no one truly finding what they hungered for? "And Maude?" she said quietly.

"Maude was heartbroken," Agnes replied, her voice catching in her throat. She turned away as if there were something on the other side of the pony trap that required her attention, although there was nothing but the grasses and the sea wind and the marsh stretching out to the horizon. "She simply ran away. God knows where she went, but about a month later we received a postcard from Granada, in the south of Spain. There were only a few words on it. I remember. 'Going to Africa. Will probably stay. Maude.' "

123

And Bedelia had said she never wrote again. Was that true? "Until she returned a few days ago?" Grandmama asked aloud.

"That's right."

"Why did she come back, now, after all these years?"

Agnes shook her head and rubbed her hand over her eyes. "Perhaps she knew she was dying? Maybe she wanted to be buried here. People do. Want to be buried in their own land, I mean, their own earth."

"Did she say anything like that?"

"She did say something about death. I can't recall exactly what it was. But she was sad, that much was clear. I . . . I wish I had listened. My mind was on Lord Woollard's visit, and how anxious we all were that it should go well." Guilt was heavy in her voice and the misery of her face. "Arthur really does deserve recognition, you know. And the amount of good he could do with it would be enormous."

"And you were concerned that Maude's behavior would be inappropriate?"

Agnes glanced at Grandmama then away again,

a mixture of impatience and shame in her face. "She had been living in extraordinary places for the last forty years, Mrs. Ellison. Places where people eat with their fingers, have no running water, where women do things that . . . I would rather not even think of, let alone speak about."

"I thought women in the Middle East were rather more modest than we are here in England," Grandmama said thoughtfully. "At least that was the impression I gained from Maude. They keep to their own apartments and don't speak to men other than those in their own families. Their clothing is certainly most decorous."

Agnes was frowning. "But Maude went unaccompanied, wandering around like a . . . like a man!" she exclaimed. "Who knows what happened to her? Her taste is highly questionable. Even her virtue, I'm afraid."

"I beg your pardon?" Grandmama said in angry disbelief, then realized she had gone too far. She must find an escape very quickly. "I'm so sorry," she apologized, the words all but choking her. "I felt so

.close to Maude because she confided in me, and I in her, that I am more offended than I have any right to be at the thought that someone who did not know her at all should question her virtue. It is quite unreasonable, and even impertinent of me. Please forgive me. She was your sister, not mine, and it is your right to defend her. I did not mean to presume." She watched Agnes's face intently, as if she were eager for pardon. She was actually extremely eager to see Agnes's reaction.

Agnes's hands froze on the reins and she stared ahead, even though they were now very close to the village of Appledore and she should have been slowing the pony.

"It is not presumptuous," she said, her face scarlet. Then she stopped again, still uncertain. "I'm sure you meant it only kindly. Perhaps we live too much in the past. Imagine too much."

"About Maude?" Grandmama had to ask. She was overwhelmingly aware of the misery in Agnes, and the knowledge that she would always be second choice. She was sorry for it—she even understood it—but it did not excuse lies, or answer justice now. They were passing the village church and she saw the festive wreaths on doors and a group of children ran past them shouting *Greetings!* What happens to people that they become bitter, and why do we not turn to each other, and help? We all walk a common path from cradle to grave, just stumble over different stones in it, trip in different holes, or drown in different puddles.

Agnes had not answered her.

"I understand," Grandmama said impulsively. "You had old memories of Maude once taking Arthur's affection, and you were afraid she would say or do something outrageous now. Perhaps even spoil his chances of receiving the peerage. So you made sure she could not be in the house when Lord Woollard was here. And now that she has died, you feel guilty, and of course it is too late to do anything about it."

Agnes turned to face her, eyes wide and hurt. She said nothing, but acknowledgment was as clear in her as if she had admitted it in so many words.

They delivered the jams and chutneys in Appledore and went on to the Isle of Oxney. The rising wind was cruelly cóld. The horizon was blurred with gathering clouds and there was a smell of snow in the air. Perhaps it would not be necessary to feign a chill after all? Although how deep the snow would have to be to make travel inadvisable she did not know. St. Mary in the Marsh was only five miles away, not even an hour's journey. Maybe a few sneezes and a complaint of a sore throat would be better? She had barely scratched the surface of what there was to detect. There were emotions, old loves and jealousies, old wrongs, but what had caused them to erupt now? Pitt had said that there was always a reason why violence occurred at a particular time, some event that had sparked the final act.

Why had Maude come home? Why not before, in all the forty years of her exile? Or next year? Why at Christmas, not summer, when the weather would be infinitely more agreeable? Whose death was it that she had been referring to? Surely not her own?

On the ride back to Snave, she deliberately spoke only of Christmas arrangements. What to eat? Goose, naturally, and plenty of vegetables—roasted, boiled, baked, and with added sauces. After there would be a Christmas pudding rich with dried fruit and covered with brandied butter, and flamed at the time of serving. And covered with cream.

But before that there were literally dozens of other things to think of and prepare: cakes, pastries, mince pies, sweets, gingerbread, and all manner of drinks, both with and without alcohol. And naturally a wealth of decoration: wreaths and boughs, garlands, golden angels, colored bows, flowers made of silk and ribbon, pine cones painted with gold, little dolls to be given afterward to the poor of the village. There were presents to be made: skittles painted as wooden soldiers, pincushions, ornaments handmade and decorated with lace and beads and colored braid. The hours of work could hardly be counted. They spoke of them together, and remembered about their own childhood Christmases, be-

129

fore the advent of cards and trees and such modern ideas that so much added to the general happiness.

$\mathcal{A}$fter luncheon Grandmama took a brief walk in the garden. She needed time alone to think. Detection required order in the mind. There were facts to be considered and weighed.

There was little to see beyond a well-tended neatness and very obvious architectural grace and skill. There were arbors, gravel walks, herbaceous borders carefully weeded, perennials cleared of dead foliage, a flight of steps that curved up to a pergola covered with the skeletons of roses, and finally a less formal woodland overlooking the open marsh.

It was very wet underfoot, and rather muddy. The long grasses soaked the hem of her skirt, but it was inevitable. In spring this would be beautiful with flowers: snowdrops, primroses in all likelihood, wood anemones, certainly bluebells, wild daisies, campion. Perhaps narcissi with their piercingly sweet scent. She saw two or three crowns of foxglove leaves. She loved their elegant spires in purples or white. One of them looked a little ragged, as if an animal had cropped it. Except that no animal would eat foxglove—it was poisonous. Creatures always seemed to know. It slowed the heart. It was used by doctors for people whose hearts raced. Digitalis. She froze. Raced . . . slowed. Stopped!

Was that it? The answer she was searching for? She bent and looked at the leaves again. There was no earthly way of proving it, but she was perfectly sure someone had picked two or three leaves. The broken ends were visible.

She stood up again slowly. How could she find out who? It must have been the day Maude was here. Had it been wet or dry? Never dry in winter in this wood, but if freezing then the ice would prevent anyone getting as wet as she was now, or as muddy.

Four days before, Joshua had received Bedelia's letter. Think! Windy, the noise of it howling in the eaves was clear in her mind. It had irritated her un-

131

bearably. And relatively mild. Who had come in with muddy boots, a dress soaked at the hems? A ladies' maid would know. But how to ask her?

She turned and walked briskly back into the house and went to find Mrs. Ward.

"I'm so sorry," she apologized profusely; startled that she meant it without any pretense at all. "I went walking in the garden and became distracted with the beauty of it."

"It is lovely, isn't it," Mrs. Ward agreed. "That's Mrs. Harcourt's skill. Mrs. Sullivan can paint a picture of a flower that's both lovely and correct, but it's Mrs. Harcourt who plans the garden itself."

"What a gift," Grandmama said. "And one from which we all benefit. But I am afraid that I have thoroughly muddied both my boots, and the hem of your dress. It was deeply careless of me, and I regret it now."

"Oh, don't worry! It happens all the time!" Mrs. Ward dismissed it. "Your own dress is quite clean and dry, and Nora can clean this again in no time."

"I'm sure it doesn't happen to everybody," Grandmama told her. "I cannot imagine Mrs.. Harcourt being so inelegant, or so thoughtless. You cannot name me the last time she did this!"

Mrs. Ward smiled. "Certainly I can! The very day Miss Maude came home. Went looking for some nice branches to add to the flowers in the hall. Woodland branches can be most graceful in a vase. Please don't think of it, Mrs. Ellison."

"Really?" Grandmama's heart was racing. So it was Bedelia. But she should be certain. "I expect she and Clara were in quite a state, with Lord Woollard expected as well."

"Certainly. She also went out on an errand and came back as muddy as you like. Poor Nora was beside herself. Then Mrs. Sullivan the day after. At least I think it was. I'll find Nora and send her up to you."

"Thank you. You are most considerate." Grandmama left with her mind whirling. So who had boiled up the leaves? Where? How could she find that out? Perhaps they were simply crushed and steeped, as one makes a cup of tea! That could have

133

been any of them. She must think more—pay attention. And be careful!

$\mathcal{I}$n the afternoon Grandmama offered to help Bedelia in some of the last-minute preparations. Of course Cook would see to the meal itself, and most of the other things that required the use of the kitchen. But there was still much sewing to be done, lavender bags that were not finished, ornamental roses to be made, and definitely more decorations for the great tree in the hall.

"I could have sworn that we had more than this last year!" Bedelia said, looking at it with dismay. "It seems almost bare, don't you think, Mrs. Ellison?"

Grandmama regarded the huge tree, its dark green needles still fresh and scented with earth and pine. It was liberally decorated with ribbons and ornaments, and there was a handsome pile of parcels beneath, and smaller ones with lace and flowers hanging from the branches. It was far from bare, but certainly there were places where more could be hung. It was important that she make herself necessary.

"It is very handsome," she answered judiciously. "But you are quite right, of course. There are still one or two places to be filled in. I am sure it would not be difficult to find the materials to make a couple of dozen more ornaments. One needs only a child's ball, perhaps two of different sizes would be even better, paste, and as many different colors of paper as possible, beads, dried flowers, ribbon, lace, whatever else can be spared that is pretty. Sometimes an old gown can provide an amazing variety of bits and pieces. It's not difficult to make tiny dolls, or angels." She had rather run away with herself, but it was all in the growingly desperate cause of detection. Very definite ideas were crystallizing in her mind, but she needed more time!

Christmas was supposed to be a time of forgiveness, but surely there could be no healing without honor, no real peace without change of heart? And no change without truth.

"It is not a lack of materials," Bedelia told her. "I have not the time, and I doubt the maids have the skill."

"I should be happy to help you, if I may?" Grandmama offered. She had not been so courteous in years, and in spite of her amusement at herself, she was rather enjoying it. It was like a step outside her own life, a curious freedom from the expectations of others, or the chains of past failure.

"I should be delighted to contribute something to such a glorious tree," she continued eagerly. "And also a sort of family tradition. The Barringtons have been in this village for so many generations there are bound to be scores of people who will call in to wish you season's greetings and share your hospitality." That was certain. Tradesmen always paid their respects this time of year and partook of mince pies, candied fruit and nuts, and of course a cup of punch.

Bedelia accepted, and half an hour later they

136

were sitting in the sewing room at opposite sides of the table cannibalizing an old evening gown, cutting off beads, braid, fine silk and velvet pieces, and the paler ribbons and lace from two old petticoats that had also been found.

"There is too much dark red," Bedelia said critically. "All of the silk and velvet is the same shade."

"That is true," Grandmama agreed. "What we really need is something else bright in a completely different tone." She looked at Bedelia with a frown. "I have a very daring idea. Perhaps you would find it offensive, but I have to ask. If it grieves you, I apologize in advance."

"Good gracious!" Bedelia was intrigued. "I am not easily shocked. What is this idea?"

"Maude said that she traveled in many strange and exotic places."

A faint distaste flashed in Bedelia's eyes but she masked it. "Is that helpful?"

"No doubt she wore some . . . strange clothes," Grandmama said tentatively. "Possibly of colors we would not choose."

137

Bedelia understood instantly and her face lit with pleasure.

"Oh! But of course! How clever of you. Yes, certainly, some of them might be cut up for the most excellent Christmas ornaments."

Grandmama felt a chill at the thought of cutting up any of Maude's clothes, things she had worn in the places that she had obviously loved so far from home. She might have stood in the sunset in some Persian garden and smelled the perfume of strange trees and the wind off the desert and looked up to unimaginable stars. Or perhaps there would be scarves of silk she had bought at a noisy, multitudinous bazaar in Marrakech, or some such city. They should all be treated with tenderness, folded to keep in the odor of spices and strange fruit, oils and leathers, and the smoke from the campfires.

"You are so clever, Mrs. Ellison," Bedelia was saying. "Of course most of her things are here and we have only to unpack them. And it is unlikely that any of them are things that anyone else would wear.

I really do not care to offer them, even to the poor. It would be . . ."

"Disrespectful," Grandmama filled in, meaning it, and enjoying forcing Bedelia to agree. She hated herself for doing it, but truth required some strange sacrifices. "This way they will be totally anonymous, and give pleasure for years to come." Forgive me, Maude, she thought to herself. Detection is not easy, and I refuse to fail. She stood up. "I suppose we should begin. See what we can find." That was crass. She had not been invited to look into Maude's effects, but she was most curious to see if there was anything helpful. No one else who knew that she had been murdered would ever have such an opportunity.

If Bedelia were offended she did not show it.

Upstairs in the box room, where the luggage had been stored, they set about opening the two trunks Maude had brought back with her. Grandmama found herself with the one packed with ordinary blouses and skirts, underclothes, and sensible, rather scuffed boots. They were of moderate quality linen, cotton, and some of raw, unbleached wool. She wondered in what marvelous places Maude had worn these. What had she seen, what emotions of ·joy, pain, or loneliness had she felt? Had she longed for home, or had she been at home wherever she was, with friends, even people who loved her?

She glanced across at Bedelia and studied her face as she pulled out a length of silk striped in purples, scarlets, crimsons, and tawny golds mingled with a hot pink. She drew in her breath sharply. At first it seemed to be pleasure, excitement, even a kind of longing. Then her mouth hardened and there was hurt in her eyes.

"Good heavens above!" she said sharply. "What on earth could she have worn this for? Whatever is it?" She shook it out until it billowed and appeared to be a sheet with very little distinctive shape. "One can only hope it was a gift, and not something she purchased for herself. No woman could wear such a thing, even at twenty, never mind at Maude's age! She would have looked like something out of the circus!" She started to laugh, then stopped abruptly. "A very good thing we looked at this first, Mrs. Ellison. If the servants had seen it we should be the talk of the village."

Grandmama felt her fury flare up and if she had dared she would have lashed out verbally in Maude's defense. But there were bigger considerations, and with intense difficulty she choked back the words. She forced herself to look as close to good-natured as she could manage, which effort cost her dearly. "Instead they will be talking about the gorgeous and perfectly unique ornaments on your tree," she said sweetly. "And you will be able to say that they are a remembrance of your sister."

Bedelia sat rigid, her eyes unmoving, her face set. It could have been grief, or the complexity and hurt of any memory, including anger that would never now be redeemed, or regret for forgiveness too late. Or even debts uncollected. The only thing Grandmama was certain of was that the emotion was deep, and that it brought no ease or pleasure.

They took the silks downstairs and Bedelia cut

into them with large fabric shears. Bright clouds like desert sunsets drifted across the table and onto the floor. Grandmama picked them up and began to work on the papier-mâché and paste to make the basic balls before they should be covered in the bright gauze. After that they would stitch little dolls to dress in the gold and bronze and white with pearls. She smiled at the prospect. It was fun to create beauty.

But she was not here to enjoy herself. This silk in her hands had been a wonderful, wild, garish robe that Maude had worn on the hot roads of Arabia, or somewhere like it.

"I imagine Maude must have known some very different people," she said thoughtfully. "They would seem odd to us, perhaps even frightening." She allowed the lamplight to fall on the purple silk and the brazen red. "I cannot imagine wearing these colors together."

"Nor could anyone else outside a fairground!" Bedelia responded. "You see why we could not have her here when Lord Woollard stayed. We allowed him the courtesy of not shocking or embarrassing him."

"Is he a man of small experience?" Grandmama inquired with as much innocence as she could contrive.

"Of discreet taste and excellent family," Bedelia said coolly. "His wife, whom I have met, is the sister of one of Her Majesty's ladies-in-waiting. An excellent person."

Perhaps even a week ago Grandmama would have been impressed. Now all she could think of was Maude's Persian garden with the small owls in the dusk.

There was a knock on the door and Agnes came in. A brief conversation followed about parties, games to be played, especially blindman's bluff, and of course refreshments.

"We must remember some lemon curd tarts for Mrs. Hethersett," Agnes reminded her. "She is always so fond of them."

"She will have to make her own," Bedelia responded. "She will not be coming."

"Oh, dear! Is she unwell again?" Agnes asked sympathetically.

"She will not be coming because I have not invited her," Bedelia said tersely. "She was unforgivably rude."

"That was over a year ago!" Agnes protested.

"It was," Bedelia agreed. "What has that to do with it?"

Agnes did not argue. She admired the rapidly progressing baubles, and returned to the task of organizing pies and tarts.

"How very unpleasant," Grandmama sympathized, wondering what on earth Mrs. Hethersett could have said that Bedelia still bore a grudge a year later, and at Christmas, of all times. "She must have been dreadfully rude to distress you so much." She nearly added that she could not understand why people should be rude, but that was too big a lie to swallow. She could understand rudeness perfectly, and practice it to the level of an art. It was something she had never previously been ashamed of, but now it was oddly distasteful to her.

144

"She imagines I will forget," Bedelia responded. "But she is quite mistaken, as she will learn."

Grandmama bent to the stitching again, blending the bright colors with less pleasure, and wondered what Maude had done to Bedelia that old memories lingered so long in unforgiveness.

Why had Maude returned now? Was it possible Grandmama was completely mistaken? Had she allowed her bored and lonely imagination to conjure up murder where there was only an unexpected death, and grief that looked like anger? And a proud woman who would not allow another to see that she was bitterly ashamed of having turned away her sister for fear that her behavior was socially inappropriate, and now regretted it so terribly when it was too late? Was Grandmama making a crime out of what was only a tragedy?

*D*inner was tense again. As on the first night there was the palpable undercurrent of emotions that perhaps there always is in families: knowledge of weaknesses, indulgences, things said that would have been better forgotten, only there is always someone who will remind.

Aloud they recalled past Christmases, particularly those when Randolph had been a boy, which necessarily excluded Clara. Grandmama studied her face and saw the flicker of hurt in it, and then of annoyance.

The others were enjoying themselves. For once Arthur joined in the laughter and the open affection as Bedelia told a tale of Randolph's surprise at re- ceiving a set of tin soldiers in perfect replica of Wellington's army at Waterloo. It seemed he had refused to come to the table, even for goose. He was so enraptured he could not put his soldiers down. Bedelia had tried to insist, but Arthur had said it was Christmas, and Randolph should do as he pleased.

Grandmama found herself smiling also—until she saw the hunger in Zachary's eyes, his look at Bedelia, Agnes's look at him, and remembered that Randolph was the only one among all four of them

146

likely to have a child. He was forty. Clara, strong-willed and ambitious, was a great deal younger. When would they have children? Or might that be another grief waiting in the wings?

She would have liked to have had more children herself; a daughter like Charlotte might have made all the difference, or even like Emily. A lot of work, a lot of frustration and disappointment, but who could measure the happiness?

It would be better if she did not think of the past anymore. Far better to treasure what you have than grieve over what you have not.

She looked around their faces again. Why does anybody hate someone enough to kill them, with all the risk involved? You don't, if you are sane. You kill to protect, to keep what you have and love: position, power, money, even safety from scandal, the pain of humiliation, or loss, or the terror in loneliness. She could easily imagine that. Perhaps we were all as fragile, if one found the right passion, the fear that eats at the soul.

She looked at the light from the chandeliers glittering on the silver, the crystal, at the white linen, the lilies from the hothouse, and the red wine, all the different faces, and wondered if she really wanted to know the answer.

Then she remembered Maude's laughter, and the memories in her eyes as she described the moonlight over the desert. There was no escaping the answer. That would be the ultimate, irredeemable cowardice.

$\mathcal{T}$he following day the scullery maid cut her finger so badly she could not use her hand, and the kitchen was in pandemonium. Agnes had been going to take the pony trap to deliver gifts to the vicar's widow in Dymchurch, and now all plans had to be rearranged.

Without a thought for her own competence for such a task, Grandmama offered to go in her stead. The stable boy could drive her and she would call, with explanations, upon Mrs. Dowson and give her the already wrapped gifts for herself, and one or two other families.

Her offer was accepted, and at ten o'clock they set off, she feeling very pleased with herself. It was a bitter day with clouds piling slate gray on the horizon, and the wind had veered round to come from the north with ice on the edge.

Grandmama sat with the rug wrapped tightly around her knees and tucked in under her, hoping profoundly that it would not snow before she returned to Snave, or she might find that the chill she had considered pretending could be only too real. She had no desire whatever to spend Christmas in bed with a fever!

And then another thought assailed her, even more unpleasant. What if she discovered beyond doubt who it was that had picked the foxglove leaves and distilled their poison, and could prove it? And that person became aware of the fact! Then it might be a great deal more than a chill that afflicted

149

her. She wondered if it was painful to die of a heart slowing until it stopped altogether. She could feel it bumping in her chest now with fear.

If she died, would anyone miss her enough to be sorry? Would anyone's world be colder or grayer because she was not in it?

She thought of Maude alone in the house of strangers who had taken her in out of kindness, or worse, a sense of duty. Or pity? That was even worse again. Had Maude felt obliged to work hard to be charming, hide the rejection she must feel inside in order to win their warmth? Had she even known that Grandmama liked her, genuinely liked her?

Now, that was a lie. Her face was hot in spite of the knife-edge wind. She had loathed Maude, even before she arrived, because Maude would displace her as the center of attention. She had realized only after Maude was dead how much she had liked her, admired her, found her exciting to listen to, freeing the imagination and awakening dreams. She wished now with a desire so strong it was like a physical ache that she had allowed Maude to see that she liked her, more than anyone else she could think of.

They were going toward the sea and she could smell the salt more sharply. Dymchurch was not far from St. Mary in the Marsh. She could not return home until she had solved this. It would be a betrayal not only of Maude, but of friendship itself. The length of it was irrelevant, it was the depth that mattered.

She ignored the great ragged skies, clouds streaming across its vastness like the torn banners of an army, spears of ice not far behind. As they drove into the village itself she could hear the roaring of the surf on the shore and the tower of the church seemed to stand aloft against the racing darkness coming in on the storm.

They pulled up to a small cottage with bare vines covering the arch over the gate and the stable boy announced that they had arrived. He said he would take the parcels in for her, as soon as they had ascertained that Mrs. Dowson was at home. Then he

151

would take the pony and trap around to the stable to shelter until she was ready to leave again. He looked anxiously at the sky, and then smiled, showing gapped teeth.

Grandmama thanked him and with his help alighted.

Mrs. Dowson was at home. She was a lean woman with narrow shoulders and bright eyes. She must have been closer to eighty than seventy, but seemed to be still in excellent health. There was a color in her cheeks as if she had recently been outside, even in this darkening weather.

Grandmama introduced herself.

"My name is Mariah Ellison, Mrs. Dowson. Please excuse me for calling unannounced on Mrs. Harcourt's behalf, but I am afraid I have accepted their hospitality in the wake of tragedy, and the whole family is bravely making the very best of a hard situation. I offered to come on this errand for her. I feel it is the least I can do."

"Oh, dear. I'm so sorry. Very kind of you, Mrs. Ellison." She looked at Grandmama curiously but without apprehension. "May I offer you tea, and perhaps a mince pie or something of the sort?" She did not ask what the tragedy had been. Was that extreme discretion, or had word somehow come this far already?

"Thank you," Grandmama accepted, wondering if there were a third possibility, that she simply did not care. "I admit, it is remarkably cold outside. I do not know this area very well. I live in London and am merely visiting, but I find something most pleasing about the sea air, even when there is so very much of it."

Mrs. Dowson smiled. "It pleases me, too," she agreed, conducting the way into a small but very pretty sitting room. It was low-ceilinged, with furniture covered in floral chintz, and a fire burning in the hearth. She rang the bell, and when the maid came, requested tea and tarts.

"Now, my dear," she said when they were seated, "what is the trouble with poor Agnes now? I imagine it is Agnes, is it not?"

How interesting, Grandmama thought. Aloud

153

she said, "I am afraid it is all of them. Did you ever know the third sister, Miss Maude Barrington?"

Something hardened in Mrs. Dowson's face, and her eyes were chill. "I did. But if you have come to say something uncomplimentary about her, I would thank you not to. I know she was a little unruly, and perhaps she threw herself too fully into things, but she had a good heart, and it was all very long ago. I think one should take one's victories very lightly, and one's losses with silence and dignity, do you not agree, Mrs. Ellison?"

How curious! Not at all what Grandmama had expected. Mrs. Dowson's eyes might be bright and cold, but they kindled a sudden new warmth in Grandmama's mind.

"Indeed I do," she said heartily. "That is one of the reasons I felt an affection for Maude the moment I met her. It is one of the great sadnesses of my life that I knew her such a very short time."

"I beg your pardon?" Mrs. Dowson said huskily, her face now filled with alarm.

Even a week ago Grandmama would have made

154

a condescending reply to that. Now all she wanted to do was find some kinder way of telling the news.

"I am so sorry. Maude arrived home from abroad and because of other family commitments at her sister's house, she came and stayed with her cousin, Mr. Joshua Fielding, who is also a relative of mine, hence my presence there. Maude died, quite peacefully in her sleep, three days ago." She saw the undisguised pain in the old lady's face. "I felt so very grieved I chose to take the news to her family in person, rather than merely send some written message," she concluded, "which is how I come to be still staying with them now. I am doing what little I can to help."

"Oh, dear," Mrs. Dowson said, shaking her head a little. "I assumed it was no more than another of Agnes's chills, or whatever it is she has. How stupid of me. One should not assume. This is a deep loss." Suddenly the tears filled her eyes. "I'm so sorry," she apologized.

Grandmama did not find it absurd that after forty years Mrs. Dowson should still grieve so

155

keenly. Time does not cloud certain memories. Bright days from youth, laughter and friendship can remain.

But crass as it seemed, it was also an opportunity that she could not afford to ignore. "Did you know her well, before she left to travel abroad?" she asked.

"Oh yes," Mrs. Dowson smiled. "I knew all the girls then. My husband was a curate, just young in his ministry. Very earnest, you know, as dedicated men can be. I rather think Maude overwhelmed him. She was so fierce in her love for Arthur Harcourt. And of course Arthur was quite the dashing young man-about-town. He was extraordinarily handsome, and he knew it. But he could hardly fail to. If he'd crooked a finger at any of the girls in the south of England they'd have followed him. I might have myself, if I'd thought he meant it. But I was never very pretty, and I was happy enough with Walter. He was genuine. I rather thought Arthur wasn't."

"Sincere? Was he simply playing with Maude?"

Suddenly Grandmama's liking for Arthur Harcourt evaporated as if she had torn the smiling mask off and seen rotten flesh underneath.

"Oh no," Mrs. Dowson said quickly. "That was where Walter and I disagreed. He thought Arthur loved Bedelia. He called them a perfect match. Something of an idealist, my husband. Thought beauty was bone deep, not just a chance of coloring and half an inch here and there, and of course confidence. Self-belief, you know? Imagine how the map of the world might have been changed if Cleopatra's nose had been half an inch longer! Then Caesar might not have fallen in love with her, or Mark Anthony either."

Grandmama was carried along in a hurricane of thought.

"I'm so sorry," Mrs. Dowson apologized again. "Walter always said my mind was totally undisciplined. I told him that was not so at all, simply that it moved in a different pattern from his. Bedelia Barrington could twist him around her little finger! And half the men in the county, too. Poor Zachary never got over it, which is such a shame. Agnes was the better girl, if only she could have believed that herself!"

Grandmama did not interrupt her. The tea arrived. Mrs. Dowson poured, and passed the mince pie and jam tarts.

"Bedelia thought she was glamorous, Agnes was dull, and Maude was plain and eccentric. Because of her confidence, far too many people believed that she must be right."

"But she was not . . ."

"Certainly she was," Mrs. Dowson contradicted her. "But only because we allowed her to be. Except Maude. She knew Bedelia's beauty was of no real value. No warmth in it, do you see?"

"But she fell in love with Arthur? So much so that she could not bear it when he came to his senses and married Bedelia after all?" Grandmama deliberately chose her words provocatively.

"I used to think he lost his senses again," Mrs. Dowson argued. "I was furious with Maude for not fighting for the man she loved. Fancy simply giving up and running away like that! Off to North Africa, and then Egypt and Persia. Riding horses in the desert, and camels too, for all I can say. Lived in tents and gave what was left of her heart to the Persians."

"She wrote to you!" Grandmama was astonished, and delighted. Maude had had a friend here who had cared for her over the years and kept her in touch with home.

"Of course," Mrs. Dowson said indignantly. "She never told me why she left, but I came to realize it was a matter of honor, and must not ever be discussed. She did what she believed to be the right thing. But I don't think that she ever stopped loving Arthur."

New ideas began to form in Grandmama's mind. "Mrs. Dowson, do you know why Maude chose to come home now, after so long?" she asked. "Did she have any . . . any anxieties about her health?"

"Not that she confided in me." Mrs. Dowson frowned. "She was certainly afraid, a little oppressed by the thought of returning after so long.

159

But the gentleman she had cared for in Persia, and who had loved her, had died. She told me that. It grieved her very much, and it also meant that she had no reason for remaining there anymore. In fact she implied that without his protection it would be unwise for her to do so. I do not know their relationship. I never asked and she never told me, but it was not regular, as you and I would use the term."

"I see. Was Bedelia aware of this?" Was that the scandal she was afraid might come to Lord Woollard's ears—even perhaps quite frankly told by Maude, in order to shock? After Bedelia's coolness over the years, and the fact that it was she Arthur had married, whatever his reason, it would not be unnatural now if Maude had been unable to resist at least preventing her sister from becoming Lady Harcourt. She asked Mrs. Dowson as much.

"She may have been tempted," Mrs. Dowson replied. "But she would not have done it. Maude never bore a grudge. That was Bedelia."

"Was Bedelia not very much in love with Arthur,

even before Maude returned from caring for her aunt?" Grandmama asked.

"Maude did tell you a great deal, didn't she?" Mrs. Dowson observed.

Grandmama merely smiled.

"However much Maude had despised Bedelia, she would never have hurt Arthur," Mrs. Dowson continued. "As I said, she never stopped loving him. And I refer to that emotion that seeks the best for the other, the honor and happiness and inward spiritual journey; not the hunger to possess at all costs, the joy for oneself in their company and the feeling that they are happy only when they are with you. That is Bedelia, all about winning. And poor Agnes was concerned she was always going to be no more than second-best."

"Then why was Arthur so foolish?" Grandmama marveled. "Was he really blinded by mere physical . . . oh." A far simpler and more understandable answer came to her mind. She saw that Mrs. Dowson was watching her intently. She felt

161

the heat in her cheeks as if Mrs. Dowson could read her thoughts.

"I do not know," Mrs. Dowson said quietly. "But I believe Maude did, and that is why Bedelia was very happy that she should remain in Persia for the rest of her life."

The idea became firmer in Grandmama's mind. It made sense of what was otherwise outside the character and nature of the people she had observed. Looking at Mrs. Dowson, she was certain she had guessed the same answer. She smiled across at her. "How very sad," she said gently, aware of what an absurd understatement that was. "Poor Arthur." She hesitated. "And poor Zachary."

"And Agnes," Mrs. Dowson added. "But above all, I wish that Maude had not . . . not suffered so."

"But she made the best of it," Grandmama said with an intensity of feeling, an absolute conviction that welled up inside her, driving away all doubt.

Mrs. Dowson nodded. "Maude always knew how to live. She knew the worst was there and she accepted the pain as part of the truth of things, but

162

she chose to see the best also, and to find the joy in variety. She did not close herself off from the richness of experience. I think that was her gift. I shall miss her terribly."

"Even though I knew her only briefly, I shall miss her also," Grandmama confessed. "But I am profoundly grateful that I did know her. And . . . and gratitude is something I have not felt lately. Simply to have that back is a . . ." She did not know how to finish. She sniffed, pulled her emotions together with an effort, then rose to her feet. "But I have something to do. I must return to Snave and attend to it. Thank you very much for your hospitality, Mrs. Dowson, and even more for the understanding you have given me. May I wish you the joy of the season, and remembrance of all that is good in the past, together with hope for the future."

Mrs. Dowson rose also. "Why, how graciously put, Mrs. Ellison. I shall endeavor to remember that. May I wish you joy also, and safety in your journey, both in the body and in the spirit? Happy Christmas."

163

Outside it was beginning to snow, white flurries on the wind. So far it was only dusting the ground, but the heavy pall of cloud to the north made it apparent that there was a great deal more to come. Whether she wanted to or not, Grandmama would be unlikely to be able to return to St. Mary in the Marsh today. That was a good thing. What she had to do would be best done in the evening, when they were all together after dinner. It would be uncomfortable, extremely so. She felt a sinking in her stomach as she sat in the pony trap, wrapped against the snow. The biting wind was behind her and the roar of the sea breaking on the shore growing fainter as they moved inland between the wide, flat fields, beginning to whiten.

She was afraid. She admitted it to herself. She was afraid of unpleasantness, even physical attack, although she expected any attack to be secret, disguised as the one on Maude had been. Even more than that, and it surprised her, she was afraid of not doing it well.

But then, like Agnes, she had regarded herself as

a failure most of her life. She had lived a lie, always pretending to be a highly respectable woman, even aggressively so, married to a man who had died relatively young and left her grieving since her late forties, unable to recover from the loss.

In truth, she had married wretchedly, and his death had released her, at least on the outside. She had never allowed herself to be released in her own mind, and worse still, in her heart. She had kept up the lie, to save her pride.

Of course no one ever needed to know the details, but she could have been honest with herself, and it would slowly have spread through her manner, her beliefs, and in the end the way she had seen and been seen by others.

Maude Barrington had suffered a monstrous injustice. She had borne it apparently without bitterness. If it had marred an earlier part of her life, perhaps when she first went abroad, she had healed her own spirit from the damage and gone on to live a passionate and adventurous life. Perhaps it had never been comfortable, but what was comfort

165

worth? Bitterness, blame, and self-hatred were never comfortable either. And perhaps they were also not as safe as she had once imagined. They were a slow-growing disease within, killing inch by inch.

It was snowing quite hard now, lying thick and light on the ground, beginning to drift on the wind-ward side of the furrows left in the fields after their winter plowing, and on the trunks of the trees. The wind was blowing too hard for the snow to stay on the branches as they swayed against the sky. There was little sound from the pony's hooves because the ground was blanketed already, just the deep moan of the wind and the creak of the wheels. It was a hard, beautiful world, invigorating, ice-cold, and on every side, sweet and sharp-smelling from the sea, infinitely wide.

She arrived back at Snave before she was really ready, but there was no help for it. And maybe she would never feel as if it were time. She allowed the stable boy to assist her, and to his surprise thanked him for his care.

Inside she took off her cape and shawl and was

very glad to be in the warmth again. Her hands were almost numb from the cold and her face was stinging, her eyes watering, but she had never felt more intensely alive. She was terrified, and yet there was an unmistakable bubble of courage inside her, as if something of Maude's vitality and hunger for life had been bequeathed to her.

She was too late for luncheon, and too excited to eat much anyway. Cook had prepared a tray for her with soup and new, warm bread, and that was really all she required. She thanked her sincerely, with a compliment, and after finishing it all, went upstairs with the excuse that she wished to lie down. In reality she wanted to prepare herself for the evening. It was going to be one of the biggest of her life, perhaps her only real achievement. It would require all the nerve and the intelligence she possessed. There was in her mind no doubt of the truth now. Proving it would be altogether another matter, but if she did not attempt it, whatever it cost her, then she would have failed the last chance that fate had offered.

She dressed very carefully, in the housekeeper's best black gown, and thanked the maid. It seemed appropriate. She was going to be a different person from the woman she had been as long as she could clearly remember. She was going to be brave, face all the ugliness, the shame, and the failure, and be gentle toward them, because she understood them intimately. She had been a liar herself, and every stupid ugly corner of it was familiar. She had been a coward, and its corroding shroud had covered every part of her life. She had tried to touch other people's lives with her own meanness of spirit, her belief in failure. There was no victory in that. One could spoil others, dirty them, damage what could have been whole. Now she could touch all their wounds with pity, but none of them could deceive her.

She regarded herself in the glass. She looked different from the way she was accustomed. It was more than the dress that was not her own; the face also was not the one that had been hers for so long.

There was color in her skin. Her eyes were brighter. Most of all the sulk had gone from her lips, and the lines seemed to be curving upward, not down.

Ridiculous! She had never been pretty, and she wasn't now. If she did not know better, she would think she had been imbibing rather too freely of the Christmas spirit, of that nature that comes in a bottle!

She straightened her skirt a last time, and went down to join the family for dinner. Tomorrow she would leave. She would probably have to, even if the snow were up to the eaves! There was something exhilarating, and a little mad, in casting the last die, crossing the Rubicon, if she were remembering her schoolroom history correctly. It was war! Triumph or disaster, because she could not stop until it was over.

PART THREE

. . . .

SHE WAS A FEW MINUTES LATE, AS SHE HAD
intended. There was very little time before dinner
was announced and they all went into the dining
room. It was now looking even more festive, with
scarlet berries intertwined in the wreaths and the
swags along the mantelpiece, all tied with gold ribbons. There were scarlet candles on the table, even
though they were not yet lit, and everything seemed
to be touched with light from the chandeliers.

"I hope you are recovered from your journey, Mrs.
Ellison?" Arthur asked with concern. "I'm afraid the
weather turned most unpleasant before you were
able to return."

"I should not have allowed you to go," Bedelia

added. "I had not realized it would take you so long."

"It was entirely my own fault," Grandmama replied. "I could have been back earlier, and I should have, for the stable boy's and the pony's sake, if nothing else. To tell you the truth, the ride back was very beautiful. I have not been out in a snowstorm for so long that I had forgotten how amazing it is. The sense of the power and magnitude of nature is very marvelous."

"What a refreshing view," Arthur said, then suddenly the sadness filled his eyes, overwhelming him. "You remind me of Maude." He stopped, unable to continue.

It was the greatest compliment Grandmama had ever received, but she could not afford to stop and savor it now.

She continued with what she had intended to . say, regardless of their responses. She even ignored the butler and the footman serving the soup.

"Thank you, Mr. Harcourt. The more I learn of Maude, the more I appreciate how very much that means. I know that for you it is as profound as it could be, and I wish more than you can be aware of to live up to it."

Bedelia was startled, then her mouth curled in a smile more of disdain than amusement. "We all grieve for Maude, Mrs. Ellison, but there is no requirement for you to cater to our family perception with such praise." She left the implied adjective "fulsome" unsaid, but it hung in the air.

"Oh, I'm not!" Grandmama said candidly, her eyes wide. "Maude was a most remarkable person. I learned far more of just how amazing from Mrs. Dowson. That, I'm afraid, is why I stayed so long."

Bedelia was stiff, her shoulders like carved ivory beneath her violet taffeta gown. "Mrs. Dowson is sentimental," she replied coolly. "A vicar's widow and obliged to see the best in people."

"Perhaps the vicar did," Grandmama corrected her. "Mrs. Dowson certainly does not. She is quite capable of seeing pride, greed, selfishness, and other things; cowardice in particular." She smiled at Agnes. "The acceptance of failure because one does

175

not have the courage to face what one is afraid of, and pay the price in comfort that is sometimes necessary for success."

. The blood drained from Agnes's face, leaving her ashen. Her spoon slithered into her soup dish and she ignored it.

Zachary started to speak, and then choked on whatever it was he had been going to say.

It was Randolph who came to her rescue. "That sounds extremely harsh, Mrs. Ellison. How on earth would Mrs. Dowson be in a position to know anything of that sort about anybody? And what she did know must have come to her in a privileged position, and therefore should not be repeated."

"Most un-Christian," Clara added.

"It can be very difficult to recognize the right . thing to do, at times," Grandmama continued, grateful for the extraordinary ease with which the opportunities she needed were opening up for her. "But I must not misrepresent Mrs. Dowson. Actually she said nothing, except to praise Maude's love of beauty, her laughter, and above all her courage to

176

make the best of her life, even after so great a sacrifice, which was given silently and with the utmost dignity."

Zachary looked totally confused. Arthur was pale, his breathing seemed painful. Bedelia was as white as Agnes now and her hands on her lap were clenched. No one ate.

"I am not sure what you imagine you are referring to, Mrs. Ellison," she said icily. "It appears you are a lonely woman with nothing to do, and you have concerned yourself in our family's affairs in a way that exceeds even your imagined duty to Maude, whom you barely met. Your meddlesomeness has run away with you. I think we had better find a way to return you to St. Mary in the Marsh tomorrow, regardless of the weather. I am sure that would be better for all of us."

Randolph blushed scarlet.

It was Arthur who spoke. "Bedelia, that is unnecessary. I apologize, Mrs. Ellison. I don't know what Maude told you, but I think you must have misunderstood her."

177

"She told me nothing," Grandmama said, meeting his eyes. "She would never betray you like that! And surely by now you must know beyond any question at all that she would not betray Bedelia either! She did not come here to cause any kind of trouble. The man who had loved her and protected her in Persia died, and she could no longer remain there. She came back home because she wished to. Perhaps she even imagined that after all these years she would be welcome. Which of course was an error. Quite obviously she was not."

"You have no right to say that!" Clara cut in. "She had been living in the desert, in tents and by campfires, like a . . . a gypsy! And with a foreign man to whom she was not married! We could hardly have her in the house at the same time as Lord Woollard! My father-in-law has given more to society than you have any idea. This peerage would have been not only a just reward but an opportunity to do even more good. We could not jeopardize that!"

"And it would, in time, have made you Lady Harcourt," Grandmama added. "With all that that means. Of course you did not wish to lose such a prize."

"Oh, no . . . I . . ." Clara faded into silence. She had the grace to be ashamed.

"Stuff and nonsense!" Bedelia snapped. "You overstep yourself, Mrs. Ellison. Your behavior is disgraceful!"

"She came home because she had nowhere else to go?" Agnes asked, her face pinched with sorrow. "We should have forgiven her, Bedelia. It was a very long time ago." '

"Bedelia does not forgive," Grandmama answered Agnes. "Not that there was anything of Maude's that needed pardon. Tragically there are some people who can never forgive a gift, especially from someone who is aware of their vulnerability. Sometimes it is harder to forgive a gift than an injury, because you have incurred a debt, and in your own eyes you have lost control, and your superiority."

There was an electric silence.

"Those who themselves do not forgive find it impossible to believe that others do," Grandmama went on. "So they expect vengeance where there is none, and strike out to defend themselves from a blow that existed only in their own guilty imaginations."

Arthur leaned forward. "I think you had better stop speaking in riddles, Mrs. Ellison. I have very little idea of what you are talking about . . ."

"Neither has she!" Bedelia said tartly. "Really Arthur, you should have more sense than to encourage her. Can't you see that she has been drinking? Let us speak of something civilized and stop descending into personal remarks. It is extremely vulgar." She spoke as if that was the end of the matter.

Arthur drew in his breath, but it was Agnes who answered. She looked at Grandmama directly. "Was Maude ill? Did she know she was going to die, and that was why she came home at last? To make peace?"

"No," Grandmama replied with authority. "As I said, there was nothing to keep her in Persia anymore, nor was it safe."

"She had made enemies, no doubt," Bedelia observed. "You did not say that this man was married to someone else, but knowing Maude, I have no doubt that it was true."

"Oh, Bedelia, you should forgive her that!" Agnes pleaded. "It was forty years ago! And she is gone now. It's Christmas!"

"Don't be so feeble!" Bedelia accused her. "Wrong does not suddenly become right just because of the season."

Agnes blushed scarlet.

"Of course it doesn't," Grandmama agreed vehemently. "Some debts can be forgiven, but there are some that have to be paid, one way or another."

"I don't care for your opinion, Mrs. Ellison," Bedelia said frigidly.

"There is no reason why you should," again Grandmama agreed with her. "But you care about your family's opinions. In the end it is really all you have. That, and the knowledge within yourself, of course. Perhaps that is why Maude was happy, in the deepest sense. She knew she was loved, and no matter what the cost, she had done the right thing."

"I have no idea what you are talking about!"

"Yes you do. You are probably the only one who does." Nothing was going to stop Grandmama. "When you were a young woman, and even more beautiful than you are now, Mrs. Harcourt,"—she glanced at Zachary—"he fell in love with you. And like many young people, you did not deny yourselves the pleasure of love."

Bedelia hissed in her breath, but the shame in Zachary's face made her denial impossible.

"But then Mr. Harcourt came along, and he was a far better catch, so you went after him instead," Grandmama continued relentlessly. "And you caught him, at least his admiration for your beauty, and a certain physical appetite. You also did not deny yourselves. After all, you fully intended to marry him. Which would all have gone very well, had not Maude returned home, and Mr. Harcourt fell truly in love with her."

Bedelia's eyes on her were like daggers.

Grandmama ignored them, but her heart was pounding almost in her throat. If she were wrong, catastrophically, insanely wrong, she would be ruined forever. Her mouth was dry, her voice rasping. "You were furious that Maude, of all people, should take your lover, but there was worse to follow. You learned that you were with child. Mr. Sullivan's of course. But it could have been Mr. Harcourt's, for all he knew. That gave you your perfect weapon for regaining everything. You told him. Being a man of honor, in spite of his lapse of self-control, he broke off his relationship with Maude, whom he truly loved, as she loved him, and he married you. He paid a bitter price for his self-indulgence. So did your sister, rather than allow you to be shamed."

There were gasps of breath, the clink of cutlery, even a broken glass stem. "That is what you cannot forgive—that you wronged her," she went on regardless. "And she sacrificed her happiness for yours— and perhaps for Mr. Harcourt's honor. Although I believe it was actually Mr. Sullivan's, in fact."

Arthur stared at Bedelia, a stunned and terrible look in his eyes. "Randolph is not mine, and you know it," he said very quietly.

183

"Are . . . are you sure?" Agnes asked. Then she looked more closely at Bedelia, and did not ask again.

"What does she mean that you could not forgive?" Arthur asked Bedelia.

"I have no idea!" Bedelia replied. "She is an inquisitive, meddling old woman who listens at doors and hears half stories, gossips with other old women who should know better, and apparently listened to Maude's self-delusions of her own romantic youth."

"It wasn't a delusion," Arthur told her very quietly. "I loved Maude as I have never loved anyone else in my life, before or since. But I could not marry her because you told me that you were carrying my child. I can't blame you for that, it was my doing as much as yours. Nor can I blame Zachary. He was no worse than I, and by heaven you were beautiful. But Maude was funny and kind. She was brave and warm and honest, and she was generous with life, with her own spirit. Her beauty would have lasted forever, and grown with time rather than fade. I

184

knew it then, and I was proved right when she came back, even after forty years, which were like a lifetime while she was gone, and nothing at all once she returned."

"Oh, Arthur!" Agnes breathed out. "How terrible for you."

Zachary was looking at Agnes with amazement.

"I found the rest of the peppermint water," Grandmama said in the silence.

"I beg your pardon?" Arthur frowned.

Grandmama wavered for an instant. Should she tell them, or was this enough? But would it last? There would be no further chance. She turned to Bedelia and saw the fury in her eyes.

"You told Maude when you gave her the macadamia nuts, which are so indigestible to some of us, that you had very little peppermint water, just the end of one bottle, sufficient for a single dose. But actually you had plenty. There is some in my room, and some in the other guest rooms also. A nice courtesy, especially over a festive season when we will all eat a little heavily."

185

"What has that to do with anything at all?" Clara demanded. "Why are we talking about peppermint water? Are you quite mad?"

"I wish I were," Grandmama answered. "It would be so much less ugly an answer than the truth. I don't eat macadamia nuts myself. They give me indigestion . . ."

Zachary was staring at her as if he could not believe his ears.

Agnes looked appalled.

"But peppermint water would help," Grandmama carried on. "Unless of course, it were laced with foxglove leaves. Then it would kill. Most of us who have ever arranged flowers know that. There are a few one must be careful of, especially with children about: laburnum, monk's hood, belladonna, and of course foxgloves. Such handsome flowers, but the distilled juice can cause the heart to fail. It is used in medicine to slow it down if it is racing, but only a very little, naturally."

"That is a wicked thing to suggest!" Clara was horrified. "How . . . how dare you?"

Randolph touched her gently. "There is no need to be afraid, my dear. She could not possibly prove it." He gulped. "Could you?"

Grandmama looked at him and realized it was a question. "I don't know," she replied. "I had not considered trying to, although it might not be too difficult. I don't think that is what matters. It is knowing the truth that is important. It gives you the freedom to do whatever you choose to, knowing right from wrong." She turned to Arthur, waiting for him to speak.

But he was not looking at her. His gaze did not move from Bedelia's face, and he read in it the fear and the hatred that betrayed her. Whatever she had said, he would know what she had done.

Randolph was staring at his mother with horror and pity in his face, and a revulsion he could not hide. He turned swiftly to Zachary, then embarrassed, away again. Zachary was looking at him with wonder, and an intensity quite naked in his eyes.

Arthur sighed. He spoke to Grandmama as if Be-

187

delia had ceased to exist. "You mentioned a garden in Persia that Maude described to you as if she loved it. Have you any idea where it was, exactly?"

"No, but I believe Mrs. Dowson would know," Grandmama replied. "Maude wrote to her quite regularly. I imagine she would be happy to tell you."

"Good. I have a great desire to see it, since she loved it so much. You made it sound marvelous also, Mrs. Ellison, and for that I shall always be grateful to you. The truth you have shown us is terrible, but deep as it cuts, a clean wound will heal, in time."

"You . . . you can't go to Persia now, Papa . . . I mean . . . ," Randolph faltered and stopped.

Arthur smiled at him, gently and with great affection. "You will always be my son in spirit, Randolph, and I will always love you as such. But I can go to Persia and I will. I shall write to Lord Woollard and decline a peerage. I may return from Persia one day, and I may not. The estate will provide for your mother. Please see that Mrs. Ellison is safely returned to St. Mary in the Marsh tomorrow. Now I shall wish you good night." He rose to his feet. He was still a startlingly handsome man, but it was his dignity that remained in the mind. "And good-bye," he added, before turning and leaving the room without looking behind him. He did not once glance at Bedelia.

Zachary reached out his hand to Agnes, and very slowly, as if uncertain that it could be true, she took it.

Reluctantly Grandmama abandoned her dinner and excused herself also. It was quite impossible to remain. She had shown them the truth. What they did with it she should not influence, only hope.

Upstairs in her bedroom she sank down into the chair. Suddenly her legs were weak and she found she was trembling. Had she done enough? Should she have tried harder to prove something that would stand the test of trial and the law?

As it was now, the family knew the truth. There could be no denying that. Arthur would leave, per- haps forever. Bedelia would probably never see him again. People would know, in the way that they do. They would look at her and whisper. There would be

189

speculation, most of it ugly. The kindest she would receive would be pity, and that would be the most painful of all to a woman like Bedelia. She would see it in their glances in the street, the half-hidden smiles.

Gradually perhaps even some of the truth would emerge, but imagination would be more colorful, and crueler. Agnes and Zachary would be happy with each other at last, and perhaps with Randolph too, and Clara. Old Mrs. Dowson would understand a great deal. She might be discreet, but Bedelia would know that she knew, and would never allow Maude's name to be blackened.

Bedelia would be provided for, waited on, but starved of friendship or admiration. No one would care how beautiful she had been, or how clever. She would be alone, a woman unloved.

At a glance, that was a gentler punishment than trial, and possibly the gallows, or possibly a verdict of innocence. But it would be more certain, and far, far longer. She would taste it for the rest of her life.

But the others would be happy, perhaps for the first time in their lives.

Grandmama stopped shaking and sat still, slowly beginning to smile, even if there was sadness in it, and pity.

$\mathcal{I}$n the morning Zachary drove her back through the deepening snow to St. Mary in the Marsh. He did not speak much, but she felt a great certainty that he had at last realized that Agnes was not a paler, second-best version of Bedelia, but a kinder if less brave person, a gentler, more generous one, who might now, at last, find the courage to be the best. And she had always truly loved him.

"Thank you, Mrs. Ellison," he said as the trap rounded the last corner through the dazzling snow and she saw Joshua and Caroline's house blazing with lights.

"I hope you will be happy," she replied, meaning it far more than the simple words could convey.

191

'I . . . I understand why you and Maude were
such good friends," he said earnestly. "Even in so
short a time. You are like her. You have such
courage to tell the truth, however difficult, and such
joy for life. I am amazed at your compassion for
even the weakest of us. I imagine you will have a
wonderful Christmas, because you will make it so.
But I wish it for you just the same."

"I will," she assured him as they drew up in front
of the door. It opened and Joshua came down the
step and across the grass to the trap to assist her. "I
shall have the best Christmas of my life," she went
on, still speaking to Zachary. "I am beginning to understand what it truly means."

"Welcome home, Mama-in-law," Joshua said with
surprise lifting his eyebrows. He gave her his arm
and she alighted.

"Thank you, Joshua." She smiled at him. "Happy
Christmas, my dear. I have wonderful things to tell
you, brave and beautiful things, when I can think
how to find words for them. About hope and honor,
and what love really means. Your aunt Maude was

192

a very wonderful woman. She has given me the greatest gift of all—an understanding of Christmas itself."

"Yes, I see that," Joshua said with sudden conviction. "It is perfectly plain. Happy Christmas, Mama-in-law."

A Christmas Secret

To all those who
would like to start again

CLARICE CORDE LEANED BACK IN HER SEAT AS the train pulled out of the station in a cloud of steam. Smuts flew and engine roared as they gathered speed on their journey northward. The rain beat against the window; she could barely see the glistening roof-tops of London. It was December 14, 1890, ten days until Christmas Eve. She had been married little more than a year, and she was far from used to being a vicar's wife. Neither obedience nor tact came to her except with a considerable effort, but she made that effort for Dominic's sake.

She glanced sideways at him now and saw him deep in thought. She knew he was concerned about his ability to rise to this opportunity they had been offered so unexpectedly. The elderly Reverend Wynter had taken a richly deserved holiday; therefore his church, in the small village of Cottisham in Oxfordshire, needed someone to stand in for him and care for his flock over Christmas.

Dominic had seized the chance. He was a widower who had abandoned a self-indulgent life and embraced the ministry somewhat late. Perhaps no one but Clarice saw beyond his startlingly handsome face and charm of manner to the doubts beneath. She loved him the more fiercely because she knew he understood his own weaknesses as well as the power of his dreams.

He looked up and smiled at her. Once again she was warmed by amazement that he should have chosen her: the awkward sister, the one with the slightly crooked nose that gave her face a wry, individual look, the one with the tactless tongue and the pungent sense of humor, rather than any of the reliable and more conventional beauties eager for his attention.

This chance to go to Cottisham was the greatest Christmas gift they could have been given. It was an escape from serving under the Reverend Spindlewood in the bleak area of industrial London to which he had been sent as curate.

How could Clarice reassure him that they expected only patience, and that he should be there to listen and comfort, to assure them of the message of Christmas and peace on earth?

She reached her hand across and touched his arm, tightening her fingers for a moment. "It will be good," she said firmly. "And being in the country will be a delight."

He smiled at her, his dark eyes bright, knowing what she meant to tell him.

They traveled for nearly two hours, most of it through gently rolling countryside, the fields now bare except for the meadows still green. The woodlands and copses were without leaf, and the higher crowns of the hills were dusted with snow. Here in the heart of England winter could be surprisingly fierce, and no doubt there was far worse weather to come.

For the most part the villages lay in the hollows, the first sight from the train windows being the steep spires of the churches, then the huddled roofs.

201

They reached the station nearest to Cottisham and hired a pony trap to take them the last few miles through winding lanes, up the brow of a long, ridge-backed hill, and down into the sloping valley.

The village was beautiful, even though it boasted little more than a wide green with a duck pond and houses all around it. Many of the dwellings were thatched, their bare winter gardens neatly tidied. Perhaps half a dozen narrow roads twisted away into the surrounding woods and the fields beyond. The church was Saxon: slate-roofed, with a square tower rising high against the wind-torn clouds.

The pony trap drew up in front of the rambling stone vicarage. The driver unloaded their cases onto the gravel and quickly drove away.

Clarice looked at the closed door, then at the fine Georgian windows. It was a beautiful house, but it seemed oddly blind, as if it were oblivious to their arrival, and they would knock on the oak door in vain. This was to be their home, and Dominic's challenge and opportunity would be to preach and to minister without the supervision—or constant meddling—of

202

the Reverend Spindlewood. Clarice knew she must behave with enthusiasm now, whatever doubt or loneliness she felt. That was what faith was about. Anyone can be cheerful when she is confident and the sun is shining.

She looked at Dominic once, then marched up to the front door and banged briskly with the lion's head knocker.

There was total silence from inside.

"Stay here with the boxes," Dominic said quietly. "I'll go to the nearest house. They must have left the keys with someone."

But before he could go more than a dozen steps a stout woman, her hair piled atop her head in an untidy knot, came bustling along the road. She struggled to hold a shawl around her shoulders against the wind.

"All right! All right! I'm coming," she called out. "No hurry! It ain't snowin' yet. You must be the Reverend Corde. An' Mrs. Corde, I take it?" She stopped in front of them and looked Clarice up and down dubiously, her blunt face skeptical. "I s'pose you know how to care for a house, an' all?" she said in a tone close to accusation. "I'm Mrs. Wellbeloved. I look after the vicar, but I can't do no more for you than a bit o' the heavy work, 'cos I've got family coming for Christmas, an' I need me holiday, too. In't good for a body to work all the days o' the year, an' it in't right to expect it."

"Of course we don't expect it," Clarice agreed, although she had in fact expected exactly that. "If you show me where to find everything and assist with the laundry, I'm sure that will be most satisfactory."

Mrs. Wellbeloved looked more or less mollified. She produced a large key from her pocket, unlocked the door, and led the way in. "Just leave them boxes. Old Will and young Tom'll bring 'em on up for yer."

Clarice followed her, pleasantly surprised by the warmth of the house, even though the vicar had been gone for a couple of days. It smelled of lavender, beeswax, and the faint, earthy perfume of chrysanthemums. Everything looked clean: the wooden floor, the hall table, the doors leading off to left and right, the stairs going up toward a wide landing. There was a large vase of branches and leaves of gold and bronze on the floor. For all her lack of grace, Mrs. Wellbeloved seemed to be an excellent housekeeper.

"You'll be liking it here," she said more to Dominic than to Clarice. It sounded something of an order. "Folks know how to behave decent. Come to church reg'lar and give to the poor. Won't be nothing for you to do but your duty. Just keep it right for the vicar to come back to. I'm sure he's left you a list of them as needs visiting, but if he hasn't, I can tell you." She opened the sitting room door to show them a graceful room with a wide fireplace and bay window, and then closed the door again. "You'll be takin' all services reg'lar," she went on, walking quickly toward the kitchen. "An' you won't be wantin' the sexton, but if you do, he's first on the right on the Glebe Road. Grave digger's two down beyond."

"Thank you, Mrs. Wellbeloved." Dominic avoided meeting Clarice's eyes and answered with as straight a face as he could manage.

"I'll be in reg'lar for the heavy stuff, 'ceptin' Christmas Day, an' Boxin' Day, o' course," Mrs. Wellbeloved continued. "You'll have enough coal an' coke an' likely enough kindlin', but if you haven't you can go walk in the woods an' pick up plenty. Works best of all, if you dry it proper first. An' you'll walk Harry, too. I can't be doin' that."

"Harry?" Dominic asked, puzzled.

"Harry." She looked at him witheringly. "The dog! Didn't the vicar tell you about Harry? Retriever, he is. Good as gold, if you treat him right. An' Etta. But you don't need to do nothin' for her, 'cept scraps and stuff, an' milk. She'll fend for herself."

Clarice made a quick guess. "Etta's a cat?"

Mrs. Wellbeloved looked appeased for their ignorance. "Right good little mouser, she is. Plain as you like, but clever. Capture 'em all in the end." She said it with satisfaction, as if she identified with the animal and were in some oblique way describing herself as well.

Clarice could not help being amused. "I am sure we shall get along excellently. Thank you for showing us in. We shall have a cup of tea, and then unpack."

"There's everything you'll need for today," Mrs. Wellbeloved said, nodding. "Game pie in the pantry, an' plenty o' vegetables, such as there is this time o' year. You'll need onions. Vicar loved 'em. Hot onion soup best thing in the world for a cold, he said. Smells worse 'n whiskey, but at least you're sober." She gave Dominic a hard, level look.

He returned it unflinchingly, then slowly smiled.

Mrs. Wellbeloved grunted. A pink blush spread up her face, and she turned away. "Handsome is as handsome does," she muttered under her breath.

Clarice thanked her again and saw her to the door. She was ready to be alone in her new temporary home and take stock of things. But first she wanted a cup of tea. It had been a long journey, and it was close to the shortest day in the year. Storm clouds were looming up over the trees, and the light was fading.

The house was everything she could have hoped. It had charm and individuality. The furniture was all well used, but also well cared for. Nothing really matched, as if each piece had been gathered as opportunity arose, and yet nothing appeared to be out of place. Oak, mahogany, and walnut jostled together, and age had mellowed them all. Elizabethan carving did not clash with Georgian simplicity. Everything seemed to be useful, except for one small table with barley-twist legs, which was apparently there simply because it was liked.

The pictures on the walls were also obviously personal choices: a watercolor of Bamburgh Castle on the Northumberland coast, rising out of the pale sands with the North Sea beyond; a Dutch scene of fishing boats; half a dozen pencil sketches of bare trees; more winter fields and trees in pen and ink. She found them remarkably restful; her eyes returned to them again and again. Upstairs she found another sketch, this time of the ruins of Rievaulx Abbey, bare columns and broken walls towering against the clouds.

"Look at this," she called to Dominic, who was carrying the last case up to the box room. "Isn't it lovely?"

He put the box away before coming to stand a little behind her, his arm around her shoulder. "Yes," he agreed, examining the picture carefully. "I like it very much." He peered at the signature. "It's his own! Did you see that?"

"His own?" she asked.

"The bishop told me he painted," he replied. "He didn't say how good he was, though. That has both power and grace to it. At least I think so. I'm looking forward to meeting him when he comes back."

She caught the edge of ruefulness in his voice. Those three weeks would go by too quickly, and then they would have to return to London, and the Reverend Spindlewood. Before that time he must somehow show that he was wise enough, gentle enough, and patient enough in listening to care for the village alone. He must be passionate and original in his sermons, not only to hold interest but also to feed the heart with the special message of Christmas. She knew this mattered to him intensely, and that his belief in himself wavered. Only the total upheaval of his life had made him consider religious faith at all.

Empty words of assurance from her would not help. He already knew she believed in him, and took it for granted that it was born of her love more than any realism.

"I wonder if he'll do any more drawing while he's away this time," she said aloud. "I don't even know where he's gone."

She awoke the next morning to stand shivering in her nightgown and drew open the curtains onto a glistening white world. The vicarage garden was surprisingly large and backed onto the woods. The trees were dusted with snow in wildly intricate patterns like heavy lace against a lead-gray sky, and the pale light gave it an eerie, luminous quality. She breathed out slowly in amazement at its beauty, momentarily forgetting to shiver.

She stared at the scene in rapture until suddenly she remembered there was housework to be done: grates to clean out, fires to be laid and lit, and breakfast to be cooked. And of course Harry and Etta to be fed. She could not afford to wait for Mrs. Wellbeloved to come.

A little after ten o'clock, when Dominic was in the study reading some of the vicar's notes and trying to familiarize himself with the parish, there was a noise outside in the gravel drive. Harry came trotting out of the kitchen, where he had been asleep by the stove. His nose was in the air and his plumed tail was waving; however, he did not bark.

Clarice snatched off her apron and went to open the door just as the knocker sounded. She pulled it wide to see a man standing just back from the step. He was a little above average height and apparently slender, although under the weight of his winter coat it was hard to tell. His face was fine-boned, not exactly handsome, but full of intelligence and a wry, sad wit. His complexion was deep olive, and his eyes had the liquid darkness that comes from the East. When he spoke, however, his voice was as English as her own.

"How do you do, Mrs. Corde. I am Peter Connaught." He gestured vaguely behind him. "From the manor house. I wanted to welcome you to the village." He held out his hand, then glanced at the smooth leather glove and apologized, pulling it off.

"How do you do, Mr. Connaught," she replied, smiling at him. "That is most kind of you. May I offer you a cup of tea? It's terribly cold this morning."

"That would be most welcome," he said with a

nod. "I think it's going to be a hard Christmas—for weather, but I hope not for anything else."

She stepped back and opened the door wider for him. He came in, glancing around as if perhaps the vicarage might have changed since he had been there last. Then he relaxed and smiled again, reassured. Did he think they would have moved things in a night?

She took his coat and showed him into the sitting room, grateful she had lit the fire early and it was pleasantly warm. She noticed how again he looked around, smiling at familiar things, the pictures, the way the furniture was arranged, the worn chairs with their colors blending.

"If you will excuse me, I shall tell my husband you are here. Then I shall bring tea."

"Of course." He inclined his head, rubbing his hands together. His polished boots were wet from the snow. The wind had whipped color into his face.

She went to the study first and opened the door without knocking.

"Dominic, Mr. Connaught from the manor house

212

is in the sitting room. I'm just going to bring tea. It's very good of him to come, isn't it!"

He looked a little surprised. "Yes. And very quick." There was a note of apprehension in his voice.

Clarice heard it and was afraid he was anxious already that she might be too frank in her opinions, too quick not only to see a better way of doing something but also to say so. It had been known to happen before.

"I suppose I should call upon his wife. She will know all the women in the village and everything about them. He didn't mention her," she added, biting her lip and looking straight into his eyes. "But I promise I shall behave perfectly. I will find her delightful and extremely competent, I swear. Even if she is a blithering idiot with a tongue like a dose of vinegar! I really do promise."

He stood up. "Just don't expect me to be there. I couldn't keep a straight face!" he warned, touching her cheek so lightly she barely felt it. "Don't change too much. I wouldn't care to be Archbishop of Canterbury if I had to lose the person you are in order to do it!"

"Oh, if you were Archbishop of Canterbury," she said cheerfully, "I would probably say whatever I pleased! Everyone would be far too in awe of you to criticize me."

He rolled his eyes and went out to meet their guest.

She went into the kitchen happily. To be loved for herself, with all her dreams and vulnerabilities, the mistakes and the virtues, was the highest prize in life, and she knew that.

When she returned with the tray of tea and biscuits, she found both men seated by the fire talking. They rose immediately. Dominic took the tray from her and set it down. They exchanged the usual pleasantries. She poured and passed Connaught his cup, then Dominic.

"Sir Peter has been telling me a little about the village," Dominic said, catching her eye. "His family has been here for centuries."

She felt herself blush. She had not known his title and had called him *Mister* when she had asked him in. She wondered if he was offended. Normally she would not have cared, but all this mattered so much.

214

She was not impressed with people's ancestors, but this was not the time to say so. She composed her face into an expression of interest. "Really? How fortunate you are to have deep roots in such a lovely place."

"Yes," he agreed quickly. "It gives me a great sense of belonging. And like all privileges, it carries certain obligations. But I believe they are a pleasure also. I was very sad when I learned the Reverend Wynter was taking his holiday over Christmas, but now that we have you here, I am sure it will be as excellent as always. Christmas is a great time for healing rifts, forgiving mistakes, and welcoming wanderers home."

"How very well you express it," Dominic responded. "Is that what the Reverend Wynter has said in the past, or your own feeling?"

Sir Peter looked slightly surprised, even momentarily disconcerted. "My own. Why do you ask?"

"I thought it so well phrased, I might ask you if I could use it," Dominic replied candidly. "I would like to say something truly appropriate in my Watch Night sermon, which has to be as short as possible, yet still have meaning. But I cannot prepare it until I have

215

at least a slight acquaintance with the village and the people."

Sir Peter leaned forward a little, a very slight crease between his dark brows. "Did the Reverend Wynter not tell you at least a little about us, collectively and individually?"

Watching him, Clarice had the sudden certainty that the answer mattered to him far more than he wished them to know. There was a tension in the lines of his body, and the knuckles of his beautiful hands were white on his lap.

Dominic appeared not to have noticed. "Unfortunately I never met him," he answered. "The request came to me through the bishop. I gather the Reverend Wynter's decision to take a holiday was made very quickly."

"I see." Sir Peter leaned back again and picked up his tea. "That is a trifle awkward for you. Whatever I can do I shall be more than happy to. Call upon me at any time. Perhaps you will dine with me at the hall one evening, when you are settled in?" He looked at Clarice. "I regret my hospitality will offer you no female company, since my mother has passed away, and I am not married, but I promise to show you much that is of interest if you care for history, art, or architecture. I can tell you stories of all manner of people good and evil, tragic and amusing, belonging to this village down the ages."

She did not have to pretend interest. "I think that would be infinitely more enjoyable than any feminine gossip I can imagine," she replied. "And I will most certainly come."

He looked pleased, as if the prospect excited him. Obviously he was enormously proud of his heritage and loved to share it, to entertain people, fill them with laughter and a little awe as well. He looked at Dominic. "I see you have moved the chessboard. You do not play?"

Dominic glanced around. He clearly had no idea where the chessboard had been.

"You didn't?" Sir Peter said quickly. "It was already gone when you came?"

"Yes. I haven't seen one." He looked at Clarice questioningly.

"I haven't seen it, either," she said. "Did the Reverend Wynter play?"

A look of pain burned deep in Sir Peter's eyes; with an effort he banished it. He swallowed the last of his tea. "Yes. Yes, at one time. He had a particularly beautiful set. Not black and white so much as black and gold. The black was ebony, and the gold that extraordinary shade that yew wood sometimes achieves, almost metallic. Quite beautiful. Still . . ." He rose to his feet. "It hardly matters. I just noticed because it was such a feature in the room. The light caught it, you know?"

"It sounds wonderful," Clarice responded, because the silence demanded it, but her mind was filled with the certainty that his reason for asking was nothing like as casual as he had said. There was a depth of emotion in him that could not be explained by the mere absence of an artifact of beauty. What more had it meant to him, and why did he conceal it?

She still wondered as she also rose to her feet and followed him to the door, thanking him again for his kindness in coming.

218

*M*rs. Wellbeloved arrived after luncheon, carrying a large bag of potatoes, which she set down on the kitchen table with a grunt of relief. "You'll be needin' 'em," she said.

"Thank you," Clarice accepted, telling herself that Mrs. Wellbeloved meant it kindly and it would be most ungracious to tell her that she would rather have gone to the village shop and bought them herself. Three weeks was such a short time to get to know people so she could help Dominic. "Thank you," she repeated. "That was very thoughtful. We had a visitor this morning." She carried the potatoes into the scullery, followed hopefully by the dog, who was ever optimistic about something new to eat.

"Come down here, did he?" Mrs. Wellbeloved said, her round eyes wide with interest, wispy eyebrows high. "Well, I never." She picked up the long-handled broom and began to sweep the floor.

Clarice returned to the kitchen, Harry still on her heels.

"He said his family has been in the village for

219

years," she added, tidying one of the cupboards and setting jams, pickles, savory jellies in some sort of order.

"Years!" Mrs. Wellbeloved exclaimed. "I should say centuries, more like. Since the Normans came, the way he tells it."

"The Normans! Really?"

"Yes. Ten sixty-six, you know?" Mrs. Wellbeloved looked at her skeptically. How could she be the lady she pretended if she did not know that?

Clarice was amazed. "That's terribly impressive!"

"Oh, *he's* impressed." Mrs. Wellbeloved bent awkwardly and picked up the modicum of dust from the floor, carefully pushing it into the dustpan. "Come over with William the Conqueror, so he said, an' bin in this village since the year twelve hundred. Everyone knows that." She made an expression of disdain then concealed it quickly, reaching for the bucket, putting it in the low, stone sink, and turning on the tap.

"He didn't tell me that." Clarice felt a need to defend him, although she had no idea why.

"Well, there's a surprise then." Mrs. Wellbeloved turned off the tap and heaved the bucket out. She looked at the floor skeptically. "Don't seem too bad."

"It isn't," Clarice replied. "We haven't been here a whole day yet. I really don't think you need to do it."

"P'raps you're right. I'll just do the table then. Got to keep the table clean." She took the scrubbing brush off its rack, along with a large box of yellow kitchen soap. "Knew his father, Sir Thomas. He was a real gentleman, poor man."

"Why? What happened to him?"

"Went abroad, he did." Mrs. Wellbeloved began scrubbing energetically, slopping water all over the place, wetting the entire surface of the table at once. "Foreign parts somewhere out east. Don't recall if he ever said where, exact. Fell in love and married." She poked loose strands of hair back into their knot. "Then she died, when Sir Peter was only about five or six years old. Wonderful woman, she was, from all he says, an' very beautiful. Sir Thomas were so cut up by it he came home and never went back there, ever. Raised Peter himself, teaching him all about his family, the land, all that. Very close, but never got over her death. I s'pose Sir Peter didn't, either. He never married."

"There's time yet," Clarice said quickly. "He looks no more than in his forties. He'll want to keep the line going, the family, surely?"

Mrs. Wellbeloved put her weight into the scrubbing, her lips tight, soapsuds flying. She stepped sideways and nearly fell over the dog. "It's his duty," she agreed. "But he isn't doing it, for all that. Maybe that's what it was all about."

"What what was all about?" Clarice asked unashamedly.

"Used to come here often," Mrs. Wellbeloved replied, wringing out a cloth with powerful, red-knuckled hands. "Twice a week, most months. Played chess with the vicar reg'lar. Loved their game, they did. Then he stopped all of a sudden, about two years ago. Never came here since, except it were business, or with other folk. Vicar never said why, but then he wouldn't. Could keep other folks' secrets better than the grave, he could."

"You mean they quarreled?" Clarice felt a stab of

222

disappointment. It seemed such a sad and stupid thing to do. "What quarrel could be so bad, and last so long?"

Mrs. Wellbeloved jerked upright, banging her elbow on the bucket, which was still on the table. She winced. "Well, it wouldn't be the Reverend Wynter's fault, an' that's for certain. He was the best man that ever lived in the village, whether his family went back to the manor or the workhouse! Forgive anybody anything, he would, if it were against himself. Tried over and over to make it up with Sir Peter, and Sir Peter weren't having any of it." She grunted fiercely. "But the vicar would never say a thing were right if it weren't. Fear o' God's in him like a great light, it is. Mr. Corde's a very lucky man to be allowed to step in for him over Christmas." She nodded several times. "Walk a few miles in the reverend's footsteps an' he'll be the better man for it, mark my words." She savagely wiped half the table dry, lifted the bucket onto the floor, and wiped the other half, wringing the cloth out several times.

Clarice felt defensive of Dominic, but bit her tongue rather than say anything; she needed Mrs.

Wellbeloved on their side. She took a deep breath. "He seems to be a very remarkable man, even for a vicar," she said with as much humility as she could manage.

Mrs. Wellbeloved's face softened. "That he is," she agreed more gently. "Man o' God, I say. He deserves a holiday. Go off an' do more of his paintings an' drawings, that's what he needs." She looked Clarice up and down, and then turned away so her face was out of sight. "Obliged you could come." She sniffed, choking off the emotion in her voice. She picked up the bucket and threw the dirty water into the sink so hard it splashed up and a good deal of it went out again on either side, waking the cat. Etta shook herself angrily and then curled up again, nose in her tail.

Clarice considered whether to wipe the water up for Mrs. Wellbeloved, and decided against it. Better to pretend she hadn't noticed. Instead she fetched Etta a dry towel for her bed and put the kettle on for another cup of tea, and then went to dust the hall, not that it needed it.

*T*here was a sharp drop in the temperature that evening and another heavy fall of snow. Dominic banked the fires high, hoping they would stay burning most of the night, so there would be at least some warmth left in the air by morning.

At dawn he looked out of his study window and saw the bleak beauty of the pale light, but he knew it meant that no one could plow through the deep drifts to leave the village—and some would find it hard even to leave their home to fetch food. This was where his ministry could begin. He had no knowledge yet at which houses he would be welcome, however, and he could not afford even one mistake. He was an outsider, temporarily taking the place of a man he realized was deeply loved.

So far he had only one source of information, Mrs. Wellbeloved. Clarice's exact words had been: "She has opinions about everything, which she'll share at the drop of a hat. Be busy about something else, and even if she's talking complete nonsense, for heaven's sake don't argue with her. Local knowledge is her great achievement."

Clarice was probably right. Dominic had not had to deal with maids before; he'd never even considered them.

It was time he did so. He rose and went to find Clarice, who was busy in the kitchen warming two flatirons on the top of the range, ready to iron his shirts, which she had washed the day before. Cat and dog were squashed into one basket together by the stove. Dominic looked at Clarice with a deep stab of guilt. She was not beautiful in the traditional sense, except for her eyes, which were wide, clear gray with dark lashes. There was far too much character in her face, too much readiness to laugh or lose her temper. She was quick with her opinions and far too candid for a vicar's wife, and much too perceptive of the truth. He could no longer count the times she had embarrassed him. But she was also generous and swift to forgive. She was without arrogance, and he had never known her to make a promise and fail to keep it.

She could have married a man able to give her a

large house and maids to look after her every need. She could have had a carriage, fashionable clothes, and invitations in society. Could she really be as happy as she seemed, face flushed, apron around her waist, testing the flatirons for temperature?

She looked up at him and smiled.

"I'm going to see Mrs. Wellbeloved," he told her. "I need her advice as to whom I should call on in this weather. She'll know."

"Excellent idea," she said approvingly. Then she frowned. "Do be tactful with her, won't you? She's a funny creature."

He bit his lip to keep from laughing. "I had noticed that, my dear."

"Wrap up well," she advised. "It's bitter outside."

"I'd noticed that, too." He kissed her quickly on the cheek, and before she could catch his arm he turned and went into the hall.

He put on his heavy boots, a thick, woolen scarf around his neck, then his overcoat, gloves, and a hat. Even so he was unprepared for the blast of cold as he opened the front door. Instead of yesterday's chill in the air, there was a slicing wind with the cruel edge of ice on it, and the glare of light off the snow caused him to narrow his eyes. He stepped out and heard the crunch of his own footsteps. It would be very nice to change his mind and go back inside, but he could not afford to. Part of being a vicar was not listening to the tempting little voice that told you another day would do, or that there was somebody else to perform the task. He was the man people looked to here to do the work of God, and he must not fail.

He crossed the village green, seeing only a few other footprints in the snow. The pond was partially iced over, the bench beside it deserted. The air was gray. The houses seemed to huddle down, roofs pale; thin trails of smoke smeared up against the sky. Only the blacksmith's glowing forge looked inviting. Beyond the village, the woods were tangled branches of black, here and there denser where the evergreens clustered, pale-patched where the snow clung.

He passed an old woman with a bundle of sticks and called "good morning" to her, but her reply was mumbled and he could not make out her words. He increased his pace and finally felt the warmth return to his body.

Ten minutes later he was knocking on Mrs. Well-beloved's door, and was relieved when she opened it and invited him in. He stepped over the threshold into a dark, warm hallway smelling of floor polish and smoke.

"Well, now, Mr. Corde," she said briskly. She refused to call him *vicar.* "What can I do for you? 'Fraid you'll have to manage the housework yourselves today. Got company coming, like I said."

"I need your advice, Mrs. Wellbeloved," he replied, watching her expression change immediately and guarding himself from smiling.

"Ah, well, that I can do, Mr. Corde. What is it you need to know? Come in an' sit a moment; it's my duty to spare you that long." She led the way into a neat front parlor where a fire was just beginning to burn up. Mr. Wellbeloved, a sturdy man with a weathered face and a shock of gray hair, was sitting whittling a piece of wood into a whistle. There was a pile of shavings on a piece of brown paper on the floor in front of him. Painted blocks were neatly stacked beside him.

When introductions were made, and he had explained that he was carving Christmas presents for the grandchildren, Dominic asked Mrs. Wellbeloved for advice about whom he should visit. He wrote down her answers, with addresses, in the notebook he had brought with him.

"An' you'd best ask Mr. Boscombe to add to that," her husband put in helpfully. "Lives at the end o' the lane as you come in from the south. A big house with three gables. He was vicar's right hand till about six months ago. Knew everything there was, he did."

Mrs. Wellbeloved nodded her agreement. "That he did, an' all. Good man, Mr. Boscombe. He'll see you right."

"Until about six months ago?" Dominic questioned.

Mr. Wellbeloved glared at his wife, then back at Dominic, his knife stopped in midair. "That's right."

"What happened then?"

Again they looked at each other.

"Don't know," Mrs. Wellbeloved answered. "That'd be between Mr. Boscombe and the vicar. Give up all his church duties, he did. But still a good man, an' very

230

friendly. Nothing whatever you could take against. You go ask him. He'll tell you all as I can't."

And Dominic had to be content with that. He thanked them and made his way reluctantly out into the bitter air again. With the directions they had given him he walked briskly the half mile against the wind to the large, thatched house where John and Genevieve Boscombe lived with their four children.

He was welcomed in shyly, but with a gentle warmth that made him immediately comfortable. John Boscombe was a lean, quietly spoken man with fair hair, which was thinning a little. His wife was unusually pretty. Her skin was without blemish, her smile quick, and the fact that she was a little plump and her hair was definitely untidy seemed only to add to a sense of warmth.

Dominic heard happy laughter from upstairs, and at least three sets of feet running around. A large dog of indeterminate breed was lying on the floor in the kitchen in front of the range, and the whole room smelled of baking bread and clean linen. There was a

231

pile of sewing in a basket, the bodice of which was obviously a doll's dress.

"What can we do for you, Vicar?" Boscombe asked. "A cup of tea for a start? It's turned cold enough to freeze the—" He stopped, coloring faintly at a sharp look from his wife. "Tea?" he repeated, his blue eyes wide.

"Thank you very much," Dominic replied.

Genevieve hastily moved a pile of folded laundry from one of the chairs and invited him to sit down at the kitchen table. He did not need the explanation that this was the only warm room in the house. People careful with money did not burn more fires than they had to. He knew that with sharp familiarity.

There was the sound of a shriek and then giggles from upstairs.

"I need your advice," he said. "Mrs. Wellbeloved tells me you were very close to the vicar and could advise me as to all the people I should keep a special care for: those alone, unwell, in hard or unhappy circumstances of any kind. I'm not asking for any confidences," he added quickly, seeing the look of anxiety

232

in Boscombe's face. "Only where I should begin, and whom I must not overlook."

Boscombe frowned. "Did the vicar not tell you those things?"

At the range, Genevieve turned to look at him, the kettle still in her hand.

"No," Dominic said regretfully. "I never actually met him. The bishop directed me here. I assume the Reverend Wynter advised him rather late. Perhaps his need to take a holiday arose very suddenly—a relative ill or in need? I was given no details. I was happy to come."

"Oh!" Boscombe looked surprised, and oddly relieved. "That was very good of you," he added hastily. "Yes, of course we'll both do anything we can to help."

"Thank you. I'd like to talk to you a little about the vicar's sermons, particularly past Christmases. I don't want to repeat his words, or his exact message, but I'd like to be . . ." Suddenly he was uncertain exactly what he meant. Familiar, but original? Encouraging and new, but not disturbing? That was nonsense. He needed to make up his mind, decide between the safe and the daring. Was Christmas supposed to be safe, comfortable? Nothing more than the restating of old beliefs?

"Yes?" Boscombe prompted.

Dominic smiled self-consciously. "Appropriate." This short time in Cottisham mattered so much, and he was making a mess of it, being trite.

Boscombe seemed to relax. "Of course. Anything I can tell you. But I haven't been . . . in the vicar's confidence for the last few months. At least, not as closely as I used to be. But I'm sure I can help. What advice did Mrs. Wellbeloved give you? I'll see what I can add. I've been here awhile, and Genevieve was born here."

And indeed he did, giving Dominic the color and flavor of the village life, and in particular those who might have a need—or the reverse: be willing and able to help. He spoke of them all with kindness, but a clear-eyed view of their vulnerabilities. He also summarized several of the vicar's more notable sermons.

But when Dominic sat beside his own fire with Clarice that evening, hearing the wind moan in the eaves, rising shrill and more insistent, and Harry snoring gently next to the hearth, it was Boscombe's anxiety that came to his mind. He tried to explain it to her, but put into words it sounded so insubstantial—a matter of hesitations that could as easily have been shyness, or even a matter of discretion—that he felt foolish to have remembered it at all.

He asked after her day: how she was finding the house, and if the work was onerous. He knew she would say it was not, whatever the truth of it. He admired her for that, and was grateful, but it only increased his sense of guilt that he could not give her the standard of comfort she had been used to before they were married.

"Oh, very good," she said wearily. "It's a lovely house." She drew in her breath to add something, then changed her mind. He knew what she had been going to say—that she wished they could stay there. It was far nicer than the grim accommodation they had in London. Of course Spindlewood and his wife had the vicarage. In the back of Dominic's mind he was always aware of how callous he had been to his first wife in the long past. He had not thought of it as a betrayal at the time, but it had been, deeply and bitterly so. Perhaps if he had been loyal to her, with or without love, she would not have been murdered.

He did not deserve such a second chance. Looking at Clarice sitting in the chair opposite him, the cat in her lap, her face grave, he was overwhelmed with gratitude.

"Except for Harry," she said, still answering his question. "He's fine now, but he's been sulking on the back doorstep half the day."

"Perhaps he wanted to go out." He started to rise to his feet.

"No, he didn't! I know enough to let a dog out now and then," she protested. "He'd only just come in. He sat there most of the time, or wandered around the kitchen pawing at the doors, all of them, even cupboards."

"Could he have been hungry?" he suggested.

"Dominic! I fed him. He tries the hall cupboard and the cellar, not just the cupboards with food in. I think he really misses the vicar."

He sat back in his chair again. "I suppose so. I expect he'll settle. The cat's certainly happy."

236

She gave him a quick smile, stroking Etta, who needled her lap happily with her claws then went back to sleep.

Dominic leaned forward and poked the fire, sending sparks up the chimney. Clarice was right—it was a lovely house. There was almost a familiarity about it, as if at some far distant time he had lived here before and he would know instinctively where everything was. It was like coming home to some origin so far back, he had forgotten he belonged here.

The third morning it was even colder. Clarice could see the village pond from the front door when Dominic went out to begin his visiting. The surface was icing over, and a dusting of white snow made most of it indistinguishable from the banks. Harry went charging out into it and had to be brought back, his chest and tummy caked with snow, and then dried off in front of the kitchen stove, loving the attention.

Clarice did not expect Mrs. Wellbeloved today.

After feeding Harry and Etta she set about the sweeping and dusting straightaway, as much to keep warm and busy as from any need for it to be done. The sitting room fire would have to be cleaned out and relit, of course, but since the ashes were still warm, it would be foolish to remove them before time. It was a waste of coal to light it simply for herself, when she could perfectly easily sit in the kitchen.

One day soon she would have to clean out the kitchen stove completely, polish the steels with emery paper, bath brick, and paraffin, black-lead the iron parts and then polish them, then wash and whiten the hearthstone. But it did not have to be today. Such a job should really be begun at six in the morning, so she could get it set and relit in time for breakfast.

She was still thinking about it with dislike when the doorbell jangled and she went out into the hall to answer it.

A woman was standing on the step. She was muffled in a heavy, well-cut cloak and had a shawl over her head, but from what Clarice could see of her, she was about forty. She had a handsome face with wide brown eyes, a short upper lip, and a round, rather heavy chin.

"Mrs. Corde?" she inquired. She had a pleasant voice, but not the local accent.

"Yes. May I help you?"

"I rather thought I might help you," the woman replied. "My name is Mrs. Paget. I know the Reverend Wynter, and I know the village quite well. I imagine many people are willing to do all they can, especially at Christmas, but you might not know who is good at which things—flowers, baking, and so on."

"Oh, thank you," Clarice said gratefully. "Please come in. I would be most obliged for any advice at all." She held the door open wide.

Mrs. Paget stepped in as if it was all very familiar, and Clarice had the sudden feeling that perhaps she had been here many times. Possibly since John Boscombe had withdrawn from his church duties, she had in some practical ways taken over.

Clarice led the way to the kitchen, explaining that she had not lit the sitting room fire yet, and offered a cup of tea. Etta bristled at the intrusion and shot past Clarice and up the stairs. Mrs. Paget gave a little cry of surprise.

"I'm sorry," Clarice apologized. "She's a very odd cat. I think both animals miss the Reverend Wynter. The dog is in and out like a fiddler's elbow, and nothing seems to satisfy the cat. I've fed her, given her milk, set up a warm place to lie, but she just sits there like an owl."

"I'm afraid I don't know animals very well." Mrs. Paget took off her cloak and shawl and arranged herself on one of the hard-backed chairs by the table, adjusting her skirts. "I can't offer any advice. I expect you are correct and they are missing the Reverend Wynter. He is a wonderful man, very charming and utterly trustworthy. He knows everybody's secrets, all their private doubts and griefs, and never whispered a word to anyone. I was happy to help him in any way I could, but even to me he never gave so much as a hint of what needed to remain unsaid."

"Admirable," Clarice agreed, filling the kettle and setting it on the hob. "And absolutely necessary. All I really would like to know is who is gifted at what practical skill—and of course who is not!" She gave Mrs. Paget a quick smile.

"Oh, quite!" Mrs. Paget eased quickly, smiling back with a flash of understanding. "That can be every bit as much a disaster. At all costs avoid Mrs. Lampeter's baking and Mrs. Porter's soup! Never give Mrs. Unsworth the flowers. She only has to touch lilies and they go brown."

They both laughed, then settled in to discuss matters of skill, tact, need, and general usefulness.

"I imagine you'll want to have a celebration for the whole village 'round about Christmas itself, Boxing Day perhaps?" Mrs. Paget said firmly.

Clarice understood immediately. "Of course," she agreed. "It would be the best possible thing. I would appreciate your guidance as to how it has been done here in the past, and what people like. Not every place is the same."

Mrs. Paget smiled with satisfaction. "I'd be delighted. Mince pies, naturally, with plenty of raisins, sultanas, and candied peel, plum pudding and cream, best be discreet with the brandy, but a bit is always nice, gives a good flame when you light it. And cake, naturally."

Clarice's heart sank at the prospect of so much cooking. In the home she had grown up in, her mother had enjoyed a full kitchen staff to attend to such things.

Mrs. Paget's brown eyes were watching her intently. "If you would allow me to, I'd be happy to help," she offered. "It's a lot for one person, and I enjoy cooking."

Clarice felt a weight of anxiety slip from her. "Thank you," she said sincerely.

Harry remained sulking in the corner, and Etta never reappeared.

Dominic returned for luncheon, then went out again. Clarice spent the afternoon going through various cupboards seeing what polishes, brushes, and so on she could find, and if she could repack them a little more tidily so as to make more room. It was annoying to open a cupboard door and have the contents slide out around your feet or, worse, fall on top of you from the shelf above.

In the middle of the afternoon she cleaned out and lit the fire in the sitting room to warm it for Dominic's return; he was bound to be frozen. Earlier she had made hot soup—better, she hoped, than Mrs. Porter's!

She was tidying the bookshelves behind the sofa in the sitting room when she came across a leather-bound Bible. Its pages were gold-edged, but very well used, as if it was someone's personal possession, rather than one for general reference. She opened it and saw the vicar's name on the front page, dated some fifty years ago. She ruffled the pages and saw tiny handwritten notes in the margins, particularly in the book of Isaiah and the four Gospels of the New Testament. She had to carry them to the window for enough light to read them. They were very personal. There was a passion and an honesty in them that made her stop reading. They were too intimate; a man's reminder to himself, not to others.

She stood in the fading winter sun, the light graying outside, the fire burning up behind her. Why had he not taken this with him? An accidental omission, surely? It did not belong in this room: in his bedroom, if not with him. He must have left it out to pack, and somehow overlooked it.

She should find his address and send it on to him.

The postal service was good; it would get to him in a day or two at the outside. Her mind made up, she went into the study and looked for the address of the Reverend Wynter's holiday dwelling. It took her only ten minutes. She was surprised: it was an area of Norfolk she knew quite well, with beautiful wide skies and open beaches facing the North Sea. It would be a wonderful place for him to create more of his pictures. It was famous for its artists. She smiled, imagining him drinking in its splendor, and then striving to capture it on paper.

Then she read the address again. It was a small hotel in one of the seaside villages. But she had been there herself two years ago—and the hotel was closed, turned into a private house. He could not be there. It must be a mistake, an address from a previous holiday—although she had seen no pictures in the house that could be from that region. She would have to put on her coat and boots and go and ask Mrs. Wellbeloved. No doubt she would have the correct address. She must send him his scriptures.

But Mrs. Wellbeloved had no idea where the vicar

might be, if he was not at that hotel. She was very sorry, and not a little annoyed also to have been misled. Clarice should try Sir Peter. She could think of no one else.

The light was waning in the winter dusk, but to the northwest the clouds had cleared. As she approached the manor house, the sun burned low and spread a tide of scarlet across the snow. She came to the gates: formal wrought iron between magnificent gate quoins with heraldic gryphons on each. She tried them, and they opened easily. She walked up the curved gravel driveway until she came around the clipped trees and saw the magnificent façade of the early Tudor house with its mullioned windows and cloistered chimneys. The gardens were formal: herbs, flowers, and low hedges carefully nurtured into the complicated patterns of an Elizabethan knot garden. *I bet there's a maze somewhere to the back,* she thought, *beyond the old cedars at the side, and the oaks.*

She felt a little presumptuous walking up and knocking on the front door uninvited, but her reason was compelling. The Reverend Wynter would need his Bible: his own copy, not something lent to him by a stranger—something with his passions, his dreams, and his understandings written in over the years.

She knocked and waited. The purple cloud banners were a pall over the embers of the setting sun. Nothing happened. Then in the fast-fading light she noticed a gryphon's head to one side and realized it was an elaborate bellpull. She tried it, and a few moments later a butler appeared. He was an elderly gentleman with white hair and a thin, ascetic face with a surprising flash of humor in it. "Yes, ma'am? May I help you?"

She stood on the step shivering. "I am Clarice Corde, wife of the vicar who is taking the Reverend Wynter's place this Christmas," she began.

"Indeed, ma'am. Sir Peter spoke of you. Would you care to come in? It's a distinctly chilly evening."

"Distinctly," she agreed through chattering teeth. "Yes. I need to ask Sir Peter's advice, if I may?"

"Of course." The butler stepped back, took her cloak and shawl, and conducted her into the withdrawing room, which was paneled in oak with a coffered ceiling. A magnificent arras hung on the wall, and the fire burning in the hearth was big enough to have roasted a pig on a spit above the flames. Sir Peter was sitting in a huge leather armchair by the blaze, and he stood up the moment she came in.

The butler offered her tea, which she accepted. She took the seat opposite Sir Peter.

"What may I do to help?" he asked her.

She told him of finding the Bible, and then the address that she knew could not be correct. "I wondered if you know where he had really gone," she finished. "I think he will miss his own scriptures, and I would like to send them to him."

"Indeed," he said, frowning now. "How odd that he should forget to pack such a thing. No doubt it was an oversight. He will be searching for it already. But I am afraid I don't know where he went. In fact I did not even know he was going. It was a surprise to me. I would have wished him a good journey. I am sorry I didn't." There was gentleness in his voice and a softness of genuine regret in his eyes.

Looking at him, Clarice was suddenly aware of

247

how deeply fond of the Reverend Wynter he must have been, and that perhaps he was more hurt by the rift between them than he admitted.

"You have no idea where else he goes?" she pressed. "I could at least write a letter; if he writes back, I shall know where to send the Bible. I must not risk losing it."

"No!" He leaned forward. "You must keep it safely. Please, don't risk it unless you are absolutely certain where he is. Family Bibles matter intensely. So many memories. Could you not be mistaken about this hotel?"

"No." She had no doubt about it. She had been sorry and inconvenienced to find it changed herself. She told him of her experience. She did not mention that it had been the vicar's personal Bible, not a family one.

A shadow flickered across his face with its delicate lines.

"I see. No, there seems to be no room for error. I'm sorry; I really don't know where else he might have gone. I wish I could offer help."

The branch of the tree burning in the grate settled a little, and a shower of sparks flew up the vast chimney. She looked around at the age and beauty of the room and wondered how many generations of Connaughts had sat here, hearing the stories of the village, helping, protecting, disciplining, governing, and probably using and taxing as well. Walls like these had seen England's history unfolding since before the Spanish Armada had sailed in the time of Queen Elizabeth. Perhaps even Henry VIII had visited here with one of his six wives. Or Walsingham had sent out his spies. There would be a priest hole behind that fireplace for fugitive Catholics when they were hunted and burned. Which side had the Connaughts been on in the Civil War? Or the Bloodless Revolution?

Sir Peter was smiling at her, his eyes bright again in the firelight. "Would you like to see the house?" he asked. "It would be my pleasure to show you."

"I'd love to," she said sincerely.

He guided her through it all with a kind of gentle pride she found endearing. He did not boast except once, and then immediately apologized for it as though it had been a breach of good manners.

"You have a right to be proud," she said honestly.

"It is so beautiful, and obviously it has been loved over the centuries. Thank you for your generosity in showing me."

He looked pleased, even a little self-conscious. "Are you sure you wish to walk home alone? It is now quite dark."

"Oh, certainly," she said with confidence. "It is only a mile or so."

"Still, I would rather accompany you, at least as far as the village green. I would be happier."

She did not argue. When she was within sight of the vicarage lights, which were already familiar to her, he bade her good night and turned back toward the manor. Clarice went another few yards, then saw the dark outline of a figure coming toward her, leaning into the wind and huddling a shawl around her. It was so small and walked with such tiny, hurried steps, it had to be a woman.

"Good evening," Clarice said clearly, thinking the woman had not seen her and was in danger of bumping into her unless she moved off the path into the snow.

"Oh! My dear, you gave me a fright!" the woman exclaimed. "I was quite lost in my own thoughts.

250

Since I don't know you, you must be the new vicar's wife."

"Yes, I am. Clarice Corde." Clarice held out her hand.

"How do you do," the woman responded. Her voice was husky and a little cracked, but it must have been rich in her youth. "My name is Sybil Towers," she went on, holding out a small hand in a woolen mitten. "Welcome to Cottisham. I am sure you will be happy here. We all love the Reverend Wynter, and we will make you comfortable, too."

"Mrs. Towers," Clarice said impulsively. "You don't know where the Reverend Wynter went for his holiday, do you? I have found something he left behind, and I would very much like to send it after him, but the only address I have is not for this year."

"No! I'm afraid I have no idea," she responded. "In fact, I didn't even know he was going away. I'm so sorry."

It would be inexcusable to keep the old lady standing outside in the rising wind any longer, so Clarice dismissed it, wished her good night, and hurried on to the vicarage.

Dominic was at home and intensely relieved to see her—so much so that she found no suitable opportunity to tell him about the Bible, or the fact that she could find no one who knew the vicar's holiday address.

$\mathcal{T}$he morning was milder, and thick wet snow blanketed everything. Even the air swirled in white flurries, blocking out the village green so that the houses at the farther side were all but invisible. It was a world of movement and shadows seen through a haze.

Dominic left to go visit the sick and the lonely, and Clarice began the necessary duties of housework. There was no point in thinking of doing laundry, beyond shirts and underclothing. Nothing else would dry.

She should air the vicar's bedroom. Closed rooms, especially in this weather, could come to smell stale. She did not wish him to return to that stuffy, unoccupied feeling. The cat pattered around behind her, poking her nose into everything and giving her the uncomfortable suspicion that there could be mice here after all. Harry had gone back to sleep in front of the range in the kitchen, as if he was still sulking. He had been outside first thing with Dominic, but now he refused to wag his tail or in any other way respond.

The first thing she noticed in the bedroom—after opening the windows briefly, just to let the cold, sweet air circulate—was a stark drawing of bare trees in the snow. There was no color in it at all, and yet there was a grace to the lines that held her attention. She stared at it so long, she grew cold, then realized the window was still open. She shut it quickly and returned to the picture. It was another of the vicar's own drawings. She had begun to recognize his style even before she read his signature in the corner.

She was glad the vicarage had been designed for a family, and was large enough that they had not needed to use this room. It belonged to the Reverend Wynter, and he should not have to move his belongings to make way for them. She looked around it with pleasure, amazed that she could feel such a liking for a man she had never met. People spoke so well of him, he was obviously a man of great compassion. But that might not be personal so much as part of his calling. It was the delicacy, the simple grace of his drawings, that showed his nature. He saw extraordinary beauty in a bare branch, the tiny twigs against the light, the strength of a trunk stripped of its summer glory, powerful in its nakedness.

She gazed around the walls at the other pictures. Each was different, and yet all had the same inner qualities. She wondered if he was busy now creating more. Was he out walking in the snow somewhere in East Anglia, selecting just the right scene under the wide Norfolk skies? Perhaps he would draw the bare coastline and the sea grasses, the wind-riven skies, clouds dragged out in long streamers above the line of the waves.

Reluctantly she made certain the windows were fastened securely and then went back downstairs. She was tidying the study when she came across a carefully sharpened soft-leaded pencil sitting on top of the chest of narrow drawers near the window. Her first thought was that Dominic had unintentionally sharpened one of the vicar's pencils before realizing what it was.

She should put it away. Perhaps it belonged in one of the drawers. She opened the top one to see, and found a dozen more pencils there, all sharpened. There were also charcoals of various thickness, white pencils, erasers, and a sharp blade—in fact, all one needed for drawing. Were they extras?

She closed the drawer and opened the one below. It was full of unused blocks of watercolor artist's paper. He must have a great deal if he had this much to leave behind! Without thinking she pulled open the cupboard door. With a sudden chill she saw an easel, neatly folded. How could he not have taken it with him? This, and his pencils, were the tools of his art!

Mystified, she went back up to his bedroom and shamelessly opened the wardrobe door. There were only four pairs of boots inside: smart black boots for Sundays; a pair of brown boots; a second pair of black boots, definitely older; and stout walking boots for country wear, up to the ankles, thick-soled such as one would choose on a day like this.

There were winter clothes hanging on the rail as

well, including an extremely nice woolen overcoat—
not city wear, more casual—with a collar to turn up
against the worst weather. It was just the sort of coat
a man would like for walking in the country or by the
sea.

Why had he not taken it with him? And the boots?
And for that matter, the stout walking stick leaning
against the wall in the corner? To forget the Bible
might be an oversight, even the pencils, or paper, but
not the winter clothes as well! There was something
wrong. He had left in haste, and not for pleasure as
he had said. Was it some family emergency, or be-
reavement? Would he be gone until the situation,
whatever it was, had been resolved? Had he a brother
or sister in some kind of trouble? Possibly it was a
sudden and serious illness?

When Dominic returned home, late and cold to
the bone, she started to tell him, then realized he
was not listening to her. He heard her words, but not
their meaning. He was too deep in his own fear that
he could not find something new and powerful to say
to the people of this village for him to hear the anxi-

ety within her. And it would be Sunday in two days, and his first sermon here.

"They are good people," he said, standing in the sitting room with his back to the fire, which burned brightly, thawing the cold that chilled and numbed his flesh. "They know their scriptures at least as well as I do. The vicar has preached to them with passion and eloquence not only at Christmas but all through the year." There was a shadow in his eyes, a tightness across his cheeks. "What can I say to them that will be anything more than an echo of what he has already said?" he asked her. "Any one of them could stand up in the pulpit and tell the Christmas story as well as I can. Clarice, what can I say to make it new?"

She saw the spark of fear in his eyes, the knowledge that he might not be equal to the task that mattered to him so much. This village was old, comfortable, and secure in its habits. It was not conscious of any hunger that needed filling, any ignorance or darkness waiting for light. The townspeople wanted to stay as they were and be reassured that all was

257

·

well. Anyone could do that: pass and leave no mark at all, like wind over water.

She ached to be able to help him. She was seeing for the first time the need in him: not desire to do a job or fulfill a duty, but a hunger to succeed that would not let him rest or leave him free from pain if he failed.

"What's the best thing about Christmas?" she asked, trying to strip away the trite, all the things that had already been said. "What does it really mean to us? What . . . what is it for? It's not goodwill, a brief time of peace or generosity. It has to be more than that."

"It's the beginning of our faith," he replied. "Christ coming into the world." He said it as if it were obvious.

"I know." She felt crushed. "But what for?" she insisted. "Why was everything different afterward?"

The fire was scorching him, and he stepped away from it. "I'm not exactly sure how to answer that," he replied. "It sounds . . . it sounds too much like an academic answer, and that's not what they need, Clarice. I need a spiritual answer, a joy in the soul."

She could think of nothing better to add. She was failing him, and, feeling empty, she turned and went into the kitchen.

*C*larice woke to find a white world, silent, deep in snow. The air was motionless, and when she opened the back door into the garden to let Harry out, the bitter cold of it was sharp in her lungs. She drew in her breath in amazement at the beauty of it. The old apple tree was laden like an extravagant blossom. Other trees, soaring upward, were naked, too thin to hold the snow, shining against an enamel sky.

But it was a dangerous beauty, a cold that paralyzed, a depth of snow that soaked heavy skirts and exhausted old or fragile limbs. The low winter sun was almost blinding.

She closed the door and turned to find Dominic standing behind her, a rueful smile on his face.

"You're going out," she said, more as a statement than a question. She wished he did not have to, but if he had found excuses to stay at home she would have been even more deeply disappointed. What use was preaching or praying if one was not willing to act?

"I'll try not to be long," he answered. "But there'll be people who shouldn't go out in this, even to fetch wood, never mind to get bread or milk."

"I know." She gave him a quick kiss, hugging him tightly for a moment, then going back to the kitchen to tidy up. It was warm in there and she had hot water, which made her more fortunate than many.

However, in the middle of the morning she found with surprise that the coal bucket beside the stove was empty, and the coke scuttle as well. She would have to go down to the cellar to fetch more. What was left would not last her until Dominic returned.

She picked up the scuttle and went to the hall. The cellar door was locked, but she had the key on the big household ring, and it opened with ease. A rush of chilled air engulfed her immediately, making her shiver and step back. There was a swish past her ankles, and Etta disappeared down the steps into the darkness.

"Mice!" Clarice said in disgust. "I suppose it's your

job, but you really are a nuisance. Well, I'm not taking a candle down there. It'll blow out and then I'll not even find my way back." She put down the coke scuttle and went to look for a lantern. She knew there was one in the scullery by the back door. She found it, lit it, settled the glass to protect the flame, and then returned. Etta was nowhere to be seen.

It was no more than a ten-minute job to fill the coke scuttle, take it back up to the kitchen, and then fill the coal bucket for the sitting room fire as well.

"Etta!" she called encouragingly. "Come on, Etta! There's a nice warm fire for you up here, and I'll give you some fresh milk! Better than mice."

The only sound was Harry's feet on the hall floor. He came padding through, looking interested at last, his head on one side, eyebrows cocked.

"She's gone down there after mice," Clarice explained, then thought how absurd she was being, talking to the animal as if he understood. Actually she was ridiculously pleased that at last he was taking more notice of her. He went to the door, slithered through the opening, and disappeared down the steps.

261

"Fetch her back up," Clarice called after him. "I'm not leaving this door open all morning. It's far too cold."

She stood hopefully for several minutes, but neither of them reappeared.

"Drat!" she said fiercely. She was now thoroughly chilled and rapidly losing patience, but she really did not feel as if she could close them in. This was their home; she was the interloper. Impatiently she picked up the lantern and went down the steps again.

Neither Harry nor Etta was visible. She held the light higher and up near the far corner, which was where she found the rather narrow entrance to the second cellar. They must be in there. More mice, no doubt. She had not known that dogs ate mice, too. Or perhaps he was just curious.

She went through the doorway, her skirts brushing against the sides. Now she would be covered in coal dust. Perhaps it would brush off without staining, but then it would still need sweeping up. "Harry!" she said sharply. "Etta!" She held the lantern forward and saw them immediately, standing side by side;

Etta's tail was up and bristling, Harry's tail down unhappily. He let out a long, low wail.

Then she saw the crumpled heap beyond them, dark but quite definitely not coal. Her stomach clenched and her hand shook so the light danced unevenly. She moved forward until it was all horribly clear. An elderly man lay faceup on the rubble remains of an old coal heap. His eyes were closed; his gaunt features smeared with dust and dark with what might have been bruises. A gash was scored across his nose, but any blood had long since dried and darkened.

Clarice breathed in shakily, gasping. The heat drained out of her body as if sucked away. The cat and dog were so close they seemed to be touching each other, as though for comfort. She did not need to question if that was their master; the dog's repeated low howl of grief was answer enough. Anyway, who else could it be? Even smeared with coal dust, the white of his clerical collar was clearly visible.

There was no question if there was anything she could do for him; it was perfectly obvious there was not. Slowly, her knees wobbling, the lantern sway-ing, she fumbled her way back up the steps again and then stood gulping air at the top. She grasped the door lintel in the gray daylight. She must re-port the death. The poor old man had probably had a heart attack or something of that sort. Everyone thought he had gone away, so no one would have missed him and gone to look. What a bitterly sad way for a vicar, of all people, to die. From everyone's account, he had been a fine man, and deeply and justly loved.

She could wait for Dominic to return, but in this weather he could be a long time doing all that was necessary. She did not want to stay here alone, know-ing what was downstairs. She was perfectly capable of putting on boots and a cape and going to find the doctor herself. She knew where he lived; that was one of the things Mrs. Wellbeloved had told her. It was a stiff walk, but along open road all the way. She would make it in half an hour, even in the snow, and he might have a pony and trap for the way back.

Extinguishing the lantern, she left the cellar door

wedged open so Harry and Etta could come out if they chose, or stay and mourn if that was their nature. Perhaps that was more fitting anyway. She rather hoped they would. Then she put on the boots, wrapped herself around in her cloak, and set out, her mind so filled with pity she scarcely noticed either the cold or the way the deep snow dragged at her feet.

"*H*eart attack I expect, poor man," Dr. Fitzpatrick told her, coming back up the steps and closing the cellar door behind him. The cat and dog had come upstairs again, persuaded with some difficulty, and were now sitting side by side in front of the kitchen stove. "Only comfort is he probably felt very little," Fitzpatrick went on. He was a fussy man with a large mustache. "Are you all right, Mrs. Corde? Horrible experience for you. What on earth were you doing down there?"

She had already explained to him, or she thought she had. Perhaps she had been more incoherent than

265

she supposed. "I went to fill the coke scuttle, and the cat came, too, and then I couldn't find her."

He nodded. "Smelled something, I suppose. Or perhaps just after the mice." He held up his coal-smeared hands.

"Oh, I'm sorry," she apologized quickly. "Please come into the kitchen and wash, and perhaps you'd like a cup of tea?" She glanced down at his trouser legs, sodden where the snow on them had melted in the warmth of the house, then her own heavy, wet skirts.

"Yes," he said with alacrity. "Thank you."

She busied herself with water in the kettle, warming the teapot, fetching milk from a very chilly pantry, and offering him a slice of cake, which he made an excuse for accepting as well.

"I'll take care of the arrangements," he said with his mouth full. "I daresay they won't be able to hold a funeral for a few days, considering the weather and what the bishop might care to do, but I'll have the body removed and all the appropriate registrations dealt with. You don't need to concern yourself, Mrs. Corde. I will take care of it all. And I would be ob-

266

liged if you would speak of this to no one yet. There is a proper order of things, which we must observe."

"Thank you." She felt relieved, but more than a little sad. It was a lonely and undignified way to go. Not that she supposed he was more than briefly aware of it. He had lived well, very well, and in the end that was all that mattered. "Thank you," she repeated. "No doubt my husband will be in touch with the bishop. He may . . . he may wish us to remain a little longer." She realized as she said the words how much she hoped that he would—a lot longer, perhaps always.

It was ten minutes later with the doctor on his second cup of tea when Dominic came in, slamming the front door behind him and striding down the hall, shedding snow everywhere. "Clarice!" he called urgently, fear edging his voice sharply. "Clarice!"

She came to the door immediately and almost ran into him. His coat was wet, his face whipped red by the cold, his eyes frightened. As soon as he saw her he was flooded with relief. "Someone told me you sent for the doctor urgently. What is it? Were they wrong?"

267

She could not help smiling. It was wonderful, and still faintly surprising to her, that he should care so intensely. "I'm perfectly well," she said, almost all the shiver gone out of her voice. "I went for coke in the cellar and the cat got into another cellar beyond. I found the vicar's body. The poor man must have gone down there and had a heart attack. I felt the doctor was the best person to inform." She met his eyes, looking to see if he understood what she had done.

He was momentarily shocked. "Dead? The Reverend Wynter? You mean he has been down there all the time?"

"Yes. Don't look like that," she added gently. She touched his hand. "There was nothing we could have done for him."

The doctor drank the last of his tea and came into the hall.

"Fitzpatrick," he said, introducing himself. "You must be the Reverend Corde. Sad thing to happen. So sorry your poor wife had to be the one to find him." He shook his head. "But I'll take care of all the details. Perhaps you'd just give me a hand to carry the poor old man up the steps, then I can fetch the blacksmith's cart and have him taken away. My trap is rather too small, you know."

"Yes, of course," Dominic replied quickly, beginning to take off his heavy outdoor coat.

It was an awkward job up the cellar stairs, and required both men, so Clarice walked in front of them with the lantern. On the way back up she moved ahead and laid a clean blanket on the kitchen table so they could put him down gently on it. As soon as it was accomplished, the doctor went to find the blacksmith.

"I think I should clean him up a bit," Clarice said very quietly. Her throat ached, and she found it hard to swallow.

Dominic offered to do it, but she insisted. Laying out the dead was a job for women. She would wash the coal dust from his head and face and hands. She did it with hot, soapy water, very gently, as if he could still feel pain. He had had fine features, aquiline and sensitive, but they were hollow now, in death. There

269

was a bad scrape on his nose, as if he had struck it falling—and yet they had found him on his back, and to reinforce that fact, there was a deep gash in the back of his head. He must have gone down hard.

In straightening his legs, Clarice also noticed that his trousers were slightly torn at the shins, and the skin underneath abraded and bruised.

"How did he do that?" she said curiously.

"It happened before he died," Dominic said quietly. "People don't bruise after the heart stops. He must have stumbled as he went down the steps. Perhaps he wasn't feeling very well even then."

"I wonder why he went down at all," she said thoughtfully, pulling the fabric straight. "The buckets of coal and coke were all full."

"I expect Mrs. Wellbeloved filled them," he pointed out.

She looked at him almost apologetically. "If she'd gone down there, and he had the buckets with him, then why didn't she find him?"

"What are you suggesting, Clarice?"

"I don't know," she admitted. "I just wondered why he went down there, and nobody knew."

"They thought he had gone away on holiday," he answered. "We all did."

She frowned. "Why? Why did the bishop think he was going on holiday?"

"Because he wrote and told him," Dominic said.

She said nothing. Something made her more than sad, but she wasn't sure what it was.

There was a voice at the door, calling out urgently. Dominic turned and went back to the hall. "What is it? Can I help?"

"Oh, Vicar!" It was a man's voice, deep and unfamiliar. "Poor Mrs. Hapgood's had bad news, and she's that upset, I don't know what to do for her. Can you come? Dreadful state she's in, poor thing."

Dominic hesitated, turning back toward Clarice.

She knew how much it mattered; this was their chance to prove they could do everything that a parish needed. "Yes, of course you can," she said firmly. There was no need to tell this man that the Reverend Wynter was dead. He had his own griefs to aid first. "There's nothing here I can't take care of."

"Oh, bless you, ma'am!" the man in the hall said fervently. "This way, Vicar."

271

The doctor came back with the blacksmith and his cart, and the two men carried the body out quickly and discreetly, wrapped in a blanket. After they had gone Clarice went back to the kitchen and washed the few dishes they had used, her mind whirling. There was something wrong. She could not put her finger on it standing here at the bench. She would have to go down to the cellar again, and yet she was reluctant to. It was more than the cold or even the memory of what she had found.

"Come on, Harry," she said briskly. "Come, keep me company." She relit the lantern and the dog, surprisingly, obeyed her. It was the very first time he had done as she'd asked. Together they went to the door and opened it. She went first down the steps, very carefully, and he followed behind. A little more than halfway he stopped and sniffed.

"What is it?" she said, gulping, her hand swaying so the light gyrated around the walls.

Harry sniffed again and looked up at her.

Swallowing hard, she retraced her steps up to him and bent to examine what he'd spotted. It was a very small piece of fabric, no more than a few threads

272

caught in a splinter of the wood. At first she thought how odd it was that the dog had noticed it; then she saw the smear of blood. It wasn't much darker than the coal-smudged steps themselves, but when she licked her finger and touched it, it came away red. Was this where the vicar had stumbled, and then gone on down the rest of the way to the bottom? How could she find out?

She held the lantern so she could see the steps closely. They were dark with years of trodden-in coal dust, each bit dropped from a bucket or scuttle carried up full. No matter how closely she looked, all she could distinguish were the most recent marks, a heel dent, and the smear of a sole. They could have been anybody's: Dominic's, the doctor's, even Mrs. Wellbeloved's.

She went to the bottom and looked again, not expecting to find anything or knowing what it would mean even if she did.

Then she saw it: a small, neat pattern of marks she understood very easily—cat prints. Etta had been this way. She walked after the marks, for no real reason except that they led to the second cellar. They

273

were easy to read because they were on plain ground, as if someone had swept all the old marks away with a broom. Why would anybody sweep just a single track, no more than eighteen or twenty inches wide? It was not even clean, just brushed once. Several times it was disturbed at the sides by footprints.

Then she understood. It was not swept—these were drag marks. Someone had pulled something heavy, covered in cloth, from the bottom of the stairs over into the second cellar.

Could the Reverend Wynter have fallen, struck his head and become confused, mistaken where he was and dragged himself in the wrong direction?

No. That was idiotic. There were no handprints in the dust. And his hands would have been filthy when they found him. They weren't: only smudges here and there—the backs as much as the palms.

She was in the second cellar now. When she had found him, he had been lying on his back. But his nose had been scraped, as if he had fallen forward. And there was coal dust on his front as well as his back. The hard, deep wound was on the back of his head.

"Somebody killed him, Harry," she said softly, putting her hand out to touch the dog's soft fur. "Somebody hit him on the head and dragged him in here, and then left him. Why would they do that? He was an old man whom almost everyone loved."

The dog whined and leaned his weight against her leg.

"I don't suppose you know, and even if you do, you can't tell me." She was talking to him because it was so much better not to feel alone. "I'll have to find out without you. We'll have to," she corrected. "I'll tell Dominic when he comes back. Right now, in case anybody calls, I think we should pretend that we don't know anything at all. Come on. It's cold down here, and we shouldn't stay anyway. It isn't safe."

$\mathcal{W}$hen Dominic returned from his visits, tired and cold, she had no alternative but to tell him immediately. It was already midafternoon; there would be little more than an hour before the light began to fade and the ground froze even harder.

"What?" he said incredulously, sitting at the kitchen table, his hands thawing as he held the cup of tea she had made. "Are you sure?"

"Yes, I am sure," she said looking at him steadily. "I'm not being overimaginative, Dominic. Remember the marks on his face and head? Remember how little coal dust there was on his hands? Or on his knees? But there was a tear on the shin of his trousers, and dust where he had been dragged. Go down to the cellar and look. It's still there."

He hesitated.

"Please," she urged. "I don't want to be the only one who saw it. Anyway, I don't think the doctor is going to listen to me."

*S*he was perfectly correct—Dr. Fitzpatrick did not believe either of them.

"That suggestion is preposterous," he said irritably, pulling on his mustache. "It is a perfectly ordinary domestic tragedy. An elderly man had a heart attack and fell down the cellar stairs. Or perhaps he simply tripped and then the shock of the fall brought on an attack. He was confused, naturally, perhaps hurt, and he mistakenly crawled in the wrong direction. You are trying to make a horror out of something that is merely sad. And if I may say so, that is a completely irresponsible thing to do."

Clarice took a deep breath, facing his anger. "What did he go into the cellar for?" she asked.

"My dear Mrs. Corde, surely that is perfectly obvious?" Fitzpatrick snapped. "Exactly the same reason as you did yourself! For coal!"

She met his gaze steadily. "I took a lantern and a coal bucket, and I left the door open at the top," she replied.

"Then perhaps he went for some other reason," Fitzpatrick said. "Didn't you say something about the dog? He must have gone to look for it."

"Why would you go to look for anything in a cellar without a lantern?" Dominic pressed. "It doesn't make sense."

"He probably stood at the top and called." Fitzpatrick was becoming more and more annoyed. His face was tight, lips thin. "Reverend, you are a guest

277

here. In view of poor Wynter's death, it will possibly be for far longer than you had originally intended. You are now required to guide the village through a sad and very trying time. As shepherd of the people, it is your calling to sustain, comfort, and uplift them, not indulge in what, I have to say, is idle and vicious speculation on the death of a deeply loved man. I am sorry that it falls to my lot to remind you of this. Don't make it necessary for me to take it further."

Dominic's face flamed, but he turned and left without retaliation. He could not afford it, as the doctor had reminded him.

Clarice went with him, not daring to meet Fitzpatrick's eyes in case he saw in hers the rage she also felt toward him. He had humiliated Dominic, and that she had no idea how to heal, so she could not forgive him for it. As she went out into the snow, she remembered her father telling her that if you sought wealth or fame, other people might dislike you for it, but if you sought only to do good, no one would be your enemy. How wrong he was! Good held a mirror to other people's hearts, and the reflection was too often unflattering. People could hate you for that more than for almost anything else.

She caught up with Dominic and linked her arm through his, holding on to him when he tried to pull back. He was ashamed because he had not found a way to stand up for the truth. She struggled for something to say that would make it better, not worse. If she were to sound superficial it would be worse than silence; it would be patronizing, as if she thought him not strong enough to face their failure. Yet she ached to comfort him. If she could not at least do that, what use was she?

"I'm sorry," she said a trifle abruptly. "I shouldn't have urged you to speak to him so quickly. Perhaps if we had waited until tomorrow, and thought harder, we might have persuaded him."

"No, we wouldn't," he said grimly. "He doesn't want to think that anyone would kill the Reverend Wynter."

"I don't want to, either!" she said hotly. "I hate thinking it. But I have to follow what my sense tells me. And I don't believe one goes into the cellar alone in the dark to fetch coal, to look for a cat or dog, or anything else. If he'd fallen down, then Mrs. Wellbeloved would have found him. The door would have been open—"

"Maybe when she came in the front door, the wind slammed the cellar door shut?" he suggested. ·

"It faces the other way," she pointed out. "It would have blown it wider open."

"Well, what do you think did happen?" he asked. They were walking side by side along the road, their feet making the only tracks in the new snow. In the east the sky was darkening.

"I think someone came in and said or did something to make him go into the cellar, then pushed him," she answered. "When he was at the bottom, perhaps crumpled over, stunned, they hit him on the back of the head, hard enough to kill him, whether they meant that or not. Although I can't see why they would do it unless they intended him to die. They could hardly explain it away." Her mind was racing. The rising wind was edged with ice, and she blinked against it. "Then they dragged him into the other cellar, so he wouldn't be found too soon—"

280

"Why?" he interrupted. "What difference would it make?"

"So nobody would know when it happened, of course." The ideas came to her as she spoke. "That way nobody could have been proved to be here at the right time. Then they closed the door, and probably took his cases away, so people would think he had already gone on his holiday. Only they forgot about his painting things . . . and his favorite Bible."

He was frowning. "Do you really think so? Why? That doesn't sound like a quarrel in the heat of some . . . some dispute. It's perfectly deliberate and cold-blooded."

"Yes, it is," she agreed reluctantly. "I suppose he must have known something about one of the people here that was so terrible to them, they couldn't afford to trust that he would never tell anyone."

"He couldn't tell," Dominic argued. "They would know that. Not if it was confessed to him. No priest would."

"Then maybe it wasn't confessed to him." She would not let go of the idea. "Perhaps he found it out some other way. He knew lots of things about all

281

sorts of people. He would have to. He's been here in Cottisham for ages. He must have seen a great deal."

"What could possibly be worth killing over?" He was putting up a last fight against believing.

"I don't know," she admitted.

"But he wrote to the bishop saying he was going on holiday," he pointed out. "So he obviously intended to. Is that coincidence?"

"Did he?" she asked. "Or did someone else write, copying his hand? It wouldn't be too difficult, and if the bishop didn't look closely, or compare it with other letters, it would be easy enough. And plenty of people in the village could have letters or notes the Reverend Wynter had written at one time or another."

Dominic said nothing, trudging steadily through the snow. The light was fading rapidly; the shadows under the trees were already impenetrable.

"That's what we have to find out," she insisted quietly, her voice heavy with the burden of what she was thinking. She would very much rather have been able to say they should let it go, pretend they had never known, but it would be a lie that would grow sharper all the time, like a blister on the tender skin

282

of one's feet. "Christ was kind; He forgave," she went on. "But He never moderated the truth to make people like Him, or pretended that something was all right when it wasn't, because that would be easier. I think the Reverend Wynter was killed for something he knew. What do you think, really?" She took a deep breath and let it out slowly. "I'll do whatever you decide." That was so difficult for her to say.

He gave an almost jerky little laugh. "You can't do that, Clarice. You'd grow to hate me. I think he was probably killed. Either way, I can't pretend I don't know. The Reverend Wynter deserves better; and if someone did kill him, then they deserve better, too. They need justice more than he does. Justice heals in the end, if you allow it to." He walked a few more yards in silence. "I suppose we need to find out what he knew, and about whom."

A wave of relief swept over her. "We'll begin in the village," she said. "We can't get out of it now anyway."

"Whom do we trust?" he asked, glancing at her quickly.

"No one," she said simply. "We can't afford to. We have no idea who it was."

They spent a long, quiet evening by the fire. Neither of them talked very much, but it was one of the most companionable times she could remember, despite the ugly task that awaited them the following days. The fire crackled and the coals grew yellow hot in the heart of it. The snow deepened in blanketing silence outside, except for the occasional *whoosh* as it grew too heavy on the steep roof and slid off to the ground. There was nothing to discuss—they were in agreement.

Sunday morning was awful. Dominic was so anxious, he barely spoke to her as he ate breakfast before church. He picked up books and put them down again, found quotes, then discarded them. One minute he wanted to be daring, challenge people to new thought; the next to be gentle, to reassure them in all the old beliefs, comfort the wounds of loneliness and misunderstanding, and say nothing that might awaken troubling ideas or demand any change.

A dozen times Clarice drew in her breath to say

that he had no time, in three short weeks, to stay within safe bounds. No one would listen; certainly no one would remember anything about it afterward.

She nearly said so. Then she saw his slender hand on the back of the chair, and realized that the knuckles were white. This was not the right time. But she was afraid there never would be a right time. The next sermon would be for Christmas. One pedestrian sermon now, safe and colorless, might be all it would take to lose the congregation's sympathy, and their hope.

"Don't quote," she said suddenly. "Don't use other people's words. Whatever they are, they'll have heard them before."

"People like repetition," he said with a bleak smile, his eyes dark with anxiety and the crushing weight of doubt Spindlewood had laid on him.

In that moment Clarice hated Spindlewood for what he had done with his mealy mouth and grudging, time-serving spirit. "Do you remember how terrible it was when Unity Bellwood was murdered, and how the police suspected all of us?" she said quietly.

"Of course!"

285

"Tell them what you said to me about courage then, and how it's the one virtue without which all others may be lost," she urged him. "You meant it! Say it to them."

He did so, passionately, eloquently, without repeating himself. She had no idea whether the congregants were impressed or not. They spoke politely to him afterward, even with warmth, but there was no ease among them. She and Dominic walked home through the snow in silence.

*O*n Monday, the wind sliced in from the east like a whetted knife. Straight after breakfast Dominic set out to make his calls.

Clarice started where she had traditionally been told lay the root of all evil, although actually she thought it was far more likely to find its roots in selfishness—and perhaps self-righteousness, which was not such a different thing when one thought about it. Still, money was easier to measure, and she had ready access to the vicar's ledgers both from the church and from the household.

She had barely begun examining them when she was interrupted by the arrival of Mrs. Wellbeloved carrying two hard white cabbages and a string of very large onions. She looked extremely pleased with herself, stamping her feet and shedding snow everywhere.

"Said as it would be cold. Tree fell over with the weight of it an' the road south's blocked." She announced it as a personal victory. " 'Less you want to go all 'round Abingdon an' the like. An' there's no saying you can get through that, either. Could all be closed."

"Then we are very fortunate to have coal and food," Clarice replied warmly.

"Onions." Mrs. Wellbeloved put them on the table. Not that anyone could have mistaken them for something else.

"Thank you." Clarice smiled at her. She already knew from the brief glance at the accounts she had taken that Mrs. Wellbeloved had done all the shopping for the vicar. She wanted to tell her of their discovery of the body in the cellar, but Fitzpatrick had asked them not to, and his implication had been clear enough. Still, Clarice felt guilty saying nothing. "That's very kind of you," she added.

Mrs. Wellbeloved smiled, her face pink. She began to take off her overcoat and prepare to scrub the floor.

It was half past eleven before Clarice could return to the ledger and read through it carefully. She had gone through it twice before she noticed the tiny anomalies. They were sometimes of a shilling or two, but more often just pennies. The mistakes seemed to be in the Reverend Wynter's own money, which he accounted very carefully, as anyone on a church stipend had to. Clarice herself knew where every farthing went. The expression *poor as a church mouse* was not an idle one.

The church accounts, including the donations signed for by John Boscombe until a few months ago, and more recently by a man named William Frazer, were accurate, then inaccurate, then accurate again. The final sum was always as it should be.

Clarice could understand how people ended up

chewing pencils. It made no sense. Why on earth would anyone steal tuppence, or even less? She was convinced it was not carelessness, because the same figures kept recurring in what she realized was a sequence. She placed them side by side, according to date, and then she saw the pattern. The few pence went missing from the church accounts, then from the Reverend Wynter's personal account. Finally the church accounts were correct again. Someone was taking tiny amounts from the collection for the poor box, irregular and always very small. The Reverend Wynter was replacing them from his own money.

But why? Would it not have been the right thing to do to find out who was the thief—if that was not too serious a word for such petty amounts? Might it be a child? Perhaps he did not want to have such an accusation made if it could become uglier than a simple question of family discipline.

Whom could she ask? Perhaps William Frazer, who had taken over the bookkeeping, would know, or have an idea? He lived next to the village store, and even in this weather she could walk there quite easily. Of course she would not go across the green. One could barely see where the pond was, never mind avoid treading on the ice beneath the snow, and perhaps falling in.

But Frazer had no idea. "I'm so sorry, Mrs. Corde," he said earnestly as she sat in the small, crowded room by his parlor fire, still shivering from her journey in the snow. The wind seemed to find its way through even the thickest cloak, and a hat was useless to protect the neck or ears. Now she was almost singeing at the front, and her back was still cold from the draft behind her.

"Your records are immaculate," she said as flatteringly as she could. "At the end of the day the money is always correct, but somewhere along the way a few pennies disappear, and then turn up again. It looks as if the Reverend Wynter made up the difference himself."

Frazer looked startled, his thin, bony face pale with anxiety. "Why on earth would he do such a thing?" he demanded. "John Boscombe never said anything to me, and he's as honest as the day. Ask anyone. If there'd been any irregularities, he'd have told me."

"Perhaps if the Reverend Wynter knew who it

290

was, he might have asked Mr. Boscombe not to say anything," she suggested, puzzled herself.

"Why would he do that?" Frazer's voice was sharp, his big hands were clenched in his lap. "More like the old gentleman lost a few pence here and there." He nodded. "Can happen to anyone. Got the wrong change by mistake, p'raps. Or dropped it in the street and couldn't find it. Done that myself. Only pennies, you said?"

"Yes."

"Don't worry about it. Daresay you'll keep better books yourself, being younger and seeing a good bit clearer. Should have had spectacles, maybe."

"Perhaps." But she did not agree. She thanked him and went out into the bitter wind to walk all the way to John Boscombe's house. In the summer there was a shortcut through the woods, when the stream was low and the stepping-stones clear. But the current was strong and deep now, and would pull a person under its dark surface like greedy hands.

It was a long walk, but she found the man at home, kept from his work in the fields by the smothering snow.

"Come in, come in!" he said warmly as he almost pulled her into the hallway and slammed the door against the wind behind her. "What a day! It's going to be a hard Christmas if it goes on like this. You must be frozen. Let's dust the snow off you before it thaws and gets you wet." He suited the action to the word without waiting for her to agree, sending snow flying all over the hallway. Fortunately the floor was polished stone, so it would mop up well enough. "Come into the kitchen," he invited, satisfied with his work and turning to lead the way. "Have some soup. Always keep a stockpot on the simmer this time of year. The children are out playing. They've built a snowman bigger than I am. Genny! New vicar's wife is here!"

Genevieve Boscombe stood in the middle of the kitchen with her hands in a big bowl of flour and pastry. She was smiling, but she did not make any move to stop what she was doing. "Welcome," she said cheerfully. "I'll not shake your hand or I'll have you covered. John'll get you a dish of soup. It's just barley and bones, but it's hot." There was a faint flush of defiance in her cheeks, from more than just the exertion of rolling the pastry.

One was not defensive unless one was vulnerable. Clarice knew that from experience. She was conscious of her own clumsiness, where her sisters and her mother had been graceful. The comparison, even made in what was intended as humor, had sometimes hurt her sharply. Once or twice when she had fancied herself in love, she had felt it even more.

She smiled at Mrs. Boscombe, deliberately avoiding looking around the kitchen, though she had noticed that the good linen sheets over the airing rail had been carefully cut down the worn-out middle then turned to be joined at the sides—to give them longer life. The china on the dresser was good, but a few pieces were chipped, one or two even broken and glued very carefully together. They had had money and were now making do and mending. Even Genevieve's dress indicated the same thing. It was of good quality but had been up-to-date ten years ago.

"Thank you. I would like that very much." She thought of adding something about barley being very light and pleasing, and decided not to; it would so easily sound patronizing. "Actually I called because I hoped Mr. Boscombe might be able to help me with a

293

little of the church bookkeeping," she said hastily. "I do so much wish to be accurate. I tried Mr. Frazer, but he was unable to offer any assistance."

"What is the difficulty, Mrs. Corde?" Boscombe said with concern.

Boscombe served the barley soup into a blue-and-white bowl and set it on the table in front of Clarice, who thanked him. Suddenly she realized how difficult it was to explain her problem without lying, at least by implication.

Boscombe was waiting, eyes wide.

She must speak. "I . . . I was going through the Reverend Wynter's account books and I found certain . . ."

He was staring at her, something in his look darkening.

She could think of nothing to excuse what she had done, except the truth. Fitzpatrick had no authority to order her silence. Everyone would have to know at some time, perhaps even by tomorrow. She plunged in. "The Reverend Wynter is dead," she said very quietly, sadness overwhelming her. "We found his body quite by chance . . . in the second cellar. I went for coal and the cat followed me down. I . . ." She looked at him and saw the shock in his face, followed immediately by a terrible regret. He turned to look at Genevieve, then back at Clarice.

"I'm so sorry," he said a little huskily. "What happened? I . . . I hadn't heard."

"No one has," she said quietly. "Dr. Fitzpatrick asked us not to tell anyone until the bishop has been informed, but . . ." This was the difficult part. "But we disagree upon what happened. However, I would be grateful if you would not let people know that I told you, at least not yet."

"Of course not," he agreed. "That is why you were going through the account books?" He still seemed puzzled, but there was an inexplicable sense of relief in him, as if this wasn't what he had feared.

"Yes." She knew she had not yet said enough for him to understand. It was unavoidable now. "You see . . ." What she had planned sounded ridiculous.

"Yes?"

Genevieve also had stopped her work and was listening.

Clarice felt the heat burn up her face. "You see,

I don't believe he died by accident," she said. She hated the sound of her voice. It was wobbly and absurd. She cleared her throat. "I think someone hit him. He had injuries both on his face and on the back of his head. They may not have meant to kill him, but . . ." She was telling them too much. ". . . but there was someone else there, and they didn't tell anyone." She turned from Boscombe to Genevieve. "He was lying all by himself in the second cellar, but he had no lantern," she went on. "Who'd go into a cellar without a lantern?"

"No one," Genevieve said quietly. "But why would anyone quarrel with the Reverend Wynter? He was the nicest man . . ." She stopped.

For a moment they all were silent: Clarice and Boscombe at the kitchen table, Genevieve standing with the bowl still in her arms.

"Do you think it's the money in the church accounts?" Boscombe asked finally, his face smooth, his eyes avoiding Genevieve's. "Surely there's hardly enough there to provoke a quarrel?"

"No," Clarice agreed. "It's only pennies missing, a

shilling or two at the most. But it happened a lot of times, over six months or more."

Genevieve was looking at Boscombe; staring at him.

Boscombe sat still, his back stiff.

He knows, Clarice thought, the conviction growing in her mind. *He knows the Reverend Wynter was putting the money back.* But had the vicar known who was taking it? Was that what he had been trying to find out all those months, and had at last succeeded? And was killed for? No, that was absurd. As she had said before, it was pennies!

Boscombe was watching her, his face tense with concentration, waiting.

"You knew, didn't you?" Clarice said very softly. "Is . . . is that why you stopped working with the Reverend Wynter? Because you knew he was protecting someone who . . ."

His eyes were wide, his face almost comical with disbelief.

"You didn't . . . ," she went on, answering her own question.

"No! Oh, I knew there were pennies missing here and there," he assured her, shifting a little in his seat. "At first I thought it was just that the Reverend Wynter was a bit careless, or even that he wasn't very good at his sums. Then I realized that in the end the figures were always exactly right, so he knew someone was taking bits and pieces. But I didn't object to his dealing with it in his own way."

"Did he know who it was?" she asked.

Boscombe smiled. "He didn't tell me."

She knew he was speaking the literal truth, but there was a real truth, a more whole and honest one, that he was concealing. "But he knew," she insisted. "As you did?"

"No, I didn't. But even if I had, Mrs. Corde, I'm not sure that I would be free to tell you."

She leaned forward a little across the table, her elbows on its pale, scrubbed wood. "I think the Reverend Wynter was killed by someone, Mr. Boscombe. They may not have set out to, but they hit him, and when he was dead, or dying . . ." She saw him wince, but she went on. ". . . they dragged him into the farther cellar and took the lantern to go back upstairs, leaving him alone there in the dark, for days. It may not have anything to do with the money—it's so small it's meaningless. But it has to do with something!"

· Genevieve shivered. "If that's true, John, then an awful thing has happened. Perhaps you should tell the Reverend Corde, even if you can't tell Mrs. Corde."

He looked at her at last. "The Reverend Wynter knew," he admitted. "At least I believe he did, but it was something else, something bigger behind it, and he wanted to know what that was. The greater sin."

"Do you suppose he found out?" Clarice asked him.

He bit his lip. Now his face was pale. They were talking about something so dark it had caused the death of a good man, and perhaps the damnation of another.

"I prefer to think not," he said slowly. "At least for as long as I can think it."

"But, John . . ." Genevieve began, and then her voice trailed away.

"I don't know," he said again. "And that's the truth."

Clarice could draw no more from him. She thanked them both and left as the children trooped in from the garden, bright-faced, eyes dancing, skin glowing from the exertion. In the sudden confines of the warm kitchen with its scrubbed table and floor, its familiar, precious, but mismatched china, and the smell of drying linen and herbs, their voices were louder than they realized. *Violence* seemed like an offensive word—and utterly inappropriate.

$\mathcal{I}$t was early afternoon when Dominic decided to call again at the manor house. He had to put his trust in someone, or else simply abandon the idea of finding out exactly how the Reverend Wynter had died. It still seemed an absurd idea that anyone could have killed him.

It was below freezing, even at this hour, and his feet crunched on the snow. He walked as quickly as he could, his mind also racing. The decision he made now could affect the rest of his life, and—of more urgent importance to him—Clarice's life also. She had given up much to marry him, and he wanted passionately that she should never regret that. He found to his surprise that as he learned to know her better with each passing month, he loved her more. She had an honesty of mind that was brighter, more translucent than any he had imagined. He kept thinking he knew her, and then she said or did something that surprised him. She made him laugh, even when he did not want to. She never complained about the lack of money, or about the small, grubby accommodations she had to make to poverty or Spindlewood's petty officiousness.

Then she would blow up with temper over an injustice, and put into irretrievable words exactly what he had been thinking, only been wise enough not to say. Or was that *cowardly enough*? Or was he simply older and more acquainted with the infinite possibilities of failure?

He did not want to disappoint her. She was still so much in love with him. He could see it in her eyes, the sudden flush to her skin if she caught him looking at her with his own emotions too naked in his face. Could he ever live up to what she thought of

301

him? Sometimes being handsome was not a blessing. It led people—women—to hope for more from one than one could live up to; it ignited dreams that were too big for the reality of what any man could be.

The manor house loomed up ahead, rising out of the virgin snow as the dark trees of the driveway parted. That was a dream in stone. Did Peter Connaught ever feel the weight of past glory crushing him? Did the ghosts expect too much?

Was Clarice building a drama of murder out of a simple domestic tragedy, weaving together facts into a picture that would create sorrow and injustice, not solve it?

Dominic thought again with a shiver of his earlier acquaintance with her family, and the murder of Unity Bellwood. He had been a curate staying in her father's house to further his studies. The Reverend Ramsay Parmenter had been a good mentor, but a conventional man of passionately orthodox views. When Unity Bellwood, modern-thinking, pregnant, and unmarried, was pushed down a stairway to her death, the Reverend Parmenter became a major suspect.

But it was Clarice's beautiful, selfish, and deadly mother who had been at the core of it with her obsessive fantasy that Dominic was as much in love with her as she was with him.

It had been a time of grief, shock, and fear for the whole family. Clarice had been the bravest of them, the most willing to see and face the dreadful truth, whatever the pain, or the price.

He lengthened his stride. He would believe her this time. Better to have pursued it and been proven wrong than to run away into blind comfort. That would lie between them always.

He reached the great oak front door and pulled the bell. It was beginning to snow again, huge white flakes falling like petals.

The door opened, and the butler welcomed him in. Sir Peter was in his office, but he appeared within moments, smiling, offering tea and crumpets, apologizing because he thought there was almost certainly no cake.

"We should have mince pies," he said, shaking his head. "I'll make sure we have them next time you come."

"Just tea would be excellent, thank you," Dominic answered, following Peter's elegant figure into the huge withdrawing room. "And a little of your time." The warmth engulfed him like an embrace. The dog in front of the hearth stood up and stretched luxuriously, then padded over to see who he was and make sure he should be allowed in.

"What can I do for you?" Peter asked when they were seated. "How are you settling in?"

"I'm afraid I have very hard news indeed," Dominic replied. "I have been told not to break it yet, but—"

"You are not leaving?" Peter said in alarm.

"No. Not in the foreseeable future. I would like not to leave at all, but that is up to the bishop." Dominic was startled by how passionately he meant that. He longed to stay here, to be his own master, free to succeed—or fail—on his own beliefs, not Spindlewood's.

"I don't understand," Peter replied, confusion clear on his dark face.

As briefly as possible, Dominic told him what had

happened, including Fitzpatrick's admonition to tell no one yet, and his own reasons for not obeying.

"Oh, dear," Peter said quietly. He looked crushed. "I liked him enormously, you know."

Dominic believed him; he did not even have to weigh it in his mind. The sorrow in Peter's face was real—a pain one could sense in the room almost like a third presence.

"The more I learn of him, the more I realize how much he was loved," Dominic said gently. "I feel a loss myself, and I never even met him. That is why I intend to find out what happened. I don't know whom to trust, or where to begin." He smiled ruefully, a trifle self-conscious. "I have a brother-in-law who is a policeman, a detective. Suddenly I appreciate how appallingly difficult his job is. I have no real authority to ask anyone questions. I am an outsider here, no matter how much I want to belong, but I feel a duty to find the truth of how the Reverend Wynter died."

Peter frowned. "Do you not think perhaps it was an accident more than deliberate, and someone panicked, felt guilty for provoking a quarrel, and so denied it, even to themselves?" His voice dropped to little more than a whisper. "We can be at our ugliest when we are frightened. I have seen men act quite outside what one had believed their character to be."

"Certainly," Dominic agreed. "But there is a cowardice in that, and a certain brutality in allowing him to lie there undiscovered, which speaks of a terrible selfishness. I don't intend to allow that to go unaddressed. It . . . it would seem as if I were saying it doesn't matter, and it does."

"Of course it does." Peter lifted his eyes and met Dominic's levelly. "What can I do to help? I have no idea as to who could or would have done such a thing."

"Or why?" Dominic asked.

Peter's mouth pinched very slightly. "Or why," he conceded. He drew in his breath as if to add something, and then changed his mind and remained silent.

Dominic wondered what he had been going to say. That it must be a secret the Reverend Wynter had learned, possibly even by accident, but that someone

306

cared about so passionately, with such fear of loss, that they had killed rather than risk it being known? It was the obvious thing, if a priest was murdered. Could Peter have failed to say this for any reason except that he knew, or feared, it was true?

His own secret, or someone else's?

What secret could the elegant, charming, and secure Peter Connaught care about enough to commit murder? Or who was the friend for whom he would condone such an act?

Anything? Anyone? The most ordinary countenance could hide stories of pain the outsider would never imagine. Peter had quarreled with Wynter himself to the point that, despite their very real affection, he had suddenly stopped calling at the vicarage, and Wynter had put away the chess set and apparently never played again.

Dominic considered challenging the man but decided not to, at least not yet. "I might be able to narrow it to some degree by knowing who called on him after the last time he was seen alive," he said aloud.

Peter relaxed fractionally. The difference in his posture in the big chair was so slight, it was no more than an easing in the tiny wrinkles in the way his jacket lay. But Dominic was aware of it.

A log settled in the fireplace, sending up a shower of sparks. Peter stood up and added another, then waited a moment to make certain it was balanced. The flames reached higher to embrace it.

"That seems like a good idea," he said, taking his seat again. "If I can help, I should be happy to. I might even be able to make some discreet inquiries myself."

"I should be most grateful," Dominic replied. He had no idea how far to trust him, but sometimes one could learn as much from a lie as from the truth. Even omissions could tell a person something. "Thank you," he went on with warmth. "I hope that, as you say, it may turn out to be no worse than a grubby accident someone failed to report."

Peter smiled. "A weakness not easy to forgive, but not impossible."

Dominic remained another fifteen minutes, and then took his leave out into a fading afternoon, now even more bitterly cold. Some of the clouds had cleared away, and it had stopped snowing. The light was pale, with the amber of the fading sun low on the horizon. Shadows were growing longer. The edge of the wind cut like a blade, making his skin hurt and his eyes water.

His feet slipped a little on the ice as he trudged down the drive. Other than the thud of the mounded snow on the evergreens overbalancing onto the ground below, there was silence in the gathering gloom.

Beyond the trees the village lights shone yellow, making little golden smudges sparkling against the blue-gray of twilight. Someone opened a door onto a world of brilliance. A dog scampered out then back in again, and the light vanished.

Dominic's hands and feet were numb. Hunching his shoulders from the cold, he stopped for a moment to retie his scarf.

That was when he heard the footsteps behind him. He swung around, his breath catching in his throat from the icy air in his lungs. The figure was there, crossing the village green only a few yards away. She was bent, shivering, and very small. She stopped also, motionless, as if uncertain whether to try running away.

But who could run in the deep snow? And like Dominic, she was probably too stiff with cold even to try.

Dominic took a step toward her. "Are you looking for me?" he asked gently.

"Oh . . . Reverend Corde . . . ," she began.

"Can I help you?" he asked gently.

"No! I was just . . . well . . ."

"Mrs. Towers?" He was almost certain it was the elderly woman he had met in about this same spot a few days ago. He recognized the small hands in their woolen mittens.

"Yes . . . er, yes. No, I am just on my way home." She did not move.

"Perhaps I could walk with you?" he offered. "Just to make sure you get home safely. It's a terribly cold evening."

"Well . . . that's very kind of you." There was an eagerness in her slightly husky voice. He could barely see her face under the shadow of her hat and the scarf wound around her neck and shoulders, but he thought she might have been smiling.

He crossed the short distance between them and

offered her his arm. She took it, pulling at him very slightly to direct him the right way. Walking at her pace was hard. There was no briskness to keep the blood flowing.

"Is there anything I can do for you, Mrs. Towers?" he asked, trying to guess why she had seemed to be following him. "Do you need some wood brought in? Or coal?" The moment he had said it he wondered if he had been clumsy. Possibly she had none, and that was the real issue.

"Oh, no thank you," she said, shaking her head and shivering. "Really, I have everything. Very kind of you, but a hand not to slip is all I need." As if to emphasize it she clung to him harder.

He walked in silence for several minutes, still believing that there was something she wanted to ask him if she could work up the courage. He ought to be able to guess it and help her if it was difficult. Surely a good minister would see needs, understand them before they were voiced?

Perhaps she was just lonely. Hardly anyone would say that. *Please, Vicar, talk to me, and break the silence I live in. It doesn't matter what I say or think,*

311

ANNE PERRY

but please pretend for half an hour that it does. Listen to me, ask me; then when you go again I shall feel better.

Would she spend Christmas alone, too, apart from coming to church? He should ask her to tea. But he should invite her once before that, so the kindness wasn't so obvious. No one wanted to be asked simply for charity's sake.

"Mrs. Towers," he began, "I hope that one day soon when the snow is a little less deep, you will come to tea with us. My wife and I would be delighted to better make your acquaintance. You could tell us much about the village, its history, and the people who have lived here. Would you?"

"Oh!" She sounded thoroughly startled. "Oh, well!" She gripped his arm as if she was in very real danger of falling. "That would be very nice, I'm sure. When the weather is better, I should be very pleased to come. When there isn't so much snow, you know. Thank you so much. I am nearly home now. Just around the corner." She pulled her arm away. "Do have a nice evening. Good night, Vicar. Thank you for your kindness. So nice to see you." She doubled

312

her speed and disappeared into the gloom, swallowed by the shadows of trees and garden hedges until she was indistinguishable from the other shapes in the night.

There was no point in standing here as if she might change her mind and come back. And yet Dominic had been certain that she had wished to say something more to him. Had he put her off by speaking? He had only asked her to tea at some time in the future.

Did she already know that the Reverend Wynter was dead, or did she perhaps fear it? Had he confided in her? Or perhaps living alone with little to do, and with no relatives nearby, she watched and listened in the village. It would not be snooping, just the instinct of a lonely person with time on her hands, but she might have seen or deduced all kinds of things for herself.

He should have asked her. Could she even be in danger herself?

He was freezing in the bone-deep cold. He was beginning to shake now that he had stopped moving. He turned and began to walk back across the snow

313

toward the spires of the church, black against the first stars. He knew the vicarage lay to the right of it, invisible in the trees, its lights kept to a minimum for economy's sake.

When he opened the front door, the warmth engulfed him, and after a moment he smelled the hot pastry, oil lamps, coal, and lavender furniture polish.

"Clarice!" he called out eagerly. "Clarice?"

She was there a moment later, hugging him. She gasped when the ice on his coat touched her neck and throat, then ignored it and held him tighter.

After supper they sat by the fire opposite each other. Outside, the wind rose, whipping the branches, and now and then clattering small twigs against the glass. He told her about speaking with Peter Connaught.

"Did he tell you anything useful?" she asked, leaning forward, eyes intent upon his.

"I don't think so," he admitted.

She caught his hesitation. "You think, you aren't sure?"

He looked at her face with its large, tender eyes

and vulnerable mouth. Had he brought her into the presence of murder again, into the violence and tragedy of human hatred? He remembered how much she had been hurt the last time, and how frightened he had been himself. She had never doubted him, no matter what the facts had appeared to be. He owed her honesty, but he also owed her protection. He did not wish her to be hurt, ever. And yet if he shut her out, he was alone. He could not tell her half-truths—not without destroying the thread between them that was so infinitely precious.

"It wasn't what he said so much as a look in his face," he said, feeling ridiculous.

"He believed you!" she said, understanding instantly. "You told him the Reverend Wynter was murdered, and he knew you were right!"

He felt a warmth inside deeper than anything the fire or the room could give him. "He believes someone has a secret, and that the Reverend Wynter could have learned it," he said in confirmation. Should he tell her the rest: the impression only barely formed in his mind?

She was waiting for him to finish. She had something urgent to say also. He could see it in her eyes, in the clenching of her hands in her lap.

"I think he was almost relieved," he said. "As if he had feared it, and now that it had happened it could be faced, and he was no longer alone."

"He isn't alone," she said quickly. "And I told John and Genevieve Boscombe as well. I couldn't help it. Dr. Fitzpatrick may be furious, but I couldn't ask their help and then lie to them. They wouldn't have helped me anyway, because I had no sensible explanation for what I'd done."

He was confused, then touched by a tendril of fear, just a tiny thing, but unmistakable. "What have you done?"

She blinked with guilt, lowering her eyes.

"I wasn't accusing you!" He leaned far forward enough to grasp her hand. "Clarice! I only meant . . ." What had he meant? He gulped, and then clenched his teeth. "I was afraid for you. If someone in this village really lured the Reverend Wynter to the cellar steps and then hit him so hard he died as a result, then it would be foolish to think we are safe if we go looking for the secret that provoked them to it. Despite the snow and the peace, the kindness, Christmas in a few days, there is still something very terrible here. Just because we haven't lived here all our lives doesn't mean we are safe from it. We have made ourselves part of whatever it is. I'm sorry!"

She took his hand, closing her fingers around it. "Don't be. The only way to be safe is not to be alone at all. I shall be very careful."

"No you won't!" he contradicted her sharply. "I know you! You'll go charging in, doing whatever you think is right. Safety, or anything to do with sense, will be the last thing on your mind!"

She sidestepped the issue. "I looked at the books," she told him. "Very carefully."

He was confused. "What books?" It appeared to be irrelevant.

"The ledgers!" she said impatiently. "The accounts!"

"Oh. Why? I'm sure we can manage until the bishop makes a decision." He heard the unhappiness in his own voice. He had not meant to allow himself to care so much, certainly not to let Clarice know.

317

But he wanted to belong here, have his own church, his own congregation to teach, to care for, and to learn from. Already he dreaded going back to the Reverend Spindlewood and his gray, sanctimonious ways, his tediousness of spirit.

"The accounts are not right!" Clarice said firmly. "There are inconsistencies in the last seven months or more." Her voice was low and tense, and she was staring at him, demanding his attention. "Someone was stealing tiny amounts from the church collections. Just pennies quite often, never more than a shilling or two. The Reverend Wynter was putting the amount back from his own money. His own ledgers were balanced to the farthing, except for those amounts. If you look carefully, they tally up."

He frowned, trying to understand. "Why?"

"I don't know, and neither does John Boscombe, but there is something bigger behind it, something they really care about. The Reverend Wynter was hiding it for a reason, until he could find what that is. John Boscombe didn't say so, exactly, but I saw the moment in his face when he knew it. I will be careful, Dominic, I promise, but we have to find out

318

what it is. How could we stay here and just pretend this hasn't happened, or that we don't know? We do know!"

"But maybe . . ." He stopped.

Her look was withering. "If there really is a God—and I can't bear to believe that there isn't, despite anything Mr. Darwin says—then He knows that we know. In the end that's all that counts, isn't it?" Now she needed an answer, not just to that question but to all that was wrapped within it, for all of their lives.

He closed his eyes for a second, two seconds, and three. She had a way of smashing through pretense that left one nowhere to hide. "Yes, of course that's all there is," he answered her. "We must find the truth and deal with it. But please be careful, Clarice. Whoever it is has a secret, which to them is so terrible they will kill a priest to keep it. It could be anything—even another death we don't yet know of. Or something that to us seems trivial, but to them is so grave, they cannot bear it. If anything happened to you, it would be unbearable to me. I love you so much I don't know how I would be any use without

319

you, to myself or to others. I might once have worked alone quite well, but not since I've known you. I've known something too good to forget."

She smiled, and her eyes were full of tears, but shining tears. "I'll be careful," she promised, sniffing and blinking hard. "I'm much too happy to let anyone take it away from me, either."

*T*he morning was bright, with a cold, hard wind. They had been in Cottisham little more than a week. It seemed longer. Clearing away breakfast dishes and wondering if Mrs. Wellbeloved would come today or not, or if Mrs. Paget would still consider, after the Reverend Wynter's death, that they should cook for a Christmas party, Clarice felt as if it were months ago that she and Dominic had first walked into this comfortable hallway and she had been so immediately at home. There had been not the slightest shadow of tragedy then. The whole vicarage had been warm with the memories of generations of families living here.

They would have had their joys and griefs like everyone, but also a security of faith in this small community, under the shadow of the church and the sound of its bells.

How could she have imagined that below there, in the darkness of the cellar, the vicar himself was lying alone, growing colder and colder each day? Would it ever get really warm again? Not until they had found the truth and faced it.

Dominic had gone out again to see Dr. Fitzpatrick. It was not a duty he was looking forward to, but there were many issues to be dealt with. The village must be told officially of the Reverend Wynter's death. Dominic would have to remain silent while the doctor passed it off as natural. He had written to inform the bishop, of course, but whether the letter had reached him depended on the snow not being too deep for a horse and trap to get out of the village. Even the main roads could be impassable if it had drifted, and he might have to hold the funeral regardless.

Clarice stood in the middle of the kitchen floor, towel in her hand, overtaken by surprise at how

321

much she dreaded being replaced. It would be crushing. She wanted to stay here, not only because Dominic wanted it so much, but also for herself. Despite what she had found in the cellar, she wanted to live in this house, see spring come to this garden. She wanted to see the village pond unfrozen, and with the spring ducklings on it, their funny little flat feet on the new grass. She wanted to see the apple trees in blossom, and children flying kites. She wanted to be here for Easter, and summer, and Harvest Festival. It could be a fulfillment she had never known before, for both of them. There was good work to be done. Dominic would become as loved as the Reverend Wynter had been, and she would watch it, and help.

First, though, they must learn who had killed the vicar, and why. They could not find the light if they had not the courage to explore the darkness. Everyone had secrets: it was within the nature of life, whether they were acts of wickedness or merely of foolishness. Guilt and embarrassment could look alike. But which one had provoked murder?

She thought about her visit to the Boscombes yesterday as she put away the crockery and cleaned the top of the range. She restoked it and then started to warm the flatirons to press Dominic's clean shirts, which were now rolled up damp in the scullery and awaiting her attention.

The Boscombes' was such a happy house, and yet she had sensed a fear there. Or was that too strong a word? Had it been no more than anxiety, and sorrow because a friend had died tragically? She knew she had not imagined the glance between them, so quick as to seem guarded, a communication they preferred not to put into words. Nor had she imagined the small but very clear signs of recent poverty.

What was their sudden misfortune, and had the Reverend Wynter known about it? She had no idea, but it was very possible. One thing she was certain about, and that was that both John and Genevieve Boscombe were aware that the Reverend Wynter knew secrets, at least one of which was dangerous. They had understood instantly what the tiny thefts were, and why he had concealed them.

Were they also protecting each other? Why did she ask herself that, when she was perfectly certain that they were?

If the Reverend Wynter had known some secret about them, what could it be?

She tested the irons on the hob. They were hot enough. She must pay attention to what she was doing. She could not afford to scorch Dominic's shirts. Apart from the fact that she had too much pride in being a good wife, they were far too expensive to replace. They came from the days of his profession as a banker, long before he decided to be a minister.

She kept a piece of extra rag to test the temperature before touching the iron to a shirt. She tried it now, carefully; only when she was satisfied did she begin to iron.

If the vicar had known something about the Boscombes, it would have to be something they cared about passionately, and she did not believe that could ever be money. What was the most precious thing in the world to them? Not material goods of any sort. Not power or prestige. They had never had either, nor would they want them. They treasured warmth

324

in their home, the laughter of children playing, the certainty of gentleness and companionship, and the good things that all people of true sanity want.

What could jeopardize those things?

The iron was getting hot in her hand. She snatched it off the collar and was flooded with relief that there was no brown mark on its white surface. The smell of warm, clean cotton filled the air.

Could there be something wrong with the Boscombes' marriage, and somehow the vicar had discovered it? Had Genevieve been underage at the time? She looked several years younger than John. Perhaps her father had not given consent, and they had run away to be married, and lied to obtain permission. Did that make their union illegal? Had she been from a wealthy family and promised to someone else? But that would not invalidate their marriage.

Were any of their children conceived or born out of wedlock? That would be scandalous, but not irrevocable. Why would the Reverend Wynter concern himself with it? It might be a sin in the eyes of the church, but it was over and done with now. Surely a confession and absolution would deal with it.

325

She could find out. She had only to go to the church itself, which was next door across the strip of grass and up the path through the graveyard. The church records would be there in the vestry: marriages, christenings, and burials. Boscombe had said Genevieve grew up here. She would have been married here, too.

Very carefully she finished the final shirt. She put both irons to cool and carried the shirts upstairs. Clarice felt rather grubby, searching the parish records for someone else's secrets, but sometimes one could feel grubby doing what was necessary to get to the truth. And if she found she was wrong, so much the better.

She put on her outdoor boots again and her heavy cape, then picked up the keys and went out. The snow was almost up to her knees in places where the land was low and it had drifted. The bare honeysuckle vine on the lych-gate was sparkling with icicles, and the path through the gravestones was slippery. The sky was ragged now, with patches of hard light making the expanse of the village green difficult to look at. The snow glared achingly white. She won-

326

dered if someone had fed the ducks. She should make sure, should take them something herself.

The church was bitterly cold inside. The stained-glass window with its pictures of Christ walking on the water cast patches of blue and green and gold light on the floor. The robe of St. Peter in the boat was the only warm color: a splash of wine. How many people down the centuries had brought their joys and their griefs here, made promises, prayed for forgiveness, or poured out their thanks?

She hurried to where the parish record books were kept. She unlocked the cupboard and found the one most likely to contain the baptism of the Boscombes' oldest child. She skimmed through a couple of years' worth of entries before finding it. It was a swift job, since the village was small: just four or five hundred people. Then she started to go backward, looking for John and Genevieve's marriage. She went through ten years but didn't find it. Twenty-three years before the birth of their first child, she came across Genevieve's own baptism. Even more carefully she moved forward. There were baptisms of two sisters of Genevieve, then the burial of both her parents.

327

The sisters' marriages were recorded, but not baptisms of any children. Presumably they had moved to wherever their husbands lived.

Then Genevieve's children were baptized, but Clarice could find no reference to her marriage.

Of course they could have been married somewhere else, but the ugly thought kept intruding into Clarice's mind that perhaps they had not been married at all. Why would that be? The only reason she could think of was that something had prevented it. The obvious thing would be that one of them was already married. If it were Genevieve, the whole village would probably know; therefore, it must be John.

Had the Reverend Wynter somehow found that out?

She closed the book and replaced it, locking the cupboard door. She walked back through the icy vestry and outside into the freezing world again. It glittered sharp on daggers of water from the earlier thaw, now hanging from every black branch.

Her feet crunched on the surface. There were gray

328

clouds looming in from the west, fat-bellied with more snow. Little shivers of wind stirred the topmost branches.

$\mathcal{W}$hen Dominic returned at lunchtime, she told him what she had found.

"She could have been married somewhere else," he said, taking a fresh piece of bread and another slice of cold mutton. "Perhaps in his village. He might have had elderly parents who couldn't travel, for example."

She passed him the rich, sharp pickle. "Possibly. But the Boscombes are in some kind of hardship. There are lots of small signs of it, if you look."

He smiled with a touch of sadness, and she saw the mounting pain in his eyes. They were not in that situation themselves, but it was not too far ahead of them if he remained a curate much longer. She regretted having said it, yet she could not deny the evidence she had seen in the Boscombes' house. Perhaps avoiding the subject of poverty was in a way making it worse, as if it were a secret too shameful to acknowledge.

"People do fall on harder times without there being a dark secret," he pointed out ruefully.

"I know." She poured him more tea although he had not asked for it. One of her pleasures was to notice his needs and meet them before he said anything. "It's just a little piece of information. But I think it fits in with the missing pennies in the ledgers, the fact that John Boscombe suddenly resigned from his position in the church, and that they are both afraid of something. None of which would matter if the Reverend Wynter were not dead. But he is, and at least for now, this is your village." Then she corrected herself. "Our village."

He frowned. "Why would their not being married, and the vicar knowing that, have anything to do with financial hard times or the petty thefts from the collection? That doesn't make any sense."

She struggled through the confusion in her own mind. "I think he knew about the petty thefts before giving up his job keeping the books. He was close enough to the vicar that they trusted each other. Then something happened, and John Boscombe left. They still go to church, as everyone does, but that's all. Could mean their sudden tightening of circumstances dates from that time, too. With children you can go through sheets quickly. You'll wash them every other week, perhaps give them a little rubbing. Middles can wear thin. Best to trim them before they actually tear."

"And what caused the hardship?" he asked. "The Reverend Wynter was blackmailing them, so they paid for half a year, and then they killed him?"

She blinked. "No! No, I don't believe that. But maybe if the Reverend Wynter found out, so did someone else. That's possible, isn't it?"

He considered for a moment, staring at his cup, but without reaching for it. "Yes," he said finally. "Who would that be?"

"His first wife," she said without hesitation. "Or, really, his only wife."

"Why didn't she come forward and accuse him openly, if he deserted her?"

"Oh, Dominic!" she said in exasperation. "Don't be

so otherworldly. Much better to ask him for money to keep quiet about it than admit to everyone that he ran away from her to be with someone else. Except that if Genevieve doesn't know, or didn't at the time, then he probably ran away just because she was ghastly."

He tried to hide a smile, and failed. "Clarice, you don't just run away because your husband or wife is appalling, or there would hardly be a married person in England living at home."

She raised her eyebrows very high. "Thank you. I hadn't thought of running away . . . yet."

He shook his head. "I'm so glad," he said drily. "It's cold out there. Do you really think the Boscombes have a secret?"

She wrinkled her nose.

"Yes. And I really do think it could have to do with their marriage. That is the only thing of sufficient importance to them that they might fight very hard to protect it." She met his eyes and hoped he could see in hers that she understood the Boscombes perfectly. She, too, would have fought with every weapon she had to protect her marriage. For her, too, it was the most precious thing she had.

He reached across the table and touched her fingertips gently. "I agree," he answered. "And I am beginning to think that Sir Peter Connaught also has. something about which he is less than honest."

She was startled. "Sir Peter? Are you sure? You don't think he's just . . . grieved? He seemed to be very fond of the Reverend Wynter, and they never made up their quarrel before he died. That makes people feel very guilty, you know."

He fiddled with his knife. "I thought of that, but it's more a matter of little things that don't fit: discrepancies in his stories about his parents. Perhaps they don't even matter, but I noticed them." He seemed about to add something further, then changed his mind. He looked unhappy.

"What is it?" she asked. "What are you thinking?"

He gave a slight shrug. "I don't know. People do boast sometimes, exaggerate their abilities, or money, all sorts of things. But Sir Peter doesn't seem in any need to do that. He is obviously a man of great wealth, or he could not maintain a place like the manor house. And it is superbly kept. He gives generously to the village; I know that from the Reverend Wynter's remarks in the notes to his accounts. And the whole Connaught family is above reproach. Their history is pretty well public."

"They could still have secrets," Clarice pointed out. "Almost every family does." She bit her lip. "We certainly do, for heaven's sake. I would go to great lengths to prevent anyone in Cottisham knowing about my mother." She felt hot with shame even saying it to Dominic, who already knew everything about it. She understood what secrets could cost and what lengths people could be driven to by love, and fear. "Dominic, it is possible the Connaughts also have something they would pay a great deal to keep unknown," she went on. "It is very hard to live with people prying through one's affairs. Perhaps that was at the root of his quarrel with the Reverend Wynter. They used to be close; we know they played chess every week."

He looked at her unhappily. "The Reverend Wynter quarreled with Peter Connaught, and with John

Boscombe. Are you saying that he was behind some kind of extortion or threat of exposure?"

"I don't know. Sometimes 'the wicked flee where no man pursueth.' Maybe just his knowledge was enough."

He said what they were both thinking. "Or he used his special knowledge in the most appalling betrayal imaginable: to blackmail those who had trusted him, and even turned to him for help and forgiveness?"

She gripped his hand across the table. "We didn't know him," she said urgently. "Perhaps we have imagined him the way we wanted him to be."

"Everyone speaks well of him," he pointed out, closing his fingers over hers.

"Well, they would!" she said, biting her lip. "He was a priest, and now he has died! Who is going to say he was brutal, a slimy betrayer of trust who blackmails the most vulnerable? They would only know it if they had been a victim themselves, and wished him dead, possibly murdered. Who would admit that?"

"No one," he said miserably. "Please God, I hope you're wrong. We're wrong," he corrected himself.

*D*ominic went out again to visit one of the old gentlemen who was too frail to leave his house in the snow, and afraid of what the deepening winter would bring.

He stayed a little while, assuring Mr. Riddington of his care. Regardless of who the vicar of Cottisham should be, he would always have time for going to those who could not come to the church. Then after bidding him good-bye he walked along the lane toward the green in the dusk. Again he became aware of footsteps behind him. They seemed to be gaining on him, as though the person was keen to catch him up.

He stopped and turned. He saw the brisk figure of Mrs. Paget hurrying toward him, her breath a white vapor in the freezing air. She was dressed rather smartly with a russet-brown cape, and there was a flush in her cheeks.

"I'm glad to see you, Reverend Corde," she said warmly as she reached him. "Have you been to see Mr. Riddington? Poor old soul can't make it even to his front gate anymore. Afraid of slipping and breaking a leg. Very wise he stays in. Broken bone at his age can be nasty. Don't let me hold you up. I'll walk beside you." Without waiting she started forward again, and he was left to keep step with her.

"Mrs. Blount next door drops in every day," he told her.

"Not the same as having the vicar call." Mrs. Paget shook her head. "No one else can comfort with the spiritual promises of the church."

"Believe me, Mrs. Blount is a far better cook than I am," he replied, keeping his balance on the uneven path with difficulty. "And there are times when a hot apple pie is more use than a sermon."

"You may joke, Vicar," she said seriously. "But there are dark things to fight against, darker than most folks are willing to admit."

He was uncertain how to answer her. The wind was rising again. It whined in the branches above them, and little flurries of dry snow skittered over the ice.

"I know the truth," she went on, her voice quiet

337

but very clear. "The Reverend Wynter was murdered, wasn't he? Please don't try to spare me by denying it. It doesn't help to close one's eyes. That's how evil flourishes, because we want to be kind and end up being cruel."

He wanted to argue, but she was right. He asked her the question that filled his mind. "How do you know that, Mrs. Paget?"

Now it was she who was silent. They were out of the lane and starting across the open green. The pond was almost invisible: just a smooth white surface a little lower than the slope of the grass. The air was darkening, color staining the west with fire and the shadows growing so dense the houses blended into one another. He began to think she was not going to answer.

"The Reverend Wynter was here in Cottisham well over thirty years," she said at last. "He knew a lot about people, sometimes things they'd rather no one did. He wouldn't have told, of course. Priests don't, do they." It wasn't really a question, but she stopped as if waiting for him to speak, her features indistinguishable in the shadows.

338

"No," he replied. Was she trying to find a way to tell him that the Reverend Wynter had done infinitely worse than use his privileged knowledge to manipulate and extort? The darkness felt as if it were inside him as well as beyond in the sky and the black lace of the trees.

"But those that betray don't trust anyone," she said, looking straight ahead of her.

"Is that why you believe he was murdered, Mrs. Paget?" he asked. "Just that he knew people's secrets? All priests do."

"What are most village secrets?" she asked. "A few silly mistakes, a little spite. All things you can repent of." Suddenly her voice dropped and became bitter. "Cottisham's different. But here there are things that are against the law of God, and a priest can't overlook or forgive them."

"God can forgive all sins, Mrs. Paget," he pointed out.

"After you've paid," she said harshly. "Not while you're still committing them, and the innocent are suffering. Don't tell me that's God's way, 'cos it isn't. I know that, and so do you, Vicar."

339

"Yes," he said a little tartly. "And the Reverend Wynter would have pointed that out to anyone who was continuing to do what was wrong."

"Exactly," she agreed, staring at him. "But what if that person didn't want to stop? What if they weren't going to stop, no matter what?"

He didn't want to know, but he couldn't avoid it simply because it was uncomfortable. If a priest refused to address sin, what use was he to anyone? He was here precisely to deal with weakness: physical or spiritual. He must face it, wherever it led him. He started to walk again, trusting his instincts though he could only dimly see the road.

"What you say is true, Mrs. Paget. But I imagine you expect me to do more than agree in theory?"

"You didn't know the Reverend Wynter," she said after another few steps. The emotion was carefully controlled in her voice now, and he could not see her face. It was dark all around them; only the yellow gleam of a few uncurtained windows shone warmly here and there, illuminating short distances, touching branches with gold and making the night beyond seem deeper. "He was a good man," she went on. "He

340

was brave and honest. He knew right from wrong, and he didn't flinch from doing what he had to, even though he didn't like it."

"Did he know things about more than one person?" he asked. He was trying to evade the issue and he knew it. Perhaps she did, too.

"He might have known things about a lot of people," she admitted. "But he knew that John and Genevieve Boscombe are living together in sin. He walked out on his first wife. Left her alone to fend for herself. Vicar never told a word, but I don't come from Cottisham, and I know one or two other places as well. I recognized him."

"And told the Reverend Wynter?" he asked, shivering a little.

"No, I didn't," she said stiffly. "But if I had, I'd have been doing those poor children a service."

"Branding them as illegitimate?" he said, disbelief making his voice hard. "The scandal would ruin the parents and make them all outcasts. How is that a service, Mrs. Paget?" They crossed the road together, side by side.

"Only if the vicar told people," she answered with

exaggerated patience. "And he wouldn't do that. You said so yourself." There was triumph in her, but thin and shivery, full of hurt. "You haven't been a vicar very long, have you," she observed.

He felt the heat burn inside him, despite the bitter edge of the wind. "No. What do you suppose the Reverend Wynter intended to do?" He wanted to know for himself, but also because it might lead him toward whoever had killed Wynter.

"Face them," she said simply. "Tell them they have to put things right. Go back and face Mrs. Boscombe, the real one, and care for her, make some restitution to her for what her husband did. Perhaps if he's lucky, she'll divorce him for his adultery with her that calls herself his wife now. If all that happens, then they can marry and make their children legitimate at last, by adoption or however it's done. Not their fault, poor little souls."

He felt an intense pity, more than she could have understood. His own first marriage had been less than happy, as he understood happiness now. He had not left his wife, but he had certainly betrayed her more than once. She may well have expected it, but that excused nothing. He still had a guilt to expiate, and he knew and accepted it. That certain knowledge made him far quicker to forgive others, to understand ugliness and stupidity and try to heal it rather than destroy the perpetrator.

"You are quite right," he said to her gently. "That would be the correct thing to do, even if not the easiest."

"He never lacked courage." She kept walking at a steady, even pace into the wind. "Takes courage to be a priest, Reverend Corde. Can't just go around being nice to people. Sometimes that isn't the real help."

"Yes, Mrs. Paget. I'm sure it isn't," he agreed.

"I'm home now. Good night, Vicar."

"Mrs. Paget!" he said quickly. "You said the Reverend Wynter knew things about many people."

"So he did," she cut across him. "But it's no good asking me what things they were, or who they were about, because I don't know. I just knew that one because I knew. I've lived in other villages, too. Good night, Vicar." This time she turned and walked away briskly up the path toward the nearest cottage.

"Good night, Mrs. Paget," he said more to himself than to her.

$\mathcal{I}$t was not a good night. He knew that after supper he would have to go see John Boscombe and ask him if what he had been told was the truth, because he felt sure that was what the Reverend Wynter was doing before he died. He had racked his brains to find another alternative, all the time knowing that there was none. Clarice had offered to come with him, and he had refused. She had no part in it, and no chaperone was necessary. She would worry, he knew that, imagining all kinds of anger and distress, but that was the burden of a priest's wife, and she did not ask to be relieved of it.

It was a hard walk to the Boscombes' house. He did not dare take the shortcut through the woods, even if the stream was frozen. His arm ached from carrying the lantern and trying to hold it against the wind. He was welcomed in. The house was warm, although not as warm as the vicarage where they could afford to burn a little more coal.

"How nice to see you, Reverend Corde," Boscombe said immediately. "It's a terrible night for visiting. What brings you? No one ill or needing help?"

Dominic almost changed his mind. Maybe this was something the bishop should deal with, or whoever was given this living permanently. But if he evaded it, Clarice would despise him. Even now he could imagine her disappointment in him.

He followed Boscombe inside to the parlor, where Genevieve was sitting sewing. She was patching the sleeves of a jacket. She put it away quickly as if to welcome him, but he saw from the quick flush in her face that she was ashamed. Were they really paying blackmail to someone? The vicar? Please God, no.

Or to anyone else, perhaps from Boscombe's home village? Even Mrs. Paget? But it was the Reverend Wynter who was dead. Mrs. Paget was very much alive.

"Genny, please get the vicar a cup of tea, or soup," Boscombe requested. "Which would you like?"

How could Dominic accept the man's hospitality, given out of their little, with what he had come to say? Guilt almost choked him. And who was he to blame a man for doing what he might so easily have done himself, had the temptation been there? Sarah was dead, however, and he was free to love Clarice as he wished, but due to luck, not virtue.

"No thank you, not yet," he prevaricated. "But I would like to speak to you confidentially, Mr. Boscombe. I beg your pardon for that, on such an evening."

"Don't worry, Vicar," Genevieve said quickly. "I have jobs to do in the kitchen. You just call when you'd like the soup."

"What is it?" Boscombe asked as soon as the door was closed and they were alone. "You look very grave, Vicar. Not more money gone, is it? Or did you find out who took it? I think the Reverend Wynter was inclined to let it go, you know. He could always see the greater picture, the one that mattered."

"Yes, I imagine he could," Dominic answered. "It seems to me he thought past today's embarrassment and saw the grief that could come in the future if present sins, however easy to understand, or even to sympathize with, were not put right."

Boscombe's face paled. His eyes were steady on Dominic's face.

"I'm sorry," Dominic said gently. "There is no record of your marriage in this parish. If I ask the bishop, will he find it in some other place?"

Boscombe's voice was husky, his eyes wretched. "No, Vicar. Genevieve is the wife of my heart, but not of the law. The Reverend Wynter knew that, and he wanted to find a way for us to make it right, but I couldn't stay on in office in the church once he knew."

·"But you could stay until then?" The moment the words were out of his lips, Dominic wished he had not said them. It was a criticism Boscombe did not need, however justified.

Boscombe blushed and looked down at his big hands. "I wasn't the one who told him. I couldn't bring myself to. I wanted to be happy," he said softly. "That was the coward's way, I suppose, but he asked me to help with the money and other tasks in the church. I couldn't refuse without telling him why." He twisted his fingers together, crushing the flesh

347

till they were white. "I didn't think you'd find out so quick."

"Did you kill the Reverend Wynter?"

Boscombe's head jerked up, his eyes wide. "No! God in heaven, man, how can you ask such a thing? He was my friend! He wanted us to put it right, and I told him I wasn't leaving Genevieve for anything, church or no church. And I wasn't going back to my first wife, either. If God sent me to hell, at least I'd have a life first. But go back and it would be hell now. And who would support Genny and my children?"

"Who supports your first wife?" Dominic asked.

"She had money of her own and no need of mine," Boscombe said bitterly. "As she often reminded me."

"If she divorced you for your adultery and desertion, you would be free to marry Genevieve and make your children legitimate," Dominic pointed out. "In the law, if not in the church. Wouldn't it still be better?"

Boscombe gave a sharp bark of laughter. "Do you think I didn't ask her to? She's not a woman to forgive, Reverend Corde. Not ever. As long as she lives she'll hold me to bondage. My only choice is to live in sin with Genevieve, the best and gentlest, most loyal woman I know, or live in virtue cold as ice with a woman who hates me, and will make me pay every day and night of my life, because I don't love her. The Reverend Wynter wanted me to make it right, for Genevieve's sake, and my children's. He told me they'd get nothing if I die, and I know that's true." He blinked several times. "I'll just have to pray I don't die. He was looking for a way for me to make it right with God, but he never found it before he died. I don't know who killed him, but I swear to you before the Lord who made the earth and everything in it, it was not me. I loved the Reverend Wynter, and I've got enough on my soul as it is without adding violence to it."

Dominic believed him. It fit with what Mrs. Paget had told him, and what he had come to know of Wynter. Boscombe might have thought, in a moment's desperation, that if Wynter were dead he could continue to live in peace. But he must have known that it would only be a matter of time before he was exposed. With murder on his hands and his heart, there would be no happiness ahead for him, or for the woman and the children he loved so deeply. Could Dominic find an answer for him? If Wynter, with a lifetime in the church, could not, then how could he, a novice? "I'll try to find a way for you to sort it out," he promised rashly. "Thank you for your honesty."

"If there were, we'd have found it by now," Boscombe said miserably. "What are you going to say to the bishop?"

"Nothing," Dominic replied, again rashly. He stood up. "I'm concerned with finding who killed the Reverend Wynter. Anything else is between you and God. Living with a woman to whom you are not married may be a sin, but it is not against the law. We will address that problem later. Perhaps after Christmas they will move me somewhere else. I hope not, but I cannot choose." He heard the roughness of grief in his own voice and was angry with himself. What had he to grieve over, when he was returning to the woman he loved, with no shadow over them or between them, except whatever he might create himself by being less than she believed of him? "First let us celebrate the birth of Christ, and leave other things until after that."

Boscombe held out his hand, blinking rapidly again. "Thank you."

Dominic gripped him hard. "But if I stay here, we will have to seek an answer one day."

"I know," Boscombe replied. "I know."

$\mathcal{T}$he morning dawned bright. The sky was a pale, wind-scoured blue, and the ice crust on the snow was hard enough to support a child's weight. The few ducks out, eager for bread, paddled across it without making a crack. Someone had been thoughtful enough to put out water for them, but it would need thawing every hour or two.

Clarice had baked bread, a skill she was very proud of because it had not come naturally to her. Dominic took a loaf to old Mr. Riddington and found him frail and hunched up in his chair. He was grateful for the bread, but even more for the company in his chilly and almost soundless world. Dominic brought in more wood and coal, making them both a cup of tea. He found it was more than two hours before he could decently leave the old man.

He went next door to check with Mrs. Blount and thank her for her kindness. Then he set out for home.

He was close to the green again when he was aware of footsteps behind him. He heard every crack and crunch of the ice. He turned to see the small figure of Sybil Towers struggling to catch up with him. Her mittened hands were waggling awkwardly as she tried to keep her balance, her cape was trailing lopsidedly, and her hat was a trifle awry.

It was the last thing he wanted to do, but he started back toward her. She looked so frantic and lonely, he had no choice.

"Good morning, Mrs. Towers. Are you all right?" He offered her his arm. "It isn't weather for hurrying, you know. Where are you going? Perhaps I can accompany you and see you don't fall."

"You are too kind, Reverend Corde." She grasped his arm as if it were a lifeline in a stormy sea. "Those

352

poor ducks. I know Mrs. Jones is putting out bread and a little lard for them, such a nice woman."

"Which way are you going, Mrs. Towers?" he asked again.

"Oh, over there." She gestured vaguely with her free arm, nearly losing her balance again. "How are you settling in? Is Mrs. Corde finding the vicarage to her liking? A home matters so much, I always think."

"We both like it very much indeed," he answered.

"A good garden," she went on. "Old trees make a garden, don't you agree?"

"Yes." He nodded. "I expect in spring they are beautiful."

She told him how many blossom trees there were, then the various other flowers in season, all the way through to the tawny chrysanthemums, the purple Michaelmas daisies, and the offer of an excellent recipe for crab apple jelly. "One of my favorites, I confess," she said with enthusiasm. "I prefer the tart to the very sweet, don't you?"

They were now well across the green and into the lane at the far side. They had passed several cot-

353

tages; the way through the woods lay ahead, winding between the trees. Presumably it led eventually to open fields and perhaps a farm or two. He had realized half a mile ago that she was not actually going anywhere. She needed to talk to him, but could not bring herself to come to the subject easily. His hands were numb and his feet so cold he was losing sensation in them also, but he felt her need as sharply as the wind rattling the bare branches above them. Did she know something about the Reverend Wynter's death? Was that what she was struggling to say?

"Of course, we will probably not be here for very long," he prompted her, surprised again by the regret in his voice. "Once the bishop finds a permanent replacement for the Reverend Wynter, we will return to London. From everything I hear, he was a most remarkable man, one whose shoes it will not be easy to fill."

"He was," she said eagerly. "Oh, he was. So kind. So very patient. One knew one could trust him with anything." She took a deep, shuddering breath. "But I think perhaps you are the same, Reverend Corde.

354

It seems to me you are a man who has understood pain." She looked away from him, and he knew she was afraid she had been too bold.

He hastened to reassure her. "Thank you. That is a very fine thing to say, Mrs. Towers. I shall endeavor to live up to it. At least I can say that I understand loneliness, and the grief of knowing that you have done something ugly and wrong. But I also know there is a path back."

They walked in silence for several yards. Crows wheeled up in the sky, cawing harshly, then circled back into the lower branches again.

"I was going to speak to the Reverend Wynter," she said at last. "I wanted to make a confession, but . . ."

"I think he knew that," Dominic said for her, still holding her arm. "Let's turn back, or we will have too far to go. All the earth is God's house. You do not have to speak in a church for it to be a sacred trust."

"No, no, I suppose not. I kept doing little things wrong, you see, to find out if he would forgive them, before I . . . before I told him the real thing."

He walked a few moments, perhaps thirty or forty

yards along the path, and then he prompted her again. "Was it you who took the pennies from the collection for the poor?"

She drew in her breath with a little cry. "It was only pennies! I made it up, always! I gave extra . . ."

He put his other hand over her arm, holding her more tightly. "That doesn't matter. The books were never short. I know that. But you wanted to speak to him, and never quite found the resolve." He did not use the word *courage*. "Perhaps now would be a good time?"

She gulped again. "I . . . I committed a . . . a terrible sin when I was young. I'm so ashamed, and it can never be undone. I wanted to confess, but . . . but I . . . he was such a good man, I was afraid he would despise me . . ."

"Then tell *me,* Mrs. Towers. I am not so very good. I understand very well what it feels like to sin, and to repent."

"I do repent, I do!"

"Then cast it on the Lord, and be free of it."

"But I must pay!"

"I think that is not for you to decide. What is it you did that is so heavy for you to bear?"

"I had a love affair," she whispered. "Oh, I did love him. You see, I am not Mrs. Towers. I never married. And . . . and . . ." Again she could not find the words.

He guessed. "You had a child?"

She nodded. "Yes." She took a few more steps. "I only saw her for a few moments, then they took her away from me. She was so beautiful." The tears were flowing down her face now. In moments the wind would freeze them on her cold skin. She must have been nearly seventy, and yet the memory was as sharp as yesterday.

He ached to do anything that would take away the pain. Could the compassion in his own heart speak for God? Surely God had to be better, greater than he was?

"Is that all?" he asked her.

"Is that not enough?" she said incredulously.

"Yes. And the penance you have already paid is enough also. More than enough. God forgave you long ago. And the Reverend Wynter would tell you that, were he here."

"I wish I'd had the courage to tell him," she said, swallowing hard.

"Did he not guess?" he asked.

"Oh, no. He knew I wished to say something, but he did not know what it was." She sounded certain.

"He knew many people's secrets," he went on. They were now almost back to the far side of the village green. "Do you not think perhaps the father could have told him?"

"Oh, no, indeed not. The father . . . never knew. It would have been quite impossible for him to marry me. There was no purpose in my telling him about it. I simply went away. It is what girls do, you know."

"Yes, yes. I do know." He did not say any more. It was an age-old story of love and pain and sometimes betrayal, sometimes simple tragedy. It had happened untold times, and would happen again. Had it been here in this village?

Whoever the father was, she had protected him all these years. She would not betray him now, and it was not part of her penance that she should.

358

Dominic was still holding her arm, and he gripped it a little more tightly as they stepped into the rutted road, icy where wheels had pressed it down, deep between ridges.

"Thank you for speaking to me," he said sincerely. "Please don't think of it any further, except with love, or grief, but never again with guilt."

She nodded, unable even to attempt words.

He left her at her door and turned to walk back toward the vicarage. He was quite certain that he had said to her exactly what the Reverend Wynter would have, and his admiration for the old man's wisdom and compassion grew even greater.

How would Dominic follow in his footsteps and guide and comfort the people of this village—be strong for them, judge wisely, know the hearts and not merely the words?

He would be here for Christmas—that much he was certain of. What could he say that was passionate and honest and caught the glory of what Christmas was truly about? It was God's greatest gift to the world, but how could he make them see that? There would be Yule logs and carols and bells, mulled wine,

359 ·

gifts, decorated trees, lights across the snow. They were the outer marks of joy. How could he make just as visible the inward ones?

He wanted Clarice to be proud of him; he wanted it with a hunger close to starvation. He must give her the gift she most wanted, too—finding the best in himself for both of them.

*O*f course he said nothing to her of what Sybil Towers had told him, and he found that a hardship. He would have liked her advice, but he never considered breaking the trust.

Instead, over luncheon, Clarice told him that Mrs. Wellbeloved had been in that morning, bringing yet more onions and another rock-hard cabbage, which with a strong wrist and a sharp knife she would be able to slice. Mrs. Wellbeloved was full of gossip about the poor vicar's death, and the fact that John Boscombe had had a terrible quarrel with him shortly before. The village was buzzing with the news, but no one had the faintest idea what the argument had been about.

"His marriage, or lack of it, I should think," Dominic replied. Since it was Clarice who had discovered it, that was not a confidence between the two of them. "Poor man."

"You sympathize with him?" Clarice said in surprise.

"Don't you?"

"I do with Genevieve, if she didn't know. Very little if she did," Clarice responded.

He smiled. "If I had been married unhappily, and met you, I might have done the same."

"Oh." She did not know whether to smile or disapprove. She tried both, with singular lack of success.

He saw the conflict in her face and laughed.

"And you think I would have lived with you anyway," she said hotly. She took a deep breath and speared a carrot with her fork. "You're probably right."

He smiled more widely, with a little flutter of warmth inside him, but he was wise enough not to answer.

At almost two o'clock he set out to go up to the manor. There were one or two favors he wished to ask Peter Connaught with regard to villagers he knew were in need, but more than that he wondered if perhaps Peter's father could have been Sybil Towers's lover. If the Reverend Wynter had known that, was it a secret worth killing him for? Did it even matter now, so many years afterward? It would be a scandal, and Peter was inordinately proud of his family and its heritage of honor and care in the village. It was not his fault, of course, but the stain would touch him. Was he protective enough of his father's name to have killed to keep it safe?

What if Sybil's daughter were known to him? She was illegitimate and had no possible claim in law, even if her heritage could be proved—which it probably could not. But in a small community like Cottisham, proof was irrelevant; reputation was all.

The weather had deteriorated. The wind was rising. Clouds piled high in the west, darkening the sky and promising heavy falls of snow that night.

He was welcomed at the hall, as always, and in the huge withdrawing room the usual log fire was

362

blazing. The afternoon was dark and the candelabra were lit, making the room almost festively bright.

He accepted the offer of tea, longing to thaw his hands on the warm cup as much as he looked forward to the drink. They addressed the business of the village. Help must be given with discretion; even the most needy did not like to feel they are objects of charity. Many would rather freeze or go hungry than accept pity. Food could be given to all, so none felt their poverty revealed. They arranged for the blacksmith to go after dark and add a few dozen logs to certain people's woodpiles.

The butler came with tea and hot toasted tea cakes thick with currants and covered with melted butter. The two men left not a crumb.

Finally Dominic had to approach the subject of Sybil Towers. He had thought about it, considered all possibilities, and found no answer that pleased him fully, but he could not break Sybil's confidence.

"I have to ask you a very troubling question," he began. He was awkward. He knew it, and could think of no way to help himself. "I have gained certain knowledge, not because I sought it, and I cannot reveal any more to you than that, so please do not ask me."

Peter frowned. "You may trust my discretion. What is it that is wrong?"

Dominic had already concocted the lie carefully, but it still troubled him. "Many years ago a young woman in the village had a love affair with a man it was impossible for her to marry. There was a child. I believe the father never knew." He was watching Peter's face but saw in it only sympathy and a certain resignation. No doubt he had heard similar stories many times before.

"I'm sorry," Peter said quietly. "If it happened long ago, why do you raise it now?"

"Because the Reverend Wynter may have known of it," Dominic said frankly, still watching Peter's face. "And he was murdered . . ."

"Did you say murdered?" Peter demanded, his voice hoarse. "That is very far from what Fitzpatrick told me!"

"I know. Dr. Fitzpatrick does not want to face the unpleasantness of such a thing. But I believe the Reverend Wynter was a fine man, and his death should not be treated with less than honesty, just for our convenience. He deserved better than that."

"What makes you think it was murder, Corde?" Peter reached for the poker, readjusted his grasp on it, and drove the end into the burning embers. The log shifted weight and settled lower, sending up a shower of sparks. He replaced the poker in its stand and added another log.

Dominic found himself shivering despite the heat. "He fell at the bottom of the cellar stairs," he replied. "There were marks of being dragged, and he was found in the second cellar, with injuries both to his face and the back of his head. The cellar door was closed behind him, and he had no lantern."

There was silence in the room. Beyond the thick curtains and the glass, even the sound of the wind was muffled.

"I see," Peter said at last, his face somber in the firelight. "I have to agree with you. As an accident, that does not make sense. How tragic. He was a good man: wise, brave, and honest. What is it you think this unfortunate woman has to do with it? Surely you are not suggesting the Reverend Wynter was the

365

father of this child? That I do not believe. If he had done such a thing—which of course is possible; we are all capable of love and hate—then he would have admitted it. He would not have lied or disclaimed his responsibility."

"No," Dominic agreed. "But I think he may have known something of the truth, and someone could not bear the thought that he would reveal it. Perhaps the vicar even wished the father to honor his responsibility in some way he was not prepared to."

"How very sad. What is it I can do to help now? I presume you cannot tell me the names of either the woman or her child?"

"I cannot tell you the name of the woman," Dominic agreed. "It has to be confidential. The name of the child I do not know, but I fear it may be someone who has returned to the village with a certain degree of retribution in her mind."

"Oh, dear! And killed poor Wynter because he was the vicar at the time, and did not do as she would have wished, or thought fair?"

"It seems possible," Dominic replied. That at least

366

was true. The more he considered it, the more likely it became. The missing money and Wynter's quarrel with John Boscombe had already been explained.

Peter was waiting for an answer to his first question.

"You must be very careful," Dominic said softly. "If it is this woman who kills, then she does it with stealth, and skill. I think it may be someone nobody suspects."

"Why should she wish *me* any harm?" Peter's eyes widened. "When Wynter first came here, I was a child myself. In fact, I wasn't even in England. That is when my parents were living in the East, before . . . before my mother died." He looked down, and a faint color touched his cheeks.

"Did your father not return to England at all during that time?" Dominic asked.

Peter looked up sharply. The whole air of their conversation had altered. There was pain in his face, and anger. His body was stiff in the chair. "Exactly what is it you are asking, Corde?"

"She could not marry him because he was far beyond her social station," Dominic told him. "It seems in Cottisham that that's most likely to have been your father."

Peter's face paled to a sickly yellow, as if the blood had drained out of his skin. He was shaking when he spoke. "My father was devoted to my mother! It is monstrous that you should make such a revolting suggestion! Who is this woman? I demand to know who has . . . no . . . I apologize. I know you cannot tell me." His hands gripped the arms of his chair. "But she is a liar of the most vile sort. It is not true!"

Dominic was startled by the vehemence of his denial. It was not so very unusual that a man of wealth and position should produce a few illegitimate children. It made Dominic wonder if perhaps Peter himself might have quarreled with the Reverend Wynter over it. Was it conceivable that, charming as he was, generous, diligent in his duties, still his family pride was such that he would have struck out in rage at the suggestion that his father had begotten any child other than himself?

"You seem inexplicably angry at the thought, Sir Peter," Dominic said gently. "It does not threaten ei-

368

ther your inheritance or your title, and it is no more than a remote possibility. I told you, in case you yourself were in some danger. Your flash of temper makes one wonder if perhaps this same suggestion was the cause of your difference with the Reverend Wynter, and you did not forgive him for making it."

Peter stared at him, and slowly the awful meaning of what he had said dawned on him. "God in heaven, man! Are you saying you think I murdered poor Wynter because he believed it was true my father begot this . . . this child? You can't!" He dragged in his breath, gulping, painfully, and then he started to laugh. It was a terrible sound, wrenched out of him with pain.

Dominic was appalled. He wanted to run away, leave this scene of naked emotion, but he must stay, find the truth, and then face it.

"Is that really absurd?" he said when Peter had gained some small measure of control.

"Yes! Yes, it is absurd!" Peter's voice rose to near hysteria. "My father could never have had an illegitimate child. Would to God he could have."

The words made no sense at all. Yet in the small

369

discrepancies in what Peter had said of his parents a tiny glimmer of light appeared. "Why would you want that?" Dominic asked.

Peter leaned forward, his face beaded in sweat, eyes dark. "You know, don't you? Did Wynter leave something that you found? He swore to me he wouldn't, but what is his word worth, eh? What is yours worth, Reverend?"

"Why do you want your father to have begotten an illegitimate child?" Dominic asked again, his voice perfectly steady now. He was still trying to untangle the confused threads in his mind. "Do you want this woman to be your sister? Do you know who she is? Did she kill Wynter?"

"I've no idea who killed Wynter, or why!" Peter said, forcing the words between his teeth. "And my father did not beget her. At least Sir Thomas Connaught didn't. He was sterile. God knows who my father was. I don't."

Dominic was stunned. Was that why Peter was so defensive of his mother, the beautiful woman who had died tragically somewhere in the East? Had Thomas found out her infidelity, and killed her? No, that was

370

impossible. If he knew he could not have fathered a child, then he would have killed his wife when he knew she was expecting, not after the child was born. It still made no sense. "He killed her?" he said, struggling for some kind of logic in it.

"You fool!" Peter shouted at him. Then he covered his face with his hands. "Of course he didn't! He never even knew her. I was an orphan, one of thousands of children who live in the streets. I was good looking, intelligent. Sir Thomas found me stealing and lied to the police to save me. He had no children, and knew he never would have. No wife, either. He adopted me. I am quite legally and honorably his heir. But I am not of his blood. I am no more a Connaught of Cottisham Hall than you are. I am illegitimate, unwanted. I have no father and no mother that I remember. Either she died, or she gave me away. It hardly matters now. I don't belong here. Wynter knew. That's what we quarreled over. He wanted me to stop boasting about my heritage." He lowered his hands slowly. "I hated him because he knew. But he was my friend, and I would never have harmed him, that I swear on the little honor I have left."

Dominic spoke slowly, weighing each word. "Did the Reverend Wynter not tell you that it was the pride of blood that was wrong? A man is great, or petty, because of who he is, not who his father was. Sir Thomas Connaught gave you the opportunity to be his son and carry on the tradition of service that his father gave to him. If you have done so, then your actions have earned you the right to be here. The respect and love of people is earned; it cannot be bequeathed by anyone else."

"You know your father!" Peter said with a raw edge of pain in his voice, almost of accusation. "You were part of him, whatever you did. That is a bond you cannot make with all the wishing in the world."

"You have no idea whether I knew my father or he knew me," Dominic said. "Actually I looked like him, so I reminded him of all that he disliked in himself." The words were still hard to say. "He greatly preferred my brother, who was fair and mild-featured, like my mother, whom he adored." He was surprised that he remembered it even now with a sense of exclusion and strange, inexplicable loss.

372

"I'm sorry," Peter stammered. "My arrogance is monumental, isn't it? As if I were the only one in the world who feels he does not belong in his own skin, his own life. Do you know who this woman is, the mother? Perhaps I could do something to help her. You could attend to it, discreetly."

"It isn't your responsibility," Dominic pointed out.

"Haven't you just been telling me that that is irrelevant?" Peter asked, smiling very faintly for the first time.

"Yes. Yes, I suppose I have," Dominic agreed. "You understand me better than I understand myself. By all means, help her. She has little in the way of possessions. Even sufficient fuel to keep her warm would be a great gift."

"Consider it done. And the others in the village who are in any need. The estate has plenty of wood, and certainly no better use for it."

"Thank you." Dominic meant it profoundly. He smiled back. "Thank you," he repeated.

*W*hile Dominic was at the manor house, Clarice took a lantern and went down into the cellar again. Though Mrs. Wellbeloved had swept the steps, Clarice knew which one had the splinter on it that had frayed the Reverend Wynter's trouser leg, as well as where he must have landed at the bottom.

Carefully she continued on down the stairs, holding the lantern high. No one could come down here without a light of some sort, and a candle would be blown out by the draft from the hall above.

If he had tripped and fallen, he would have dropped the lantern and it would have broken. What had happened to it? Had someone swept up all the shards and hidden them? And what had they done with the metal frame? She should find out from Mrs. Wellbeloved if there was a lantern missing or not.

But whom would the Reverend Wynter go into the cellar with? What excuse had they given? To fetch coal for him, on the pretext that it was heavy? No it wasn't, not very. Mrs. Wellbeloved normally did it herself. She was strong, but not like a man. And where was the coke scuttle to carry it in?

Whoever it was had dragged the Reverend Wynter's body from the bottom of the steps across the floor and into the other cellar, leaving the marks in the coal dust. Why? They had tried to scuff them out, but hadn't entirely succeeded. Why make them in the first place? He was an old man, light-boned, frail. Why not carry him?

Because the killer had not been strong enough to carry him. A weak man? Or a woman? Genevieve Boscombe? It was a sickening thought, but Genevieve had much to lose. A woman would do almost anything to protect her children. A bear, to protect her cubs, would kill indiscriminately.

She turned around slowly and started climbing back up again, glad of the light from the hallway at the top. She reached it and was facing Mrs. Paget.

"Sorry to startle you," Mrs. Paget said with a smile. "I took the liberty of coming in. The door was unlocked; the Reverend Wynter always left it unlocked, too. And it's bitter outside. That wind is cruel."

"Yes, of course." Clarice felt as if she should apologize for being less than welcoming. After all, in a

375

sense the vicarage belonged to the whole village, and Mrs. Paget had obliquely reminded her of that. "Please come in. It's warmer in the kitchen. Would you like a cup of tea?"

"That's very kind of you," Mrs. Paget said. "I brought you a bottle of elderflower wine. I thought it might be pleasant with your Christmas dinner. The vicar was very fond of it." She held out a bottle with a red ribbon around its neck, the liquid in it shining clear, pale gold.

"How very kind of you," Clarice said. She blew out the flame in the lantern and set it on the hall shelf, then took the bottle. She led the way into the kitchen and pushed the kettle over onto the hob to boil again. Thank goodness today she had cake. She must not get the reputation for having nothing to offer visitors.

Mrs. Paget made herself comfortable in one of the kitchen chairs. "I see you were down in the cellar again," she remarked. "Not to get coal." Her eyes wandered to the full coal and coke receptacles by the stove, then back to Clarice. "Hard for you that it happened right here."

Clarice was taken aback by her frankness. "Yes."

"I suppose you're working out what happened?"

Should she deny it? That would be pointless. It was obviously what she had been doing, and Mrs. Paget knew it. That, too, was clear in her bright brown eyes.

"Trying to," Clarice admitted.

"Poor man. That was a terrible thing." Mrs. Paget shook her head. "But vicars sometimes get to know secrets people can't bear to have told. You be careful, Mrs. Corde. There's wickedness in the village in places you wouldn't think to look for it. You watch out for your husband. A pleasant face can very easily fool men. Some look harmless that aren't."

Clarice decided to be just as blunt.

"Indeed, Mrs. Paget." She thought of the marks of dragging in the cellar floor. The vicar had trusted a woman he should not have, perhaps even trying to help her. "Do you have anyone in particular in mind?"

Mrs. Paget hesitated again, but it was clear in the concentration of her expression that she was not offended at being asked.

The kettle started to steam. Clarice warmed the

377

teapot then placed the leaves in and poured on the water, setting it on the table to brew. She sat down opposite Mrs. Paget, still waiting for an answer.

Instead Mrs. Paget asked another question. "What did you find down there?"

Clarice was not sure how much she wanted to answer. "Nothing conclusive."

Mrs. Paget surprised her again. "No doubt you were disturbed by my coming. I'm sorry about that. I did call out, but not loud enough for you to hear downstairs. Perhaps there is something, if we looked properly. The poor man deserves justice, and that old fool Fitzpatrick isn't going to do anything about it. I'll come with you, if you like? Hold the lantern."

Clarice felt her stomach tighten, but she had no possible excuse to refuse. And she could not bring herself to tell Mrs. Paget a deliberate lie. For one thing, it could be too easily found out if anyone at all were to go down there, and what could she say? She needed to keep the evidence; it might be the only proof of what had happened. "Thank you. That would be a good idea. I didn't really have time to look."

After tea and cake Clarice went gingerly down the

steps again with Mrs. Paget behind her, holding the lantern. Of course they found exactly what Clarice had already seen. "That was where I found him." She pointed to the doorway of the second cellar.

"So he fell here," Mrs. Paget said quietly, pointing to the bottom of the steps. "And whoever it was dragged him there—" She indicated the marks. "—over to there."

"Yes, I think so."

Mrs. Paget studied the floor. "By the shoulders, from the look of it. And those are their own footmarks . . . unless they are yours?"

Clarice stared at the distinct mark of a boot well to the side of the tracks. "It might be Dr. Fitzpatrick's," she said with a frown.

"Going backward?" Mrs. Paget asked gently, her eyes bright. "Why would he do that, unless he was dragging something? And it looks a little small, don't you think?"

She was absolutely right. It was a woman's boot, or a boy's.

As if reading her thoughts, Mrs. Paget said the same thing. "Tommy Spriggs, one of the village boys, said he saw a woman hurrying away from here the day the vicar was last seen. He'll tell you, if you ask him. Hurrying she was."

"Who was it?"

"Ah, that he doesn't know. Could've been any grown woman who could walk rapidly and wasn't either very short or very tall."

"Can you take me to him?" Clarice asked.

"Of course I can." Mrs. Paget picked up her skirts to climb back up the stairs. "Good thing you came down here, Mrs. Corde. And a good thing you're not minded to let injustice go by, simply because it's easier and, I daresay, more comfortable."

In the evening Clarice told Dominic about it, and of finding Tommy Spriggs and confirming what Mrs. Paget had said.

"Had he any idea who she was?" Dominic asked.

"None at all. What he had told Mrs. Paget was all he knew," she answered. She looked at him, both fearing the same answer. Neither spoke it.

380

Christmas Eve dawned so cold the windows were blind with fresh snow, and even inside the air numbed fingers and toes. Outside all color was drowned: white earth, white sky. Even the black trees were mantled in white. Just a few filigree branches were hung with icicles here and there, though when it had thawed sufficiently for them to melt into daggers of ice was hard to say.

Blizzards blew in from the east, and through that cold-gripped world Genevieve Boscombe came to the door and asked to see Dominic.

The study fire wasn't lit, so he took her into the sitting room. He spent several moments poking the wood and coal until the fire caught a better hold and started to give a little more heat. Only when she sat down and he looked more closely at her eyes did he realize that no hearth in the world was going to assuage the cold inside her.

"I killed the Reverend Wynter," she said quietly. Her voice was flat, almost without emotion. "I lied to you when I said he wasn't going to do anything about

John and me not being married. He was going to tell everyone, so all the village would know. I couldn't take that, not for my children."

Dominic was stunned. After what Clarice had told him the previous evening, they both knew it was horribly possible that Genevieve Boscombe was guilty. Even so, he could not easily believe it. He hated the thought. He had liked both of them. But then how good was he really at judging character any more deeply than the superficial qualities of humor or gentleness, good manners, the ability to see what is beautiful? And he sympathized with her. He well understood those who truly loved and could not bear to lose the warmth and purpose from their lives.

"I did!" she repeated, as if he had not heard her. "It's not a religious confession, Vicar. I expect you to tell the police so they can arrest me." She sat with her back straight and her hands folded in her lap. Her eyes were red-rimmed, but there were no tears in them now. He thought she had probably done all her weeping, at least for the time being.

"How did you do it, Mrs. Boscombe?" he asked,

still reluctant to accept and looking for a way for her to be not totally at fault.

She looked surprised, although it was visible as just a momentary flicker of the eyes. "I carried the coke scuttle down for him," she replied. "I hit him with it. He fell, and I pulled him into the other cellar, so he wouldn't be found too soon."

"But you knew he would be found sometime," he said.

"I didn't think. I don't remember." And she refused to say anything further, merely requesting that he report her to the constable so she could be arrested.

There was, in effect, no constable, only the blacksmith who was appointed to represent the law in the village. She insisted on going with him. After much protest, the blacksmith locked her in the large, warm storeroom next to the forge.

Dominic went straight to tell John Boscombe what had happened, trudging through the snow. He was cold inside and out, even when he stood in Boscombe's kitchen in front of him.

383

"She only said it to protect me!" Boscombe said frantically. His face was haggard, his eyes wild. "Where is she? I'll reason with her. I was the one who killed the vicar. I quarreled with him because he wanted me to get straight with the law, and the church." His voice was rising in pitch, rising desperately. "I had an accident in the summer. Could have been killed. Was then the vicar told me that if I had been, my family would get nothing, not even the house, because they weren't legal. Genny and the children would be thrown onto charity, and folks might not be that kind to them, seeing I still had a wife alive that I'd never sorted things with."

"I see," Dominic said quietly. "And did you believe that the Reverend Wynter would have forced you to do this, whatever the cost to you?"

Boscombe hesitated.

"Did you?" Dominic insisted.

"I was afraid he would." Boscombe evaded a direct answer. His eyes were angry, challenging. "That's why I did it. Genny's innocent. She didn't even know I was already married when she—" He stopped.

"Agreed to live with you without marriage?" Dominic asked.

Boscombe was caught. To deny it would suggest Genevieve did not care about marriage, and that was obviously ridiculous.

"Was the vicar blackmailing you?" Dominic asked.

"Good God, no!" Boscombe was appalled, but a tide of color swept up his face.

Dominic guessed the reason.

"Then who is?" he said. "I don't believe you killed the Reverend Wynter, nor did Genevieve. But you are each afraid that the other did, so there must be a terrible reason why it could be so. Someone is threatening you. Who is it?"

Boscombe's face was wretched—eyes full of shame.

"My wife. She's here in Cottisham. She's asking money every week. She'll bleed us dry."

All the jumbled pieces were beginning to make sense at last.

"But she's still alive, isn't she?" Dominic said gently. "Why would you kill the Reverend Wynter, and not her? Why would either of you?"

Slowly the darkness melted from Boscombe's face and he straightened his shoulders, leaning forward a little as if to rise. "It wasn't Genevieve! It was Maribelle! The vicar wouldn't have forced us to do the right thing, only helped us, but if we did, then Maribelle would get nothing! And he knew what she was doing! He wanted it all out, just like you did!"

"Maribelle?" Dominic asked, although by now he was certain he knew. His blood chilled at the thought of her alone with Clarice in the cellar where she had killed the Reverend Wynter, but there was no time to stare into nightmares now.

"Maribelle Paget was my first wife," Boscombe admitted. "And a crueler woman never trod the earth."

"Come." Dominic stood up. "We must go and face her."

"But Genevieve—"

"She's safe. We have other things to do first. She thinks you did it, and she won't back down from her confession until we've proved otherwise."

*A*fter Dominic had left with Genevieve Boscombe, Clarice stood in the kitchen staring out of the window at the snow on the apple tree, going over and over in her mind what Mrs. Paget had said in the cellar. The impression would not leave her that Mrs. Paget had expected to find the footprint where it was, almost as if she had known it was there. She had read the drag marks without hesitation, knowing what they were. How did she do that so accurately? Why did she assume that the woman seen leaving the vicarage in the wind and snow had had anything to do with the vicar's death? She could have been anyone. She had even known at which step he had fallen. She had stopped at it instinctively.

Clarice turned from the window. Taking her cape from the hook in the hall, she wound it around herself and set off in the snow toward the Boscombes' house. She must tell Dominic immediately that neither John nor Genevieve was guilty. She was afraid John Boscombe might panic, even fight Dominic when he heard what had happened, and do something that in itself would condemn him.

There was no time to waste. She took the shortcut along the path through the trees. The stream would be frozen over and safe to cross. The Boscombes' house was only just beyond.

The crust on the snow was hard. For a moment it bore her weight, then cracked and pitched her off balance. The icy breath of the wind sighed in the branches, blowing clumps of heavy snow onto the ground. Two or three fell close to her, distracting her attention. She was almost upon the three figures before she saw them, dark and blurred in the colorless landscape. It was Dominic and John Boscombe facing Mrs. Paget.

Clarice stopped abruptly. The stream was to her right, identifiable now only as a winding strip of level ground between the banks.

They must all have seen her, but it was Mrs. Paget, ten feet closer, who moved first. She plunged forward through the deep snow, flailing her arms, crossing the ground with extraordinary speed. She reached Clarice in moments, her face contorted with fury.

Clarice stepped back, but not quickly enough.

Mrs. Paget grasped hold of her, fingers like a vise, pulling her toward the stream, dragging her along. She had no time to think. She struggled, but her fists struck only the other woman's heavy cloak.

Dominic was shouting something, but another avalanche from above drowned his words. The snow was melting.

Now they were on the flat icy surface of the stream itself, where it was easier to move.

"It won't hold you!" Mrs. Paget shouted back at the man, triumph loud and high in her voice. "Step onto it, too, and we'll all go down!" She turned back to Clarice. "Struggle too hard and you'll crack the ice under us, clever vicar's wife! Believe me, the cold under there will kill you!"

Clarice stopped moving instantly.

"Good," Mrs. Paget said with satisfaction. "Now come with me, slowly, carefully. When we get to the far side, I might let you go. And then I might not. They're too heavy to come after us. Nothing they can do." She pulled again, hard, and Clarice nearly fell.

Boscombe and Dominic stopped at the brink, aware that their weight would break the ice.

Mrs. Paget laughed with a high, vicious sound. She yanked on Clarice's arm and started forward again. Clarice did all she could to resist, but her feet had no purchase on the ice. She heard it before she realized what it was: a sharp sound, like a shot, then another, more like ripping cotton.

Mrs. Paget screamed, grabbing at Clarice and clinging to her hand so hard, Clarice cried out in pain. Mrs. Paget had fallen down on her back, legs thrashing. The ice swayed and tipped, the cracks in it fanning out, the black water swirling over it, as cold as death. Her big cloak imprisoned her in its folds.

Clarice felt the water with a shock that almost took the air from her lungs. The cold was unbelievable. She could not even cry out.

Dominic started out across the ice, calling her, heedless of the danger to himself. Boscombe was in the churning ice floes of the shallows, knee-deep, then waist-deep, his whole body outstretched to hold on to Dominic's arm.

Clarice was paralyzed with the cold, her hand still gripped by Mrs. Paget's like a small animal caught in the jaws of a trap.

Dominic seized her other hand, pulling hard, but Mrs. Paget would not let go. If she drowned, Clarice would drown with her.

Dominic reached past her. There was a piece of branch in his hand. He swung out hard, striking Mrs. Paget's fingers with a force enough to break the bone. She shrieked once, drawing the black water into her lungs, and then she was gone, sucked into the current as it swept under the unbroken ice, carrying her away.

Dominic and Boscombe dragged Clarice out. She was almost unconscious, and shuddering so violently she could barely breathe. She saw lights in the gloom and heard voices, then drifted into a kind of sleep.

She woke with someone rubbing her hands and arms, then her legs. Someone else put hot tea between her lips, and she swallowed it awkwardly. It hit her stomach like fire and made her choke.

Then she saw Dominic, his face white with fear.

"Don't be so silly," she whispered hoarsely. "I'm not going to drown. I was just . . . detecting . . ."

He laughed, but there were tears in his eyes and on his cheeks.

"Of course you were," he agreed. "You have to hear my Christmas sermon."

There were murmurs of assent, and more tea, and then it all faded into a blur, distant and happy and full of kindness.

*T*he usual Watch Night service was not held, in deference to the death of Maribelle Paget. However, word rapidly spread of exactly how it had come about, if not why. Nor did anyone mention that she was really Maribelle Boscombe.

But in the morning every man, woman, and child was in the village church to celebrate Christmas Day. Even old Mr. Riddington was there, wrapped in a blanket and warmed with liberal doses of blackberry wine.

The bells rang out over the snow, carrying the message of joy across fields and woodlands, from spire to spire throughout the land. Inside the organ played the old favorites, and the voices sang—for once—in total unison.

Dominic went to the pulpit and spoke simply, passionately, knowing that what he said was true.

"Christmas is the time when we give gifts, most especially to children. Many have spent long hours making them, carefully and with love, putting into them the best that they have. There are dolls, toy trains, a wooden whistle, a new dress, painted bricks."

He saw nods and smiles.

He leaned forward over the pulpit rail. "We are the children of God, every one of us, and nearly nineteen hundred years ago He gave us the greatest of all the gifts He has, greater even than life. He gave us hope: a way back from every mistake we have made, no matter how small or how large, how ugly or how incredibly stupid, or how shameful. There is no corner of hell secret enough or deep enough for there to be no path back, if we are willing to climb up. It may be hard, and steep, but there is light ahead, and freedom."

Deliberately he did not look at Sybil Towers or Peter Connaught; nor did he look at the Boscombes with their children, or Mrs. Wellbeloved or Mr. Riddington. Only once did he glance at Clarice and saw the pride and the joy in her. It was all the reward he ever wanted.

"Do not deny the gift," he said. "Accept it for yourself, and for all others. That is what Christmas is: everlasting hope, a way forward to the best in ourselves and all that we can become."

"Amen!" the congregation replied. Then again, with passion, they rose to their feet one by one. "Amen!"

Above them the bells pealed out across the land.

Read on for a preview of

Anne Perry's

next thrilling
Christmas novel,

A Christmas
Grace

Published by Ballantine Books
Coming to bookstores everywhere

$\mathcal{E}$MILY RADLEY STOOD IN THE CENTER OF HER magnificent drawing room and considered where she should have the Christmas tree placed so that it would show to the best advantage. The decorations were already planned: the bows, the colored balls, the tinsel, the little glass icicles, and the red and green shiny birds. At the foot would be the brightly wrapped presents for her husband and children.

All through the house there would be candles, wreaths and garlands of holly and ivy. There would be bowls of crystallized fruit and porcelain dishes of nuts, jugs of mulled wine, plates of mince pies, roasted chestnuts, and, of course, great fires in the hearths with apple logs to burn with a sweet smell.

The year of 1895 had not been an easy one, and she was happy enough to see it come to a close. Because they were staying in London, rather than going to the country, there would be parties, and dinners, including the Duchess of Warwick's; everyone she knew would be at that dinner. And there would be balls where they would dance all night. She had her gown chosen: the palest possible green, embroidered with gold. And, of course, there was the theater. It would not be the same without anything of Oscar Wilde's, but there would be Goldsmith's *She Stoops to Conquer,* and that was fun.

She was still thinking about it when Jack came in. He looked a little tired, but he had the same easy grace of manner as always. He was holding a letter in his hand.

"Post?" she asked in surprise. "At this time in the evening?" Her heart sank. "It's not some government matter, is it? They can't want you now. It's less than three weeks till Christmas."

"It's for you," he replied, holding it out for her. "It

was just delivered. I think it's Thomas's handwriting."

Thomas Pitt was Emily's brother-in-law, a policeman. Her sister, Charlotte, had married considerably beneath her. She had not regretted it for a day, even if it had cost her the social and financial comforts she had been accustomed to. On the contrary, it was Emily who envied Charlotte the opportunities she had been given to involve herself in some of his cases. It seemed like far too long since Emily had shared an adventure, the danger, the emotion, the anger, and the pity. Somehow she felt less alive for it.

She tore open the envelope and read the paper inside.

Dear Emily,

    I am very sorry to tell you that Charlotte received a letter today from a Roman Catholic priest, Father Tyndale, who lives in a small village in the Connemara region of Western Ireland. He is the pastor to Susannah Ross, your father's younger sister. She is now widowed again, and Father Tyndale says she is very ill. In fact this will certainly be her last Christmas.

I know she parted from the family in less than happy circumstances, but we should not allow her to be alone at such a time. Your mother is in Italy, and unfortunately Charlotte has a bad case of bronchitis, which is why I am writing to ask you if you will go to Ireland to be with Susannah. I realize it is a great sacrifice, but there is no one else.

Father Tyndale says it cannot be for long, and you would be most welcome in Susannah's home. If you write back to him at the enclosed address, he will meet you at the Galway station from whichever train you say. Please make it within a day or two. There is little time to hesitate.

I thank you in advance, and Charlotte sends her love. She will write to you when she is well enough.

Yours with gratitude,
Thomas

Emily looked up and met Jack's eyes. "It's preposterous!" she exclaimed. "He's lost his wits."

Jack blinked. "Really. What does he say?"

Wordlessly she passed the letter to him.

He read it, frowning, and then offered it back to her. "I'm sorry. I know you were looking forward to Christmas at home, but there'll be another one next year."

"I'm not going!" she said incredulously.

He said nothing, just looked at her steadily.

"It's ridiculous," she protested. "I can't go to Connemara, for heaven's sake. Especially not at Christmas. It'll be like the end of the world. In fact it is the end of the world. Jack, it's nothing but freezing bog."

"Actually I believe the west coast of Ireland is quite temperate," he corrected her. "But wet, of course," he added with a smile.

She breathed out a sigh of relief. His smile could still charm her more than she wished him to know. If he did, he might be impossible to manage at all. She turned away to put the letter on the table. "I'll write to Thomas tomorrow and explain to him."

401

"What will you say?" he asked.

She was surprised. "That it's out of the question, of course. But I'll put it nicely."

"How nicely can you say that you'll let your aunt die alone at Christmas because you don't fancy the Irish climate?" he asked, his voice surprisingly gentle, considering the words.

Emily froze. She turned back to look at him, and knew that in spite of the smile, he meant exactly what he had said. "Do you really want me to go away to Ireland for the entire Christmas?" she asked. "Susannah's only fifty. She might live for ages. He doesn't even say what's wrong with her."

"One can die at any age," Jack pointed out. "And what I would like has nothing to do with what is right."

"What about the children?" Emily played the trump card. "What will they think if I leave them for Christmas? It is a time when families should be together." She smiled back at him.

"Then write and tell your aunt to die alone because you want to be with your family," he replied.

"On second thoughts, you'll have to tell the priest, and he can tell her."

The appalling realization hit her. "You want me to go!" she accused him.

"No, I don't," he denied. "But neither do I want to live with you all the years afterwards when Susannah is dead, and you wish you had done. Guilt can destroy even the dearest things.. In fact, especially the dearest." He reached out and touched her cheek gently. "I don't want to lose you."

"You won't!" she said quickly. "You'll never lose me."

"Lots of people lose each other." He shook his head. "Some people even lose themselves."

She looked down at the carpet. "But it's Christmas!"

He did not answer.

The seconds ticked by. The fire crackled in the hearth.

"Do you suppose they have telegrams in Ireland?" she asked finally.

"I've no idea. What can you possibly say in a telegram that would answer this?"

She took a deep breath. "What time my train gets into Galway. And on what day, I suppose."

He leaned forward and kissed her very gently, and she found she was crying, for all that she would miss over the next weeks, and all that she thought Christmas ought to be.

ANNE PERRY is the bestselling author of *No Graves As Yet, Shoulder the Sky,* and *Angels in the Gloom*; two earlier holiday novels, *A Christmas Journey* and *A Christmas Visitor*; and two acclaimed series set in Victorian England. Her most recent William Monk novels are *Death of a Stranger* and *The Shifting Tide.* The popular novels featuring Charlotte and Thomas Pitt include *Southampton Row, Seven Dials,* and *Long Spoon Lane.* Her short story "Heroes" won an Edgar Award. Anne Perry lives in Scotland. Visit her website at www.anneperry.net.